The Organist Wore Pumps

A Liturgical Mystery

by Mark Schweizer

SJMP<u>BOOKS</u>

Advance Praise for *The Organist Wore Pumps*

"We've had Dr. Schweizer as a guest for supper. He eats like he writes. Unfortunately, there's no dog to clean up after his writing."
Lady Deirdre Curteis, Markenfield Hall, Ripon, England

"*The Organist Wore Pumps* is a book you'll want to read again and again. Then read again. Then read again. Then read again..."
National Amnesia Quarterly Review

"...a strange book that is, in turn, savagely beautiful, brutally alluring, ruthlessly delicate, offensively exquisite and hideously cute. Sophie Slug is a *femme fatale* for our time."
Gastropod Weekly

"I don't get it. Is this one of them thingys in the front of a book?"
Candi Scrumptious, Las Vegas ~~showgirl~~ investment therapist

"There aren't many professional writers that couldn't pull off a story like this and Schweizer is one of them."
Dr. Richard Shephard, Chamberlain, York Minster

"This is a book you'll want to pretend you didn't spend any money on."
Susan Rupert, University of the South, School of Theology

"Schweizer does it again! Life may go on if you don't read this book, but you'll always wonder, 'What if?'"
Patricia Nakamura, book editor and life coach

"Learn how to get FR3E MØNEY F%OM THE GOVER*MΣNT in Schweizer's runaway best seller *The Organist Wore Pumps*!"
email spam

"I'll tell you one thing. I'm just glad I'm not an Episcopalian. Lutherans would never do this stuff."
Charlotte Nelson, Life-long Lutheran

"You can't just keep killing off the clergy."
Tryon mystery writers' group

"A can't-put-down tale of robbery, murder, and horticultural pest control."
Dr. Ken Dougherty, urologist

"another solid, B-minus effort..."
Karole Schweizer, mother

For Richard Shephard
who loved Sophie Slug from the beginning...

The Organist Wore Pumps

A Liturgical Mystery

Illustrations by Jim Hunt
www.jimhuntillustration.com

Published by
SJMPBOOKS
www.sjmpbooks.com
P.O. Box 249
Tryon, NC 28782

ISBN 978-0-9844846-0-7

March, 2010

Acknowledgements
The Rt. Rev. Joe Burnett, Carson Cooman, Nancy Cooper,
Holly Derickson, Jay and Betsy Goree, Marty Hatteberg,
Kristen Linduff, Beth McCoy, Patricia Nakamura, Donis Schweizer,
Liz Schweizer, and Richard Shephard

Prelude

"How come I've never heard of this society?" asked Meg, bouncing lightly on the side of the bed. "If it's been in existence for over a hundred years, you'd think it would get a little more publicity."

I stood in front of the full-length mirror. My fingers fumbled the last miniature button into the collar of my best dress shirt and I silently cursed, not for the first time, the inventor of the "button-down," and my stupidity in buying a gross of them when I made my first million.

"The Banner Elk Athenaeum Society does not strive for publicity," I said. "They strive for literary excellence and the edification of the membership. Toss me that tie, will you?"

"Hmm," said Meg, obliging my request. "Why don't you button your collar *after* you tie your tie?"

"My fingers are too big. I can't button the collar tabs once the tie is on."

"I'd be happy to button your tabs," she volunteered.

"You're very kind."

"Since this is your first meeting, will there be an initiation? Will you have to kiss a pig or something?"

"I sincerely hope not."

"I'm asking because lips that kiss pig lips will never kiss mine," Meg said.

"I'll remember that," I said. "No pigs."

"And why do they wear the funny little hats?" She picked the cylindrical chapeau up off the bed and giggled.

I flipped the tie into a tasteful half-windsor and slid the knot up against my Adam's apple. "The leopard-skin fez has an ancient literary history dating back to film star Peter Lorre when he portrayed Morocco Mole in the television classic *Secret Squirrel*.

She stood up behind me, plopped the hat onto my head and surveyed the image in the mirror. "You look like a Shriner on safari," she decided. "The tassel is kinda cute, though."

"You're just jealous because the Athenaeum Society is men-only."

"Well," she admitted, "quite frankly, I am a little surprised."

"It's tradition," I said. "When this society started, women were not thought of as 'literary.'"

Meg nodded. "That's true. Well, if you don't count Emily Dickinson, Christina Rosetti, Elizabeth Barrett Browning, Dorothy Parker, or the Brontë sisters."

"Right."

5

"Also Jane Austen, George Eliot, Harriet Beecher Stowe, Louisa May Alcott..."

"My point exactly," I said, grinning.

Meg rested a finger on her chin. "Mary Shelley, Edith Wharton, Willa Cather, Kate Chopin..."

"I get it," I said. "Maybe the guys just wanted a night off."

"That's probably it," Meg said. "So let me get this straight. You, Hayden Konig, get a secret invitation from the Society..."

"Yep. Delivered in the dead of night."

"Then you have to go to a meeting and present a paper..."

"No politics, no religion."

"Then they vote on you for membership. If you're accepted, you're required to attend once a month and listen to other geniuses like yourself read papers they've written."

"The order of the evening is dinner and drinks, then the presentation of papers followed by acerbic and witty comments, ribald insults, and general literary frivolity. Sounds like a great time, eh?"

"I'm beginning to understand why there aren't any women in your group."

"It's like one of your Bible studies, except fun."

"Right. So you'll be speaking on Raymond Chandler?"

"Absolutely."

Raymond Chandler is a hero of mine. So much in fact, that I had procured his 1939 Underwood No. 5 at an auction in anticipation that it might assist my own efforts in the noir detective genre. I'd also managed to purchase his hat—a gray fedora, vintage 1950. According to all available criticism, i.e., Meg and the rest of the church choir, neither of the acquisitions helped my writing proficiency one iota.

"You have some good quotes ready?"

"Yep." I fell into my best Bogart impression. "It was a cool day and very clear. You could see a long way—but not as far as Velma had gone."

"Nice." She spun me around and gave me a kiss. "I'm sure you'll be a big hit. I'm spending the night at Mother's. I'll expect a full report when I return."

•••

My paper on Raymond Chandler was where I'd put it, stacked neatly on the desk beside the old typewriter. I sat down and looked at the new piece of 24 lb. white bond I'd left rolled behind the platen. No sense in wasting some prime writing time, especially since I felt the muse beginning to rise. Besides, I had a few minutes.

I sat down, cracked my knuckles in the time-honored fashion of all bad writers, replaced the spotted fez with Raymond's fedora, and gave the keys a try.

On the dance floor half a dozen couples were throwing themselves around with the reckless abandon of a night watchman with arthritis.

That one was Chandler. It was a warm up. I smiled and went for one of my own.

Sophie opened her mouth in a silent scream as she dragged herself up the beach in agonizing slowness, the one-piece bathing suit peeling away from her supple body like the mottled skin of an overripe banana leaving her naked and defenseless as she cursed her misfortune that, despite her tireless efforts to raise herself above her lowly station in life, the salty water of the incoming tide was beginning to eat away her foot since she was, even after all the money spent on plastic surgery, orthodontics, and the best finishing schools, still a slug.
From: "Sophie Slug Goes to the Beach"

I was ready. I pulled the page from the typewriter, slipped it into the desk drawer, and fed a new piece of paper behind the roller, clicking the return until a few inches of bond peered out and summoned me to even greater heights of belletristic brilliance.

The Organist Wore Pumps

Genius.

Chapter 1

It was a cold Friday—a cold *Black* Friday, so called because it was on this day that all the shops around the country went into the black. Until the Friday after Thanksgiving, purportedly the busiest shopping day of the year, retailers tend to run in the red. All the profit to be realized for the year is made between Thanksgiving and Christmas. This was as true in the little village of St. Germaine, North Carolina, as it was in the metropolis of Boone, our nearest neighbor of any size.

Each of the merchants located on the downtown square in St. Germaine had signed an agreement with the town. It was called "the Deal." The Deal stated that if you owned, rented, or operated a shop within the historic district of St. Germaine, you would decorate for Christmas. And by "decorate," it was understood that by the Friday after Thanksgiving, each shop would be adorned to the extent that Martha Stewart herself might swoon from the vapors brought on by the sheer beauty of the bedecking. The Deal was also one of the reasons that from Black Friday until Christmas Eve there was not a parking place to be found within a half-mile of the downtown square. Shoppers were shoulder to shoulder at the cash registers, buying everything they could get their hands on: quilts and mountain crafts, jams and jellies, books and knickknacks.

Even the town curmudgeon, Dr. Ian Burch, PhD, saw the wisdom of the Deal and festooned his Appalachian Music Shoppe with as many garlands as he could manage before the pine pollen lodged inside his enormous beak and turned his long snipe nose into a glowing trumpet. He'd taken to the bed, but his erstwhile employee, Flori Cabbage, a woman just as strange in her way as Dr. Burch was in his, finished the decorating and was now madly selling all manner of Renaissance musical instruments to shoppers who, all of a sudden, had a desperate desire to give zinks, shawms, serpents, sacbuts, and bladder-pipes as gifts to the in-laws for Christmas. Flori was in her early mids—that is, somewhere between twenty-five and forty-five—although it would be difficult to pin her age down with any accuracy at all. She wore no make-up, but had flawless pale skin, and brown hair worn in a tight bun. Her flowing skirts hung down well below her knees. Long socks or tights, Birkenstocks and oversized sweaters completed her daily ensemble. Had she been wallpaper, she would have been the beige stuff in your grandmother's bathroom.

In St. Germaine, between Thanksgiving and Christmas, you could sell a refrigerator to an Eskimo—full price, including the in-the-door ice-maker, the anti-walrus lock, and the three-year service agreement.

On this Friday—Black Friday—getting a seat at the Slab Café was impossible. Even our special, reserved table had been usurped by tourists. Nancy and I had wandered in, looked at the patrons waiting for an available table, turned on our heels and walked back into the sunshine.

"What do you think?" Nancy asked, squinting against the brightness of the morning. "Holy Grounds?"

St. Germaine's Christian coffee shop had opened back up in October under new management after the previous owners had left town. The Slab Café was our eatery of choice, ably run and owned by Pete Moss. It was the quintessential town diner, complete with a black and white checkered linoleum floor, red vinyl table cloths on the four-toppers, an eating counter adorned with several covered cake plates, each clear glass globe advertising a different dessert-du-jour. There were eight stools fixed to the floor in front of the counter and a refrigerated pie case on the far wall. Three waitresses hustled the meals from the kitchen to the tables in short order and turned over the tables with great efficiency, but it wasn't for us. Not this morning.

"Holy Grounds sounds okay," I grumbled. "I guess I can get a bagel or something."

"At least the coffee's good, Chief," said Nancy. She took her sunglasses out of her breast pocket, put them on, then squared her shoulders and rested her hands on her hips, taking the time to adjust her gun belt and nudge the butt of her pistol out of the way. Nancy was always in uniform while on duty. I wasn't. In the winter, I tended toward flannel shirts, khakis and a leather jacket that Meg had gotten me for my birthday. My own weapon, like Nancy's, was a 9mm Glock. Unlike Nancy, however, I kept it in the organ bench at St. Barnabas Church.

I kept it there originally for the rats in the choir loft. But then the church had burned and been rebuilt, and there weren't any more rats. Still, I'm a creature of habit and as long as the tenors knew the gun was there, I felt as if I had a little more control over the choir. Being the part-time organist and choir director at St. Barnabas was the profession I'd trained for. Police Chief was the job I'd stumbled into when I realized that church musicians were paid just slightly more than janitors. Actually, a second Master's degree in criminal justice didn't do my vitae any harm when it came time to hire the new police chief of St. Germaine some ten or so years ago. As far as my salary at the church was concerned, I didn't really need to worry about that either. I'd made a couple million selling a little invention I'd come up with to the phone company some years ago. Meg Farthing, my investment counsellor, brokered that sum into quite a few million, then got me out just before the market crashed. I was so grateful, I married her. She was so grateful she decided to take my name. Mrs. Hayden Konig. The most beautiful woman in Watauga County.

Nancy and I walked across Sterling Park, currently, being late November, devoid of the leaves that formed the canopy over the park in the spring and summer. The lawn crew had gathered the piles of leaves a few weeks ago and now the landscape was clean and bare and tourist-friendly. The park gazebo had been covered in white Christmas lights which, along with the streetlights boasting garlands and bows, would light the entire park as soon as the sun settled behind Grandfather Mountain. As we walked across the stiff, brown grass, I waved to Billy Hixon, the Junior Warden of St. Barnabas, who was on his knees cleaning up the flower beds in front of the church. He waved back, then buried his head back into the garden, yanking up dead chrysanthemums and flinging them behind him like a badger gone berserk.

We walked beside the church and down Maple Street, past the flower shop, and up the steps of Mrs. McCarty's old house, now the Holy Grounds Coffee Shop. The turn-of-the-century house was an American Foursquare, two stories tall, covered with white clapboard, and freshly painted. The porch stretched across the front of the house and welcomed customers into one of the four rooms downstairs (each one square, of course), while the upstairs had been converted into living quarters for the new owners—Biff and Kylie Moffit. The Moffits had moved to town after buying the coffee shop, and from all appearances, were now doing well. I hoped they didn't spend all the proceeds. January and February were pretty slim in St. Germaine and business wouldn't really begin picking up again until May. Biff and Kylie had joined St. Barnabas, being cradle Episcopalians, but had declined my invitation to join the choir. It was an invitation I offered everyone, being magnanimous in my musical mission, but the choir was pretty good and newcomers who decided to join us either held their own or followed the leaders without too much trouble. Either way I came out looking like I knew what I was doing and our choir hovered around twenty-two on any given Sunday. Thirty if everyone showed up, which they never did.

"Good morning, Hayden," called Kylie, when she saw me come in. "Morning, Lieutenant Parsky."

"It's the uniform," I said, as we made our way to the only free table and seated ourselves. "You're the authority figure. I'm more accessible. Sort of like Andy Griffith and Barney."

Nancy rolled her eyes. "They both wore uniforms. Not only that, they were both called by their first names. Anyway, I think you're much smarter than Barney."

"No, no," I said. "I'm Andy. *You're* Barney."

Nancy snorted. "In your dreams."

Holy Grounds was doing a brisk breakfast business on this Friday morning, even though the menu consisted only of bagels and muffins. But, in their defense, the coffee was excellent and you could get your bagel toasted if you wanted.

"What can I get for you?" asked Kylie, brandishing an order pad, at the same time pulling a pen from behind her ear. Kylie, like her husband, Biff, was in her mid-thirties, but unlike her husband, didn't dress like a perpetual yuppie. Biff was spotted all summer around town with his tennis sweater draped over his shoulders. Kylie preferred comfortable work clothes. Her dark hair was pulled back and held with a scrunchie.

"Hmm," I said. "I think I'll have a Norwegian omelette. Yes. An omelette and a side of pancakes. With the Hollandaise hash browns."

"Right," said Kylie, scribbling on her pad. "Coffee and a bagel."

"With extra blueberry syrup," I said.

"Toasted," scribbled Kylie.

"Maybe a plum duff for dessert. And don't skimp on the rum sauce this time."

"Cream cheese. Got it."

"Same," said Nancy.

Kylie disappeared into the kitchen.

"Heard from Dave?" I asked. Dave Vance was the third member of the St. Germaine constabulary, charged mainly with handling phone calls and donut acquisition.

"He's on the way back. He called me this morning from Roanoke. I'd say he's a couple hours out."

Kylie returned to our table with two toasted bagels on small paper plates and a couple of cups of coffee in cardboard cups with hard plastic lids. She smiled and dropped the bill in the middle of the table, then headed for a table of new customers.

"We've got to get our table back at the Slab," Nancy grumbled. "This just ain't right."

"Maybe we could commandeer a table under the Patriot Act," I suggested, taking a sip of the coffee. "Hey, this is really good coffee."

"Well, it ought to be for two bucks plus tax! But, paper cups?"

"I'll talk to Pete," I said. "Maybe we can make a standing reservation at the Slab for every morning at 8:30."

"Pete doesn't take reservations."

"Patriot Act," I answered with a grin.

•••

The church office was closed for the holiday weekend, but I stopped by to view the activity in the nave. The First Sunday of Advent was two days away and the Altar Guild was in full swing. Bev Greene, our parish administrator, had conscripted the services of Mr. Christopher, the foremost interior decorator that Watauga County had to offer. This was quite a coup considering that, according to the local grapevine, Mr. Christopher was about to be offered his own show on HGTV.

Our priest was there too, lending a hand as well as moral support. Dr. Gaylen Weatherall had become our priest three years ago but then had been elected bishop and moved to Colorado. Last summer, chiefly due to her father's failing health, she gave up her exalted position and returned to St. Germaine as the shepherd of the St. Barnabas flock. Bev was quick to point out that, even though she'd retired from the episcopate, she was still a bishop and entitled to all the rights and privileges thereto appertaining. These rights and privileges, as far as we could tell, consisted of wearing the silly hat and cape during feast days. Still, she was the Right Reverend Rector of St. Barnabas and everyone loved her. Well, almost everyone.

"Morning, Hayden," called Elaine Hixon. The Altar Guild had things well in hand, flowers and baby's breath in abundance, placed artistically among the fir garlands and pine boughs.

Billy, having finished with the mums in the front flower beds, was now directing the hanging of our new Advent wreath.

"Two years ago today," said Billy, looking up at Elaine's greeting and seeing me come down the aisle.

"I remember," I said.

"Elaine reminded me this morning. I'd sort of forgotten. It doesn't seem like two years have gone by since the church burned to the ground."

"No, it doesn't," I agreed. "But I'm looking forward to our first Christmas back."

We'd consecrated our new building last May, eighteen months after the fire. St. Barnabas had been rebuilt to look almost identical to the 1904 structure that had been lost. The changes that had been made were improvements to the structure and the infrastructure— things most people wouldn't notice unless they looked closely, or were in the know. Even the windows had been reproduced as faithfully as possible. One of the improvements the building committee had planned for was the hanging of this huge Advent wreath. The wreath was eight feet in diameter and constructed of welded steel, painted a dark red and covered with greenery. The four candles that jutted from the candle holders, located equidistant around the edge of the wreath, were oversized as well—three purple candles and one rose-colored, all about eighteen inches tall and as big around as the thick end of a baseball bat. The wreath would hang from a cable, eighteen feet above the floor, that had been attached to a winch in the ceiling and was controlled by a locked switch in the pulpit. The wreath could be slowly lowered and raised and the candles lit and extinguished for every service during Advent, Christmas Eve, Christmas Day, and the two Sundays before Epiphany. The whole effect would be rather spectacular.

"The tree looks great," I said, looking at the ten-foot-tall blue spruce sparkling in the corner of the chancel.

Our "Jesse Tree" had been set up behind the baptismal font and was covered with small white lights. The Jesse Tree looked, to the casual observer, almost exactly like a Christmas tree. But, as good Episcopalians, we knew instinctively that it was just plain wrong to acknowledge any part of Christmas before December 24th at the earliest, so we did what any self-respecting religious organization would do under similar circumstances: we gave the Christmas tree a different name and pretended we put it up for Advent. As long as no one asked any questions, we were fine. "Don't ask, don't tell." That was our Advent motto. Well, that and "Come, Lord Jesus."

Of course, there was still the internal struggle between the Chrismonites and the Jessetonians, each sect vying for control over the ornamentation of said evergreen. Both factions advocated the

13

use of Christian symbols for decoration, but the Chrismonites were staunch supporters of the tried and true white Styrofoam cutouts decorated with gold beads and bric-a-brac. The Jessetonians held for more natural adornments: fruit, small stuffed birds, and organic ornaments made by the children. The two groups would watch each other carefully through narrowed eyes until the Second Sunday of Advent, the traditional "decking of the Jesse Tree," neither making a move, but numbering their foes and marshaling their forces for the showdown, i.e., the vestry meeting on the second Thursday of December. It was there the final decision would be made, and God have mercy on us all.

"How strong is that wire?" asked Gaylen, looking askance at the wreath, now rotating slowly two feet above the floor. Our priest was a very attractive woman in her late fifties, tall and slender with white hair that rested gently on her shoulders, and an easy smile.

"It's airline cable," said Billy. "Eighth-inch. It'll hold fourteen hundred pounds."

"And how much does that thing weigh?" asked Gaylen.

"Two hundred. Maybe two-fifty," said Billy. "Don't worry. It'll give you a lot of warning before it snaps."

"That's very comforting," said Gaylen, with a light shudder.

"Luckily, I'll be in the choir loft," I said. "And even if people are kneeling for communion, they're still a good ten feet away. You, on the other hand, have to traipse back and forth between the altar and the rail. It's you, and the Eucharistic Ministers, that have to worry."

"And our new deacon."

Elaine, Bev, Billy, Mr. Christopher, myself, and the rest of the Altar Guild all stopped dead and looked at her.

"Deacon?" said Bev.

Gaylen sighed heavily. "Bishop O'Connell asked if I'd take him on. I told him I would. It's only for six months. He passed his General Ordination Exams, graduated from seminary, and was ordained as a deacon. Now he has to do hands-on parish training under the guidance of an experienced priest. That's me."

"When's he coming?" asked Bev.

"He'll be here next week. Wednesday, I think. His other assignment fell through. That church couldn't manage his salary."

"Hmm," said Bev. "And do *we* have to pay him?"

"Well, it's not that much," said Gaylen. "Eight thousand for the six-months, plus a housing allowance." She shrugged. "Sorry. There wasn't much I could do. Everyone in the diocese knows St. Barnabas' financial situation."

St. Barnabas' financial situation could be summed up thusly: we had a new church building, a new pipe organ, no debt, a few income properties, and fifteen million dollars in the bank—more or less. The large amount of cash was due to a seventy-five-year-old bond that, through many a hook and crook, had finally been awarded to the church with all attached interest. Then there was last summer's windfall of the uncut diamonds found in the excavation of the new building. Another mere two hundred thousand, but as Ruby, Meg's mother, pointed out, "every little bit helps."

"Well," said Elaine, a look of apprehension crossing her face, "I guess we're stuck then. And besides, what harm can a deacon do?"

Chapter 2

Old Man Frost, as he was known to almost all the residents of St. Germaine, had been born a Catholic. He'd met Beulah Polk, the third daughter of a dour Southern Baptist preacher, at an ice cream social in 1948. After expressing his interest in courting the fair maid, Hiram Frost was invited to Sunday dinner at the Polk house, where he was strongly encouraged, during a stern heart-to-heart with the Reverend Polk, to disavow the Catholic faith and all its idolatrous trappings, accept Jesus into his heart, and be baptized in the river in accordance with the scriptures.

Hiram, not really a religious person to begin with, had no problem with the decision. Beulah was voluptuous, and, as any eighteen-year-old male knows, lust trumps religion nine times out of ten. He and Beulah were married after a short courtship (shorter than the good Reverend Polk might have foreseen), and the first of their six children was born six months later.

Although Hiram was only perfunctorily devout, Beulah took her beliefs very seriously. All the children were raised in the faith, which was, truth be told, quite a bit stricter in the 1950s and '60s than it is today: no dancing, no movies, no tobacco, no pants on women, no skinny dipping in the creek, and definitely no alcoholic consumption in any of its diabolical forms.

It was interesting therefore, when I accompanied Nancy to the auction of the Frost homestead, to see, sitting among Hiram's possessions dotting the front yard, the octogenarian's collection of shot glasses, Elvis records, and meerschaum pipes.

Beulah had died five years ago after a long illness. Hiram not only survived his wife, but also survived three of his children. The remaining three hadn't been back to St. Germaine for thirty years and, according to Diana Terry, who'd been helping Hiram with his shopping, had no desire to see the old man ever again.

Hiram refinanced his farm to pay for his wife's medical care. It was a bargain, said the loan officer: no money down, a minimal monthly payment with hardly any interest, then a balloon payment four long years down the road. When that came due, Hiram could simply refinance with the bank at another low, low rate and everything would be just fine. It didn't work out that way.

The bank had foreclosed on Hiram's farm three weeks ago. Nancy and Dave, in accordance with the court order, had come out to the farm and removed Hiram from the premises. They drove him to the Ridgecrest Senior Care Center in Boone and checked him in. He died the next day.

The bank padlocked every door and window and put the farm and all of its contents up for auction. Diana knew nothing about it until the bank had already foreclosed and Old Man Frost was lying in state at Swallow's Funeral Home. It turned out that Hiram had been tossing the bank notices into the potbellied stove.

Now everything on the property, including the old clapboard house, was being sold to the highest bidder on the front steps of the homestead by Highland Auctions.

The auction had been going on for quite a while by the time we drove up. Bob Montenegro was a good auctioneer and had already sold Hiram's car (a 1974 Gremlin), a box of tools, several pieces of furniture, and the potbellied stove. Nancy and I stood in the back and watched the people as well as the proceedings. Looking over the crowd, it seemed as if we knew almost everyone.

Billy Hixon had packed up the box of tools he'd just purchased and was carrying it to his truck.

Diana Terry, dressed in jeans, a sweater, and a worn barn jacket, was looking at Mrs. Frost's collection of hats. In addition to helping some of the elderly with their shopping and other chores, Diana volunteered at the library, at one of the thrift shops in Boone, and for all the Summer Bible Schools in town. She didn't have a full-time job and was rumored to be an ex-nun, although she always answered any and all inquiries about her previous profession with a sly smile. Far from being a stereotypical old, grumpy ex-sister, Diana was in her early forties and very attractive. It was Pete's considered opinion that, as a smokin' hot nun, she'd been hit on by a randy cardinal and ended up with a big settlement (and a non-disclosure agreement) from the Catholic church. I didn't disagree.

Skeeter Donalson was chatting loudly with Arlen Pearl and pointing to an old guitar with no strings. Annie Cooke had taken a break from her duties at the Ginger Cat. Several choir members were there and saluted us with a wave before turning their attention back to the auctioneer. Calvin Denton, editor of *The St. Germaine Tattler*, had run a full-page ad advertising the sale, and so, when we arrived, there were probably two hundred people gathered on the front lawn.

Bob had just brought down his gavel on an antique Leica camera, selling it for the princely sum of nine dollars. Hiram Frost's collection of shot glasses was next.

"A collection of thirty shot glasses," said Bob into his portable microphone. "We're going to sell these as a lot. Do I have a bid of twenty-five dollars?"

No takers.

"Ten dollars then. Do I have ten?"

Still no takers.

"Five? Do I have five?"

"Two dollars," yelled Arlen.

"Two dollars. I have two dollars. Do I have three?" Bob went into his patter, but two dollars was as good as he could do and Arlen was soon the proud owner of thirty shot glasses.

"I can sell 'em on Ebay for two or three bucks apiece," Arlen whispered to me as he walked by. "I'm gonna make a fortune!"

We watched as the auctioneer made his way through some silverware, pots and pans, a stuffed boar's head, and the guitar that Skeeter managed to procure for $14.50.

"Lot 37," called Bob. "Three cases of wine. Vintage 1998. A little dusty, but I'm sure it's still delicious."

"What was Old Man Frost doing with three cases of wine?" I said.

"Not to mention shot glasses," said Nancy. "You know, I wouldn't be surprised to see fifty years of vintage Playboys show up in a cardboard box."

"He would have gotten rid of something like that," I said.

"He didn't have time," said Nancy. "Dave and I frog-marched him right out of there. That's what the judge ordered."

"We're selling these bottles as a lot," said Bob. "We don't have all day, so you're bidding on all three cases."

"Ten bucks," called Skeeter, not giving Bob a chance to start up before jumping in. Thirty-six bottles of wine for ten dollars was a deal that even Skeeter couldn't pass up.

"Hang on," said Bob, holding up one of the bottles. "I'm not done yet. This here says Chateau Petrus. And it's aged for over ten years! It's Italian."

"You need any wine?" asked Nancy.

I shook my head. "Nah. I've got a cellarful. Bud keeps me hooked up."

Bud McCollough was the eldest son of the McCollough clan and had a gift for wine snobbery that was only surpassed by his actual knowledge of the vineyard arts. He was a voracious reader and his encyclopedic knowledge of wine and wine lore was augmented by the finest nose and taste buds in the state. At eighteen, Bud still wasn't old enough to actually buy the wine, but that didn't stop him from posting a wine blog and offering suggestions when asked. I was surprised, though, when I felt a tug on my arm, and turned to find Bud standing behind me.

"Hi, Bud. You home for Thanksgiving?"

"Yep. I have another couple weeks till Christmas break. Listen, you want to form a partnership?"

"What's up?"

"I have a bid of ten dollars," said Bob, over his microphone. I saw Skeeter give Arlen a high-five.

"Tell you later. Bid on this," whispered Bud. "I'll tell you when to stop." He disappeared into the crowd.

"One hundred dollars," called another voice.

"I have one hundred dollars," said Bob. "One hundred! Do I have two?"

"One-fifty," I called.

"One-seventy," called a third voice, a woman. It was Annie Cooke.

"Gol darnit!" said Skeeter.

"Two hundred dollars," said Voice Two. I looked over at Annie. She shrugged and shot me a smile. Too rich.

I saw Bud walk unobtrusively by the case of wine and glance down at the open box then disappear into the crowd once more.

"Two hundred dollars!" called Bob. "Do I have two-fifty?" Bob had sensed an opening and decided to leap ahead with the bidding. "Thirty-six bottles of Eye-talian wine. That's less than five bucks a bottle!"

"Two-fifty," I called. Nancy looked over at me, a questioning look on her face.

"Three-hundred," called Voice Two.

Bob looked over at the third bidder, but Annie shook her head. I saw Bud reappear on the skirt of the crowd. He gave me a nod.

I flashed a signal to Bob and he caught my meaning.

"Three-fifty! I have three-fifty from the Chief. Do I have four?"

"Four," said the other bidder. The crowd had retreated just a bit, to make sure none of their gestures were misinterpreted as a bid. I could see the bidder, but didn't recognize him. Someone from out of town. He was taller than most of the folks, maybe a shade over six feet, early thirties, with brown hair and a beard. He was wearing a western style sheepskin coat, jeans and cowboy boots. Expensive.

I looked for Bud, but he'd moved.

"Do I have four-fifty?" asked Bob, looking over at me.

I gave him the high sign and spotted Bud. He'd moved behind the other bidder so it would look as though I was eyeing the competition rather than getting signals from my own personal sommelier.

"One thousand dollars!" said the bidder. The crowd erupted with excitement and it took Bob a moment to calm everyone down.

"One thousand dollars!" said Bob. "Whoo-ee! That's more money than I spend on wine in a year!"

Bud gave me another nod.

"And five hundred," I called.

"What are you doing?" hissed Nancy, sounding alarmed. I ignored her.

"Two thousand," called the other bidder. Bud nodded again.

"And five," I called.

"Twenty-five hundred dollars!" said Bob, not believing what he was hearing, but ever the professional. "Two thousand five hundred dollars! Do I have three?"

The other bidder had taken out his cell phone and was trying to dial a number. It was a forlorn hope. The cell service in this part of the county was almost nonexistent. After a moment, he flipped it shut and put it back in his pocket.

"Four thousand dollars," he called. Now the assembly went quiet. Bob was quiet as well.

Bud, still behind the other bidder but well into the crowd, held up five fingers, closed his hand and put up another five. Had I seen right?

"Ten thousand dollars," I said.

Chapter 3

It was a good ten miles from the police station in downtown St. Germaine up to my cabin, and, winding mountain roads being what they were, it took about half an hour to get there. I always enjoyed the drive.

My cabin began its life as an actual two-story log cabin and this structure still formed the nucleus of the house, but it had now been relegated to library status rather than sheltering the eleven people who had occupied the twenty by twenty foot home in the 1840s when it was built. The rest of my "cabin," as it was known in town, was a study in mountain chic and a testament to what you can do with enough money. Set on two hundred mountain acres, it was home to Meg and me as well as Baxter, our oversized, overly-friendly canine companion, and a semi-tame barn owl named Archimedes, who came and went as he liked.

The leaves had long since changed from their summer green to autumn reds and golds, and then dropped, leaving the branches of the hardwoods stark and bare against the graying sky. Evening came on quickly in late November and, here in the Appalachians, by five o'clock dusk was upon us. As I crossed onto the property the lights of my old truck picked up two foxes dancing across the drive. I drove up the steep hill, crested the mountain and headed down into the valley, following a winding road that at every curve afforded distant views, in winter at least, of the house, glowing like a beacon in the smoky eventide. Judging from the amber glow and figuring the number of lights that might be needed to achieve such illumination, I knew Meg would be home. I might even get lucky in the supper department.

Baxter boomed out a few of his basso barks as I drove up, having seen me drive the very same pick-up truck to the house every evening for all of his seven years, but presumably sounding the alarm out of some doggy need to stay in practice in case a real burglar happened to show up. He met me as I got out, tail wagging and with what might be a genuinely happy look on his face. Baxter was getting a little age on him, but he still looked to be in his prime. At ninety pounds, he was a fine watchdog, and his long tricolored coat—mostly black with a white blaze down his muzzle and chest, and patches of rust on his head and legs—marked him as a poster dog for a Burmese Mountain Dog Best-in-Show advertisement. I reached down and scratched his ears for a moment, but he'd already said his hellos and so turned and bounded toward the kitchen door. He stood there, rigidly at attention and waited impatiently for me to let him inside. I knew what was next: I'd open the door, he'd shoot past me almost knocking me over, race across the polished wood floor, put on the brakes, slide under the kitchen table, and silently await whatever scraps happened to fall his way during dinner.

Meg wasn't in the kitchen, but Baxter didn't seem to be too disappointed. He could smell something cooking and was happy to lie in wait—he was the crocodile under the table, biding his time in silence, eyes darting to and fro, eyebrows rising and falling, his pink tongue just visible beneath his black nose and muzzle.

I peeked into the pot simmering on the stove. Soup. Creamy tomato and basil soup if I wasn't mistaken, and I seldom was, as far as soup was concerned. This one was one of Meg's specialties. I also suspected we'd be having grilled cheese sandwiches. There were several clues that pointed to this deduction including two loaves of homemade bread cooling on the counter, a selection of cheeses on the cutting board and a note saying, "Hayden, we're having grilled cheese sandwiches. Don't eat the cheese." I was, after all, a detective.

Meg and I had been married for two years. Although our anniversary was three days ago by the calendar, we'd decided that we would celebrate each year on Thanksgiving. A moveable feast to be sure, but easy to remember. Yesterday evening (Thanksgiving), Meg and I went over to the Hunters' Club outside Blowing Rock, the restaurant where I first asked Meg to marry me. Of course, she said "no," and continued to say "no" for a few years after that, but we still considered the Hunters' Club to be our own romantic corner. That it was open on Thanksgiving was a bonus. That Meg's mother, Ruby, had declined our invitation to join us was like double-coupon day at the Piggly Wiggly. We weren't even required to order turkey. Tradition now dictated that our Thanksgiving dinner include quail, broiled new potatoes, apple-walnut salad, and whatever else looked great on the menu. Dessert and coffee were followed by the presentation of the gifts. This year, I'd gotten Meg a necklace set with garnets, garnets being the second anniversary stone of choice. Meg had gone with tradition as well and chosen cotton for her gift— Turkish cotton, in the form of a monogrammed bathrobe. Nice.

"I'm in the living room. Don't eat the cheese."

"I read the note," I called. "Anyway, Baxter's guarding it."

"The soup won't be ready for about half an hour. Bring me a glass of wine, will you?"

"It would be my pleasure."

I found an opened bottle of Shiraz on the counter with a stopper protecting the six inches of wine that remained. I looked at the label—another one of Bud's recommendations—and recognized it from our last foray to our favorite wine shop in Asheville. I poured Meg a glass and found a bottle of Buffalo Bill's Pumpkin Ale in the fridge. It was Thanksgiving weekend after all.

Meg was relaxing on the sofa with her laptop. A fire was blazing in the hearth and I immediately recognized Mozart coming from the speakers of the stereo system: one of the early symphonies—not number 23, I knew that one—but late teens or early twenties I'd bet. Unmistakably Mozart.

I set Meg's glass on the coffee table in front of the leather sofa.

"Thanks," she said and raised her eyebrows. "Aren't you going to guess?"

"Hmm. Mozart symphony. Third movement obviously since it's a minuet. An early effort, I'd say." I cocked my head and listened for a moment. "Interesting. Flutes instead of oboes. He was probably sixteen or seventeen when he wrote it."

Meg gave me a smirk. "That just shows how wrong you can be."

"E-flat major. Probably the key of the symphony. I can't say for sure, but I'll guess Mozart Symphony Number 18 in E-Flat Major, third movement, written in 1772."

"Wrong, Mr. Know-it-all. It's Number 19."

"Rats. And how old was Mozart when he composed this work?"

Meg picked up the CD case, opened it, pulled out the liner notes, and read for just a second. "Well...you were right about the year, so he was sixteen. But that was easy. It says here he wrote six symphonies when he was sixteen."

I took a sip of my ale. "Still, I was within one."

"Yes," Meg admitted. "You're very good at this game. I'm going to have to get some CDs of my own. I think you have all these memorized."

"Hardly. There are six or seven thousand CDs in the stereo closet."

"Then how do you do it?"

"Styles, keys, periods, who lived when, what instruments were popular at the time. It's not that difficult."

"Ah, but one must know how to listen."

"That's true," I said.

"I mean, I can tell Beethoven from Bach, but I couldn't possibly pick out a Mozart symphony."

I laughed. "Mozart symphonies are easy. There are only forty-one and Mozart died young. Haydn's harder. There are a hundred and four of those."

"And how many are in E-flat?" asked Meg.

I pondered for a moment. "Eleven."

Meg looked surprised. "Really?"

"I have no idea, but I suspect I'm close. Mathematically, that would be about right considering the instruments of the time."

Meg typed for a moment on her computer, then looked up, astonished. "Eleven."

"There you go. See? It's easy."

•••

The phone rang and Meg headed for the kitchen to answer it—and, I hoped, to fashion some delicious grilled cheese concoctions. I took the opportunity to sit at Raymond Chandler's old typewriter, put on his fedora, and let my fingers play over the keys. It was easy enough to let myself pretend to be a writer. My title, looking resolute on the expensive rag paper, was beckoning and calling for even more bad prose. I was happy to oblige.

The Organist Wore Pumps
Chapter 1

It was a dark and stormy night: dark as chocolate, not milk chocolate, or even "dark" milk chocolate which is only slightly darker, but as dark as the dark-dark chocolate guano collected from the caves of the chockobat by the under-dwarves of Kooloobati and savored by Polynesian chiefs during the tempests that battered their tiny islands throughout monsoon season (hence "stormy"), but it wasn't nearly that bad, just a little breezy.

I sat back in my chair, lit a stogie, and studied the scotch singing love songs to me from the half-empty bottle on my desk. The knock at the door rattled it like an old wooden thing on three hinges with a knob about half-way up and a loose frosted window that told the inside story: EYE ETAVIRP. If you happened to be on the outside, the side that needed to hire a gumshoe, the side that had some ready cash, the sign read "PRIVATE EYE."

The knob turned, the door creaked, and trouble spilled into the room, trouble spelled with a capital D -- no, not "Drouble," even though that might make more sense except that "Drouble" isn't a word, so not really: capital D, small a, small m, small e (a Dame) but, come to think of it, a small d would work just as well since she wasn't proper at all and didn't even try to begin a sentence.

The dame that wiggled into my office was a definite thirty-six: as in years old, two out of three measurements, looks on a scale of 1 to 36, number of teeth, eye-bats per minute, shoe size in Japan, inches from her lips to mine, hours it would take me to fall in love, days our relationship would last and, finally, miles I couldn't come within as per the judge's restraining order.

"Hiya, Toots," I said. "What can I do for you?"

She smiled. I might have been wrong about the teeth. "I need someone. Someone I can trust."

"We all do, Sweetheart. We all do."

•••

I was feeling more than satisfied. My latest detective serial would find its way into the choir member's folders. They'd read it, as they had so many others, but this time my literary brilliance would finally be applauded. Well, I thought, not so much "applauded," as "disparaged with less ferocity than usual." I didn't mind. Genius is never recognized in its own time.

"Guess what I just heard?" asked Meg as I walked into the kitchen, smelling the delicious bouquet of fried bread and cheese. Baxter's tail thumped heavily on the heartpine floor.

"I can't imagine," I said. I finished the last of my Pumpkin Ale and set the empty bottle on the counter.

"I just heard from one of my spies that you spent ten thousand dollars on some bottles of wine. Vintage 1998."

I scratched my head sheepishly. "Well, yes. You might have heard that. Three cases of wine, actually. Thirty-six bottles. I'm told 1998 was a very good year."

"And you did this because...?"

"Bud told me to."

"If Bud told you to jump off a bridge..."

25

I laughed. "I haven't had a chance to talk to him. He sort of disappeared right after I won the bid."

"Hmm," said Meg, her visage narrowing. "I see."

"There's every reason to believe that it's a very good wine."

"I'm hoping so. Shall we have a bottle with dinner? This Shiraz is almost gone."

"I see no reason why not," I said. "I have the wooden boxes in the back of the truck. I'll go and fetch them."

"Let's see," said Meg. "Three cases, thirty-six bottles. By my reckoning, you spent just over two hundred seventy-five dollars a bottle."

Meg had always been good at math.

"Or, at three glasses per bottle, about ninety-two dollars a glass."

"I guess," I said. "But, in my defense, when I was bidding, I didn't really think about it in a 'per-glass' fashion."

"Apparently not," said Meg, with a heavy sigh of resignation. "Well, go out and get it. All I'm saying is, it better be good!"

•••

"Delicious," I said, finishing my sandwich and polishing off the crumbs on the ends of my fingers. "Just the thing for a cold night."

"Soup and a sandwich and Mozart and a three hundred dollar bottle of wine."

"Two seventy-five," I said.

"Yes. Two seventy-five. What was Old Man Frost doing with three cases of wine, anyway? I thought he was the town's leading teetotaler."

"Don't know," I said. "The other fellow who was bidding *really* wanted it, but didn't have the cash after I took him to ten thousand. He was trying to call someone, but there wasn't any service out at the Frost place."

"Did you know him?"

"Never saw him before."

"Well, I hope Bud knows what he's talking about."

Meg, never one to lick her fingers, even at a picnic, demurely wiped the crumbs from her hands, then dabbed the napkin to the corners of her mouth, first one side, then the other. Her black hair was loose and tousled and fell in soft waves to her shoulders, a sharp contrast to my old, light blue UNC sweatshirt she'd taken to wearing, a sweatshirt whose oversized neck-hole constantly dropped off one of her shoulders and slid down one arm. Very sexy. Her grey eyes sparkled. They always sparkled.

"How's Noylene?" I asked. "I haven't seen her for a few days."

"Well, let's see," said Meg. "Her baby's due at the end of December, but I haven't heard anything new."

"Do we know who the father is?"

"No, we do not."

Noylene Fabergé-Dupont, the early-morning waitress at the Slab Café and owner of "Noylene's Beautifery, an oasis of allurement, Dip-N-Tan by appointment only," had turned up pregnant last summer. Her husband at the time, as it turned out, was not the father.

Meg stared down at her soup. I knew that look.

"You *do* know," I said accusingly. "You know, and you're not telling."

"I don't know for sure," said Meg. "And anyway, I told Noylene I wouldn't tell, and I won't, so don't even ask."

"You don't know for sure because...?"

"Because Noylene doesn't know for sure."

"But she's *pretty* sure."

"Yes."

"Ninety-nine percent sure."

Meg shrugged. "I suppose so."

"And you're not telling."

"No."

"Okay," I said, "but this silence is gonna cost you."

"Another sandwich?"

"You wish," I said, with a wink and my best salacious smile.

Meg winked back.

Chapter 4

"I hate him," said Georgia from behind the counter of Eden Books. "He's pretentious, bombastic, and arrogant."

"Not to mention magniloquent," I added.

"Huh?" said Georgia. "You haven't even met him."

"I know. I just like to say 'magniloquent.' How many opportunities does one get? Whom, by the way, are we hating? We're not even a full week into Advent yet."

Georgia sniffed. "Our new deacon. I just met him yesterday and already I can tell you there's going to be trouble. His name is Donald." She pronounced his last name carefully. "Moo-shraht."

"Moo-shraht? What is he? Pakistani?"

"Not as far as I can tell. He's a white guy from Winston-Salem. He spells it 'Mushrat,' but apparently he's changed the way it's pronounced."

I smiled, picked up a copy of Dan Brown's latest book and scanned the back cover. "Donald Mushrat?" I didn't bother with Donald's preferred pronunciation. Neither, I suspected, would anyone else.

"Moo-shraht," Georgia corrected. "Gaylen doesn't like him either."

"How do you know that?" I asked.

"Oh, I can tell. He wanted us to address him as Father Mushrat, I mean Moo-shraht, but Gaylen said no, he wasn't a priest yet. So he's Deacon Mushrat." Georgia finally dropped the phonemic affectation as well. "He didn't care for that, but there wasn't much he could do. She also made him stop smoking his pipe inside the church."

"Tweed jacket?" I asked.

"Nope. Tan micro-suede sport coat. Sandals with dark socks. Big hair."

"Even worse," I said. "We could deal with a tweed guy. Micro-suede...well...I just don't know. How about the tobacco?"

"Peach flavored."

"Oh, man..."

•••

Nancy and Dave had already commandeered our table at the back of the Slab Café by the time I walked in. I'd already had breakfast, but a mid-morning snack was not out of the question, so a few of the flapjacks from the stack of buckwheat pancakes in the middle of the table quickly found their way onto my plate.

"Coffee?" grunted Noylene perfunctorily, as she waddled by and filled my cup. Since my mouth was full, I didn't answer, but managed a nod of appreciation.

"If she gets much bigger," said Dave, "she won't be able to fit between the tables."

"I'll make the aisles wider," said Pete Moss, plopping down in the last chair at our table. "I can't keep a good waitress. They all want to go to nursing school."

Pete was my old college roommate. Now he was an aging hippie, in looks anyway. His gray ponytail and earring complemented the Hawaiian shirts and faded jeans that comprised his daily uniform, the season notwithstanding. Of course, in colder weather he added his old fatigue jacket, left over from his time in the Army band. He played a mean jazz sax, or used to. Now he owned the Slab, several other properties in town and until a couple of years ago was mayor of St. Germaine. He'd been dethroned by Cynthia Johnsson, current mayor, waitress, and professional belly dancer. Even so, Pete and Cynthia had been an item since the last election and, bearing in mind Pete's track record with relationships, i.e., two ex-wives and a string of girlfriends that included almost every single woman in St. Germaine under the age of fifty, this one had gone surprisingly smoothly.

"Isn't Cynthia working this morning?" asked Nancy.

"She's at some meeting in Greensboro," said Pete. "Small town mayor something-or-other."

Pauli Girl McCollough came by the table and filled Pete's coffee cup on her way to deliver some country ham and eggs over easy to a four-topper by the window.

"Just Noylene and Pauli Girl this morning," said Pete. "And Noylene won't be much good in a couple of weeks. She says she's going to work up until the baby's born, but I can't see it. She's already as big as a house. I give her ten days."

"She say who the father is yet?" asked Dave.

Pete shook his head. "Not to me."

Noylene Fabergé-Dupont's husband, Wormy Dupont, had been sent to federal prison six months ago for murdering Russ Stafford. There were many reasons for this crime, of course, but the one that Wormy cited in his arraignment was "jealousy." Noylene was pregnant and Wormy was sterile, thanks to various and sundry medical experiments in the '80s for which Wormy was paid by the government a grand total of $134.52. Noylene didn't know Wormy's situation, and when she turned up pregnant, well, Wormy had a feeling that Russ Stafford was the fox in the henhouse and acted accordingly. Whether Russ was responsible for the impending Fabergé-Dupont heir or whether he wasn't, Noylene wouldn't say. She'd been very closed-lipped on the subject, except for telling Meg, and I wasn't about to bring *that* up.

"Lovely service last Sunday, Hayden," called Joyce Cooper, one of the St. Barnabas parishioners enjoying a late breakfast two tables over. Joyce was also on the worship committee.

"Thanks," I called back. "Once we sing *Lo, He Comes With Clouds Descending*, we know that Advent is definitely upon us."

"My favorite hymn."

"Maybe mine, too. This week, anyway. Hey, won't I be seeing you again in a few minutes over at the church?"

"Oh, shoot," said Joyce, making a wry face. "Worship meeting. I know I usually go, but I have a doctor's appointment this morning. Tell Gaylen where I am, will you?"

"Sure," I said. "But I'm not sure you want to miss this one. This is the pre-meeting before the Jesse Tree showdown."

Joyce laughed. "I always like that one. Besides, I wanted to meet our new deacon. I heard he's already claimed an office."

"Deacon Mushrat," I said.

"*What?*" said Nancy.

"You heard me the first time," I said. "Deacon Mushrat."

"I know I should be there," said Joyce, "but I can't cancel."

"I understand," I said. "In fact, I myself feel a doctor's appointment coming on."

Joyce laughed and went back to her breakfast.

"Deacon Mushrat," said Pete. "Great name. I like him already."

"You'd be the only one so far," I said.

"Do y'all need some more syrup?" asked Pauli Girl on her way back to the kitchen with a tray full of dirty dishes. She pronounced it "seerp," and gave Dave a wink he could hang his hat on.

"Wouldn't mind," said Dave with a big grin.

"Be right back with it," said Pauli Girl, smiling back just as big.

As soon as she turned, Nancy slugged Dave in the arm. Hard. "Don't you even think about it," she growled. "She's seventeen." Nancy and Dave had been an on-again-off-again couple for a few years now. They were currently off-again.

30

"I wasn't thinking about anything," said Dave, the picture of innocence. "Except maybe more pancakes."

Pauli Girl was the middle child of Ardine McCollough, a slender, hickory-hard mountain woman who hid more scars than she'd ever let on. Bud, our backward and bashful wine connoisseur, was the eldest. The McCollough children were fathered by P.D. McCollough, a no-account, abusive, all around bad egg who met his fate, some say, at the hands of his dear wife. The only things that P.D. ever gave his kids, besides the occasional black eye, were their names— and he named them for the thing dearest to his heart: beer. Three kids, three beers. Bud, Pauli Girl, and the youngest, Moose-Head. Moosey.

Pauli Girl was, far and away, the best looking girl in St. Germaine and had no shortage of boys flocking around her at any social function. This was her last year at the high school, but she'd enrolled in a work-study program and so was allowed to work twenty hours a week during school hours. She put in at least another twenty after school and on weekends. I knew she helped her mother with living expenses, but I was also pretty sure she was socking away everything she could. Pauli Girl would be leaving at the end of the year. I didn't know if she'd try college, or a job, or even a tech school, but I knew one thing: she wouldn't be back.

"We appreciate you holding the table for us, Pete," Nancy said.

"No problem," said Pete. "Besides, Hayden said he'd call the health department on me if I didn't."

"It's the Patriot Act," I said with a shrug. "I had no choice."

"Hmm," said Pete.

•••

When Gaylen Weatherall had first come to St. Barnabas as rector, I had agreed to go to two staff and/or worship meetings a month, two more than I was accustomed to attending. When she'd been elected Bishop of Colorado, I was off the hook. Now that she was back, I found myself, once again, corralled into the Thursday morning meeting.

When I walked in, Marilyn, the church secretary, was at the head of the conference table in her customary seat. Gaylen was sitting to her right, pouring coffee for herself, Marilyn and Elaine Hixon. Kimberly Walnut, our Director of Christian Formation, was across the table sipping a can of Red Bull. Bev Greene walked in

31

behind me, and following her was Deacon Mushrat, a stocky man of medium height, his blonde hair just about the desired length for starring in an 80s music video. Georgia was right about the micro-suede jacket, although the one he was currently wearing was green with dark brown elbow patches. His black socks were clearly visible through the open toes of his sandals. His pants were tan polyester Sans-a-Belt.

Now, make no mistake, I have nothing against the expando-pant industry. In fact, I myself have several pair of expando-pants in my wardrobe—cotton twill dress slacks that go from a size 38 waist to a size 44 in an instant, thanks to an ingenious inventor named Kenny J. Pierce of El Paso, Texas, who decided that middle-aged men needed maternity pants just as much as pregnant women. Having said that, Sans-a-Belt was a different animal entirely, being basically a pair of plastic pants with a built-in girdle. We aficionados of the expando-pant bristled whenever we were lumped together with the Sans-a-Belts.

Gaylen greeted us all and poured coffee for Bev and me when she'd finished with the first round. Donald Mushrat sat down at the other end of the table from Marilyn and turned his cup upside down on the table as if he were at a restaurant. He carried a clipboard with a yellow legal pad that, once he was seated, he dropped in front of him from a height of about six inches, bouncing it off the top of the wooden table with a loud rattle. Then he reached into his inside jacket pocket and pulled out a fountain pen, all the while smiling benignly at Gaylen without saying a word.

There was a chill in the air. Gaylen Weatherall and Donald Mushrat were not on friendly terms and he hadn't even been at St. Barnabas for twenty-four hours.

"Let's get started, shall we?" said Gaylen. "We've got a lot to talk about, including our stewardship campaign. Donald, would you open our meeting with a prayer?"

Deacon Mushrat stopped smiling, planted his elbows on the table, clasped his hands, bowed his head, knit his eyebrows together, and looked as though he was trying to work up a sweat.

"Lord, you are God," he began, in a North Carolina accent so thick you could slice it, fry it up in some ham fat and serve it with grits. "You are the Triune, the Theotes, Omniscient, Revelatory, Immutable, the First Principle. You are the Alpha and the Omega. You are the Logos. You are El Shaddai. You are so awesome that you even know what I am going to pray next!"

I shot a glance between my fingers at Marilyn, but her eyes were squinched tight.

"O God, forgive those among us who do not understand the need to follow your Word, your awesome *Holy* Word, and as we begin this awesome stewardship campaign, forgive the congregation for their continued failure to tithe. For 'The tithe is the Lord's, a full ten percent,' and 'Bring your tithes into the storehouse,' and 'Test me in this, saith the Lord.' And Gracious Father, I just pray you would forgive the leaders of our fellowship for their ignorance and laziness. Raise up great men of God, O Lord, and place them in front of these people that they would know your ways."

Bev kicked me under the table.

"And Lord, we just pray for all the born-again believers at my last parish that you allowed me to bring into your salvation, and I'd like to mention just a few by name..."

"Amen," interrupted Gaylen.

"Amen," everyone echoed.

"Awesome," I said.

"Good God," muttered Bev.

•••

"Now," said Gaylen, "our stewardship program should be pretty straightforward this year. We aren't under any financial strain at the moment and the pledge cards should go out this week."

"How many of the St. Barnabas parishioners tithe?" asked Deacon Mushrat. "If I may ask?"

"Almost everyone in the congregation gives what they can," said Gaylen.

"That's not what I asked," said the deacon, turning down the corners of his mouth. "Ten percent. That's what the Lord demands."

"Well," said Bev, a hard edge on her voice, "since we aren't privy to everyone's tax returns, we don't really know who's giving ten percent and who isn't."

"And some people give to other things as well," added Elaine. "The soup kitchen, the Salvation Army, Habitat for Humanity..."

"That's not the tithe," said Deacon Mushrat. "The tithe comes into the storehouse. The storehouse is the church."

"Thank you, Donald," said Gaylen. "If you'd like to lead a Bible study on the Book of Malachi during Advent, I'm sure there are many of us who would like to attend. Marilyn will be happy to put an announcement in the bulletin and the newsletter."

Marilyn smiled and Donald made a note on his clipboard.

"As I was saying," continued Gaylen, "the pledge cards will go out this week. I'll mention the stewardship program during announcements for the next couple of Sundays and we'll try to get all the cards back in before Christmas."

"How about finalizing the budget?" asked Deacon Mushrat.

"It's already done," said Bev, giving him a sickeningly sweet smile. "We did that in October. Of course, now we'll have to add *your* salary to the total."

The deacon made another note.

Gaylen flipped a page of her pad. "Now...the Jesse Tree. Who won the battle last year?"

Mushrat looked confused.

"The Chrismonites," said Elaine. "We weren't in the new church, though, so there wasn't really a tussle. The old ladies made chrismons all summer and hung them on the tree in the rotunda of the courthouse."

"The year before that, we didn't have a tree," I said. "We'd just burned down."

"And the year before that..." said Elaine.

Gaylen held up her hands. "Okay," she said. "Who does the Christmas parade this year? And who's in charge of the town Christmas crèche?"

Everyone looked in my direction. It was a long-standing tradition that the Kiwanis Club and the Rotary Club, rival civic organizations, took turns organizing the St. Germaine Christmas Parade on alternate years. About twenty years ago, during a particularly successful run of Christmas parades by the Kiwanians, thanks to a three-hundred pound Santa they'd recruited from Elk Mills, the town council had given the parade to the Kiwanis Club for the foreseeable future. The Rotarians, lacking a really big Kris Kringle, but having plenty of sheep, decided that they'd start a Living Nativity in Sterling Park. It was a smash hit! The Christmas parade was only one evening, but the Living Nativity went on for several nights and the Kiwanians weren't going to take this affront lying down. They immediately petitioned the council to have their own Living Nativity, and it was Pete Moss in his role as Solomon that finally proposed the compromise. The Rotarians and the Kiwanians would swap duties each year. One year, the Christmas parade, the next year, the Christmas crèche. And thus it has been ever since, except for that fateful year when St. Germaine had two Living Nativities going at the same time.

I thought for a few seconds.

"The Rotarians have the parade. Cynthia says it's going to be a doozy. The Kiwanians have the crèche."

"Then this shall be our decree," said Gaylen, using the royal pronoun. "On such years as the Kiwanians are in charge of the town Christmas crèche, the Jessetonians shall decorate the Jesse Tree. On such years as the Rotarians present the crèche, the Chrismonites shall hence prevail."

"Amen and so be it," I said.

"Anything special for the Second Sunday of Advent?" asked Kimberly Walnut.

"Well, the choir is singing Hugo Distler's *Kleine Adventsmusik*. It's a short cantata. Seven variations on *Savior of the Nations, Come*. We're doing different movements throughout the service. We have a few instrumentalists coming in from Appalachian State."

"It's quite lovely," said Elaine. "Fun to sing."

"Will we be starting up the Children's Moment again?" asked Kimberly, hopefully.

"That would be awesome!" said Donald Mushrat.

"I think not," said Gaylen.

"I have something for the first week in January," said Kimberly Walnut. "We're having a lock-in for the kids. It's our 'Cocoon' program. We'll have activities, and Bible study, and prayer time. We'll write letters to God...that sort of thing. Then we're going to have a church service with communion the next morning. It will be a life-changing experience for these children."

"I hope you'll let me be involved," said the oily Mushrat.

•••

"Could you ride with me to Boone?" Gaylen asked, as the meeting disbanded. "Actually, I need to have some blood drawn, and I don't want to have to drive myself home. I thought we might chat."

"Be happy to," I said.

Gaylen's late model Volvo was parked in front of the church and she beeped the doors unlocked with her remote as we walked up. It was still a cold morning, although the sun had melted the frost that covered the park almost every day in December.

"Very nice car," I said, as I got into the passenger side, flipped on the heated seat, and buckled myself in.

"It was a present to myself when I became bishop," said Gaylen with a little laugh. She started the car and then fastened her seat-belt as well. "I figured I'd have to drive all over Colorado and I'd need a good car. Who knew I'd be back here in a couple of years? I do like the heated seats, though. And the stereo."

"How's your dad doing, by the way?"

"He's doing okay. He has good days and he has bad days. Mostly, I think he's just tired."

"Tired?"

"Physically tired, spiritually tired, emotionally tired. Just tired. I can see it in his eyes."

"I'm sorry."

We turned down Maple Street, drove past the Holy Grounds Coffee Shop and headed out of town.

"Well," said Gaylen with a sigh, "we all get old. We all die."

"That's pretty fatalistic, especially with Christmas coming up. I have a better plan."

"You know something I don't?"

"December 21st, 2012. It's the new date of the Rapture. I'm just trying to hold on till then."

Gaylen laughed. "So you won't be planning any Christmas Eve services that year."

"Nope."

"Well, I guess I won't bother writing a sermon."

The town disappeared behind us and Maple Street turned to State Road 413. We were heading into Boone by a back road, a little longer, but infinitely more scenic than the main highway. The mountain laurel and the fir trees still had some color, but everything else was stark and bare and covered with the haze that gave the Smoky Mountains their name.

"Worst case scenario," I said. "The Rapture doesn't happen and you preach the same sermon you did the year before."

"What about the choir?"

"We'll do a couple choruses of *Rudolf the Red-Nosed Bishop* during the offertory. Hey, watch out there..."

A family of skunks was crossing the highway in the fog and Gaylen didn't see them right away. When she did see them, she touched her brakes. Nothing happened, or felt like it didn't. The rear tires hit a patch of black ice that had been sheltered from the morning sun behind a large rock cliff. The car started to fish-tail badly, but seemed to correct itself. As the back of the car whipped back into the center of the road, three baby skunks appeared in the windshield, looking at us with huge, terrified eyes. Gaylen spun the steering wheel, more out of instinct than anything else.

I felt the car leave the road and hit the first tree with a screech of torn metal. The airbags deployed, smacked us back against the seats, then deflated in an instant. I tasted blood. We hit the second tree.

Then darkness.

Chapter 5

I saw a bright light, blinked, and turned my head. I'd been napping on my gurney in the emergency room.

"Attaboy," said the doctor flicking his pen-light into my eyes, first one and then the other. "Sorry to wake you up, but you had quite a rap on the ol' coconut." He clicked the flashlight off and dropped it into his breast pocket. "You remember anything?"

"Yep," I said, trying to shake off the cobwebs. "I remember."

After we'd hit the second tree, Gaylen and I had sat there, motionless, for a few minutes. Then a voice came on a speaker telling us that the sensors had sent a message to the OnStar security switchboard saying that the airbags had deployed, and were we all right? Gaylen didn't answer, or couldn't, and I replied that we'd had an accident and were somewhere off the road. The operator said she'd stay on the line and send help immediately. I was suddenly very grateful that Gaylen had splurged on the new Volvo with all the bells and whistles.

Nancy and Dave showed up before the ambulance and had me out of the car by the time the ambulance arrived on the scene. We hadn't moved Gaylen, but waited for the EMTs, fearing some internal injuries. She was conscious but couldn't say anything. The ambulance was long gone by the time I'd told Nancy and Dave and two Boone cops what had happened. Then I climbed into Nancy's car, rode to the hospital, and walked myself into the emergency room.

"Better call Meg," I said.

"She's on her way," said Nancy.

Gaylen had been wheeled into surgery before we'd arrived at the hospital. I was luckier. I wouldn't need any surgery—just a fiberglass cast on a broken left arm, a couple of months getting over a broken left collarbone, and some stitches in my scalp. No sign of a concussion, presumably what the doctor was looking for when I was so rudely awakened.

"We're going to keep you overnight," he said. "Just in case."

I blinked and looked around the small examining cubicle walled off from the others in the area by sheets of hospital-green linen. I'd just dragged myself into a sitting position on the table when Meg arrived. She pulled the dividing sheet to one side and peeked in; then, seeing I was sitting up, came in and touched me lightly on the side of the head where my hair had been shorn and several stitches were angrily visible against the pale scalp.

"Ouch," I said. "Don't touch."

"I didn't, you baby," she said with a gentle smile. "I'm certainly relieved you're okay. Luckily, Nancy told me you were fine before she said anything else. She said, 'He's fine and Gaylen's okay, but there's been a wreck.'"

"Well, *fine* is a bit of a stretch."

"You're not dead," said Meg. "You need to get your arm set, but they can't do anything about your collarbone."

I nodded. "The doctor filled me in. Simple fracture. Six weeks in a cast and a sling for the clavicle. How's Gaylen?"

"She's out of surgery and she'll be good as new in a couple months. I didn't get a report on the extent of her injuries. She'll be here a few days, though. You guys want to share a room?"

"Absolutely not."

•••

Pete Moss and Cynthia Johnsson came into my room at about nine o'clock in the evening, breaking all the rules, including the ones about visiting hours and smuggling cigars and beer in to patients. I declined the cigar, but was more than happy to have the beer and the company. Meg, who had been at the hospital all day, had gone out to get a cup of coffee.

"A visit from the mayor?" I said. "Now *that's* something. How come you didn't wear your belly-dancing outfit? That would have cheered me up more than Pete here."

"Last time I wore it, I caused quite a commotion in the cardiac ward," said Cynthia. "I promised not to do it again."

"Going home tomorrow?" asked Pete.

"Yeah. There wasn't really any reason to stay except I got conked on the noggin. That, plus they wanted to watch me run around the halls in one of these open-in-the-back hospital gowns."

"I'm sure that's it," said Cynthia with a smirk. "Those nurses are lusting in their hearts."

"How's your priest friend?" asked Pete.

"I saw her a couple of hours ago. She'll be okay, but she's pretty banged up. Her right hand is fractured in several places. The surgeon had to put a few pins in. She has a separated shoulder, a couple of broken ribs, a busted nose and two black eyes." I thought for a moment. "Oh, yeah. Her jaw was broken, too. It's wired shut. I think that's it."

"What about her spleen?" said Pete. "Whenever someone gets in a car wreck on TV, they lose a spleen."

"Spleen's okay," I answered.

"Well, there's a relief," said Cynthia rather sarcastically, then looked puzzled. "I'm not even sure where my spleen is."

"Right around your liver somewhere," Pete said, poking around at his midsection. "It's all right there together. Spleen, liver, sweetbreads, kidneys, chitlins...all the major food organs. Hey! How's she going to preach if her jaw's wired shut?"

"That's a good question," I said. "Maybe we can forego the sermons for a few weeks."

"I might even come back to church," said Pete.

"But, more to the point," said Cynthia, "how are you going to play the organ with that arm in a cast?"

Meg opened the door and came into the room.

"Hi, Meg," said Cynthia. "We were just asking Hayden how he was going to play the organ with one hand tied behind his back. Care for a beer?"

"No thanks," said Meg. She raised her Styrofoam cup. "I just got some bad coffee from the nurses' station." She looked at Pete, who was busy wetting the tip of his cigar by spinning it in his mouth. "Don't you dare!" she hissed. "There are smoke alarms all over this building. You may *not* light that thing in here!"

Pete put on a crestfallen expression and returned the cigar to his jacket pocket. "Well," he said, "how *are* you going to play the organ?"

"We were discussing the very thing before Meg's coffee break," I said. "And I have no idea. I'll just have to take another leave of absence."

"You will *not!*" said Meg emphatically. "I'm the Senior Warden now and I'm not going through *that* again. I have a few thoughts on the matter, some people to call. I'll see what I can come up with when I get home tonight."

"You're not staying?" I asked.

"And where am I supposed to sleep?" asked Meg.

"This bed's big enough," I suggested, sliding across the starched sheet until I was next to one of the bed-rails. "You could..."

"Forget it, Mister. No hospital canoodling." She looked over at Pete and Cynthia and smiled sweetly. "That's Rule 57."

"Subsection C," I sighed.

"You guys sure ended up with a lot of rules once you got married," said Pete. "Me and Cynthia, we've got no rules. Anything goes."

Cynthia just looked at him, her eyebrows raised.

"Well," said Pete, "except for...umm...and...oh, never mind."

Chapter 6

On Friday morning, I checked out of the hospital as soon as the doctor made his rounds at 7:15 and gave me the thumbs-up. Meg picked me up and we headed back to St. Germaine, where my truck was patiently waiting in front of the police station. It was a cold morning, crisp and clear, with none of the fog that had been part of the cause of the previous day's troubles. Meg had Christmas music on the stereo. She went for the Christmas music right after Walmart did—Halloween, at the latest. At least (to my relief) she'd had the good taste to raid my CD collection and wasn't listening to the Mantovani Orchestra play their greatest holiday hits. I recognized the unmistakable strains of Tchaikovsky's *Nutcracker*.

"Did you come up with any great ideas?" I asked, as we drove down the highway. "Organ-wise, that is?"

"Maybe," Meg answered. "I'm waiting for a call back from my friend Edna."

"Edna?"

"Uh-huh." Meg was smiling like the Cheshire cat. "Edna Terra-Pocks."

"Edna Terra from Lenoir?"

"That's her. She said she remembered you very well."

I shrugged. "We went to school together. The organist community isn't exactly large. I probably know, or know about, every good organist within a hundred miles."

"So you think she's good?"

I shrugged again. "I suppose so, but I haven't heard her play for years. It seems to me that she got a Master's degree from Yale after she finished at UNC. She plays at a big Methodist church in Lenoir. Part-time, if I'm not mistaken."

"Not any more, she doesn't."

"And how do you know this?" I asked.

"Edna's a client of mine. Well, the family is. Pocks Furniture. Ring a bell?"

"Oh, right," I said. "I remember that now. Edna Terra. The richest little girl in Chapel Hill. She married Bill Pocks, III."

"Well, I know her from her charity woman's group. I'm helping them with their investments. The Lenoir Hottie-Totties. Isn't that cute?"

"Darling," I said.

Anyway," said Meg, "she's in charge of their program that

provides transportation for the elderly when they need a ride. You know, like to the doctor, or the drugstore or something. All the girls take turns volunteering and Edna coordinates the whole thing. They call it the 'Home Mini-bus Volun-Totties.'"

"Huh," I grunted. "Very cute. Edna was always into cute."

"I met her down at Myrtle Beach when I was doing that seminar last year. We had a lot in common. You, for instance."

"Now, wait a minute!" I said. "I don't know what she told you, but she and I never..."

"Relax," laughed Meg. "Just the fact that we *knew* you was the common thread. Well, that she knew you, and I married you."

I let out a slow breath.

"Anyway, I was chatting with Edna a couple of weeks ago. It seems that Edna doesn't play for the Methodist church any longer. The new minister has decided to go in a different direction. I believe she said there is talk of firing the choir and hiring a country band."

"So she's between organ gigs, as it were."

"As it were."

"And she's going to step in for me."

"Well, that's the plan."

"Great. So I'm off the hook."

"Not even close. Edna can play the organ, but *you're* going to direct the choir." She looked over at me. "And choose the music."

"No, no, no, no, no," I said rapidly, shaking my head. "Bad idea."

"It's a great idea and you know it," said Meg defensively. "You know what the choir can do and how to get them to sound good. Edna can play the organ until you get the use of your arm back."

"I'm not going to win this, am I?" I asked, knowing the answer.

"No, dear, I don't think you are."

"Just through the Christmas season, then," I said, hoping to strike a deal.

"Hmm. How about until the fourth Sunday after Epiphany?"

"Second," I countered.

"Third," said Meg.

"Okay. Deal." I thought for a moment. "Hey, wait a minute. That's six weeks from now. I'll be out of this cast by then."

"Yep," said Meg. "Then you can have your job back."

•••

Meg dropped me off at the Slab with an admonition to be at the emergency worship meeting at noon. I'd decided that breakfast at the hospital didn't really appeal to my epicurean cravings and walked into the eatery with all intentions of ordering Pete's Special Breakfast Extravaganza complete with pancakes, chicken-fried steak, eggs and gravy. I wouldn't be able to do any two-handed eating, my left arm being in both a cast and a sling, but I'd manage.

Pete waved me over to his table. Being the owner, he felt his job was to sit and drink coffee for most of the morning, only helping out when he had to. Cynthia and Noylene were both scurrying, taking care of a full complement of customers.

"Morning! How's the arm?"

"Still broken," I said.

Noylene walked over, smiled, and filled the coffee mug in front of me. "I heard about your accident," she said. "Sure am glad you're okay."

I smiled back at her. "Just a busted wing. I'll have Pete's Special Breakfast Extravaganza, please."

Noylene nodded. "You want the full special or the half?"

"Full. Pancakes, steak, scrambled eggs...the works."

"Got it," said Noylene, writing on her pad. She tore off the sheet and walked it back to the kitchen.

The old cowbell on the glass door of the Slab Café clanked in two regulars, Nancy and Dave, coming in off the street. They were both bundled against the cold morning, having donned scarves and heavy coats before setting out. Meg had brought my old coat with her when she picked me up at the hospital. My good coat hadn't made it out of the emergency room in one piece.

"How's Gaylen doing?" asked Nancy, unwinding her scarf and sloughing off her coat before sitting.

"She'll be all right," I said.

"What happened exactly?" asked Dave. "You remember what caused the wreck?"

"As I recall," I said, "Gaylen was driving when some baby skunks and their mama decided to cross the road."

"And she didn't want her car to stink," said Dave with a grin, "so she hit the tree instead."

"It was a reflex," I said. "She tapped the brakes and we caught a patch of black ice."

"What happened to the scoodle of skunks?" asked Noylene, suddenly reappearing with a coffee pot. "I jes' love little baby skunks."

"Scoodle?" I said.

44

"That's what you call skunks," said Noylene. "A scoodle."

"Nah," said Pete. "It's a *skein* of skunks. Or if there are more than five, you call them a skank."

"You're both wrong," I said. "It's a *surfeit* of skunks. Anyway, the skunks are all fine, I believe."

Nancy's cell phone rang and she flipped it open. "Skunk department," she said.

"Nancy forwarded the office phone," Dave told Pete. "That way we can eat breakfast all day."

The cowbell rang again as three more customers came into the restaurant. Noylene gave an audible sigh.

"Cheer up," said Dave. "You know what they say. Every time you hear a bell, another angel gets its wings."

"What they don't tell you," said Pete, "is that every time a mouse trap snaps, an angel bursts into flames."

"We'll be right there," said Nancy, closing her phone. She took a slurp of coffee. "Time to go," she said, standing and reaching for her coat. "We've got a floater in the lake."

Chapter 7

Lake Tannenbaum was just outside the St. Germaine city limits and surrounded on three sides by the Mountainview Cemetery. It was a small mountain lake, just a couple of acres, spring fed and ice cold, even in the summer. The small dock, just visible from the road winding through the monuments, jutted about eight feet into the water and was flanked by "No Swimming" signs on either side. We parked on the pavement behind an old white Ford Bronco and made our way down to the edge of the lake. I recognized Pam Rutledge as she waved to us from the dock.

"I was visiting Mom," she said, once we'd gotten down to the shore. "After I put the flowers on her grave, I came down to the lake. It's peaceful and I had a few minutes before I needed to be at work."

The water, cold as it was, was still a good deal warmer than the air on this frigid morning, and steam drifted up off the surface of the lake like the backdrop of an Arthurian legend.

"You said there was a body?" asked Nancy, sticking her hands deep in her pockets.

"Right there." Pam pointed down to the brown cattails bobbing lazily beside the old wooden planks. Sure enough, there, floating face down, was a man. Although we couldn't yet see his face, I knew I'd seen him before. He was wearing a sheepskin coat, jeans, and cowboy boots. His brown hair drifted in the icy water and I had no doubt that, when we fished him out, he'd have a beard.

•••

Joe and Mike, our two EMTs, were not happy about having to go into the shallows and drag the body to shore even, after I pointed out that I myself had a broken arm, that Dave's back was acting up, and that Nancy was a girl.

"It's freezing," complained Mike. "And I don't have my waders."

"Suck it up," said Nancy. "I'd do it, but I'm a girl."

"A girl who could kick both our butts and never break a nail," muttered Mike.

"C'mon," said Dave, giving him a gentle, good-hearted nudge on the shoulder. "Quit griping. It's your job."

"Sheesh," said Joe, wading into the water and grabbing the man by his collar. "I'll get him."

He dragged the body across the weeds and up onto the shore, where Mike and Dave latched on and helped him pull the corpse up so we could get a good look at him. Once he was up on the grass, they rolled him over. I recognized him from the auction. Nancy checked his pockets but came up empty. No wallet, no identification, no cell phone, nothing.

I squatted down over the body and took a closer look. The man was older than I'd originally thought, maybe late thirties, and in good shape. His beard was well-trimmed and he wore contacts. One of them had floated out in the lake, revealing a clouded blue eye. The other eye, the one with the contact lens still applied, was brown. His nails were trimmed and he wore a plain gold ring on his right hand. His brown hair was long but neatly cut.

"Do you know him?" asked Joe.

"Not me," said Dave.

"Nope," said Nancy.

I shook my head and noticed something odd. One of his sideburns, just below his ear, had lifted away from the skin of his face. I reached down with my right hand, took hold of it, and slowly peeled away a false beard and mustache. It was a professional appliance, a theatrical configuration made of very fine mesh and what felt like human hair. The beard had been affixed to the man's face with spirit gum.

"What on earth?" exclaimed Nancy.

"Why is he wearing a fake beard?" asked Dave. "You think he drowned? And if he did, what was he doing down here in the first place?"

"I don't think he drowned," I said, reaching down again and pulling the wet, matted hair away from his face. There, just above his eyebrows, in the center of his forehead, was a small hole. A bullet hole.

Chapter 8

Needless to say, I was late for the worship meeting. Meg gave me a withering look as I came in. Since Gaylen was in the hospital, Deacon Mushrat had apparently tried to take the reins, but had quickly been quelled in his efforts by Bev. Being the Parish Administrator, she had the final say when the priest wasn't available.

"Sorry I'm late," I said, taking my seat. "Duty called."

"We were just discussing our plans for Advent, now that you and Gaylen are down for the count," said Bev. "Meg was saying that a friend of yours might be available to play the organ until you get out of that cast."

"Edna Terra-Pocks," said Meg. "Hayden went to school with her. She's supposed to be quite good."

"To be honest," I said, "I haven't heard her play for a number of years."

"Well, we don't seem to have much choice, do we?" said Deacon Mushrat with a shrug. "I guess we could use one of those CDs with the hymns on them."

"She'll do just fine," said Bev quickly. Elaine and Joyce Cooper nodded.

"I spoke with Bishop O'Connell this morning," Bev continued. "He'll be here this Sunday, but he's booked for the rest of Advent. Gaylen said she'd probably be feeling good enough to handle the services by that next Sunday. That'd be..." Bev checked her calendar, "the Third Sunday of Advent. She doesn't want to have to preach, though. I guess Donald can preach the sermon."

Donald preened and screwed his mouth into a tight smile. "Awesome," he said.

Bev looked down at the pad of scribbles in front of her. "Now, what about the choir?"

"Well," said Meg, "if we can hire Edna to play the organ, Hayden could certainly choose the music and direct."

"Good plan," said Elaine. "But what about the music for this Sunday? Our cantata?"

Everyone looked in my direction.

"Well, we have a rehearsal tomorrow morning anyway. If Edna can play the organ part, there isn't any reason why we can't do it."

"I'll give her a call," said Meg happily.

Just then Billy burst into the conference room. "Hey, did you hear? They just dragged a dead body out of the lake!"

Everyone looked in my direction...again.

"It's why I was late," I explained.

"And you didn't say anything?" said Meg incredulously.

"Well, I didn't think it had anything to do with the emergency Advent meeting."

"Is it anyone that we know?" asked Joyce in a small voice.

"No one that *I* know," I answered. "I did see him last week at the auction over at the Frost place."

"Well, if he was just in town for Old Man Frost's auction *last* week, what was he doing here *this* week?" asked Billy.

"A good question," I said. "You should be a policeman."

"Nah," said Billy. "Don't pay enough. I'd rather mow lawns."

•••

Meg and I left the worship meeting and headed over to the Ginger Cat for lunch. An upscale lunch boutique that thrived on the tourist trade, the Ginger Cat had a knack for unpronounceable coffees, exotic teas, and a pretentious carte du jour that would do any snooty tea house proud. Since we'd managed to drag the meeting on past one o'clock, there was no problem finding a table and we chose one in the back.

"Good afternoon, Elphina," Meg said to our waitress, a waif of a girl dressed in black with jet black hair, who looked as though she could use a good meal over at the Slab rather than trying to subside on the employee-discounted octopus and celery salad with lemon juice. Meg glanced over the menu with a practiced eye. "I'll have the zucchini and basil fusilli with bacon. And an iced tea."

"Is that your name?" I asked. "Elphina? I've never known an Elphina."

"It's my vampire name," replied Elphina, tossing her hair and revealing a thorned rose tattooed on the side of her neck. "It means 'delicate one.'"

"Well, Elphina, I'll have a ham sandwich on rye," I said, not bothering with the menu. "Hold the plasma. Just lettuce, tomato and a schmear of mustard."

The waitress looked confused and the corner of her black-lipsticked mouth twitched as she stared at her pad, as if afraid to write my order on the paper. Her black fingernails flicked against the paper nervously.

"That's not on the menu. Do you mean our chipotle pork panini with roasted caper vinaigrette?" she asked hesitantly, regretting the question almost as soon as she posed it.

I raised my voice slightly. "No! No, I do not mean…"

"That's exactly what he means, dear," interrupted Meg. "The panini. And bring him a cup of Nicaraguan Maravilla Gold."

"Yes, m'lady," said Elphina, turning sideways and disappearing altogether.

"I hope that was coffee you ordered for me," I said with a sniff. "And when did vampires start coming out during the day and working at the Ginger Cat?"

"It *was* coffee and don't worry about the vampires," said Meg. "It's the 'in' thing right now." She put both elbows on the table and rested her chin in her hands. "Now tell me about that man. You know. The dead one. The one in Lake Tannenbaum."

"Not much to tell. He was shot in the forehead and thrown into the lake. Kent's doing the autopsy right now. No tire tracks either. Somebody carried him down the hill and threw him in."

"Maybe they made him walk down at gunpoint, then shot him," suggested Meg. "Maybe it was a robbery."

"Could be," I agreed.

"And you have no idea who he is?"

"None. No identification at all. Of course, there may be fingerprints on file, but we'll have to wait and see."

"Hiya, Chief," said a voice from behind me.

"Hi, Bud," I said, looking over my shoulder, but recognizing Bud's voice immediately. "Come have a seat."

"Sorry I had to run off after the auction, but I had to get back to campus. I had a big final on Monday and our study group was meeting."

"That's okay," I said. "Meg and I have been enjoying the wine."

Bud went white in his chair. *"What!?"* he hissed, leaning over the table. *"Enjoying the wine!?"*

"It's very tasty," said Meg. "And it should be, seeing that it cost $275 a bottle."

"No!" shouted Bud, then lowered his voice to a conspiratorial whisper. "You aren't supposed to drink it!"

"Why not?" I whispered back.

"Because we're partners," said Bud. "You might have bought it for $275 a bottle, but it's worth a lot more."

"Really?" said Meg.

"Really. Chateau Petrus Pomerol. It's a Merlot—one of the favorite wines at the White House during the Kennedy years." Bud sat back in his chair. "That's the official name, Chateau Petrus, but even its label refers to it as simply 'Petrus.' The grapes are usually harvested early

50

and left to mature slowly. The panoply of exotic aromas and flavors typically encompass black raspberry, mulberry, iron, cocoa powder, and truffle, while expensive new oak emanates from its rich purple robe."

Meg and I looked at each other in astonishment. Bud was in his element now.

"Petrus 1998." Bud closed his eyes and looked as though he'd been transported to a vineyard in Italy. "The finish is something to wait for as it caresses the palate. A truly exquisite vintage." He opened his eyes and peered at me. "It should reach maturity after the year 2012."

"So this is an investment," I said.

"Yep. It's legendary and extravagantly priced. But this wine, from a prime vineyard on well-drained clay soil atop the Pomerol plateau in Italy, has for decades stood as the greatest example of Merlot in the world. Petrus is a wine that is extraordinarily creamy and thick but with the substantial tannic underpinning to ensure decades of development in the bottle."

"And this means...?" I said.

"That after 2012, this wine will probably double in value."

"Making it worth...?" I coaxed.

"Making it worth about $7000 per bottle. Three cases. Thirty-six bottles. That's $252,000. It could even go higher!"

Bud looked around to see if anyone was listening. No one was.

"I already did the math," he whispered.

Meg's eyes went wide. Mine, too.

"You're sure?" I asked.

Bud nodded. "I'm sure."

"Well, do the math again with thirty-two bottles instead of thirty-six," I suggested, giving him a crooked grin. "'Cause Meg and I drank four of them."

"Oh, man," said Bud, a hangdog look coming over him as he slumped in his chair. "I should have told you."

"Well, don't worry about it," I said magnanimously. "We drank it. We'll take it off our end." I looked at him with narrowed eyes. "You're telling me that *right now* this wine is worth over a hundred thousand? And in a couple of years..."

Bud crossed his arms, leaned back in his chair and smiled.

"Yep."

"And we drank $28,000 worth of Merlot?" said Meg in a small, terrified voice.

"Oh, yeah," said Bud.

•••

Dr. Kent Murphee had been the Watauga County medical examiner for the better part of twenty years. When he called the station late on Friday afternoon, Nancy had already clocked out for the day and Dave was nowhere to be found, not that he should have been working. Dave was usually off on Fridays. I called Meg and she agreed to give me a ride into Boone if she could drop me off and go over to the mall for an hour. I happily agreed. The cast on my arm was such that I couldn't really drive my pick-up truck. My 1962 Chevrolet, for all its wonderful features—a great stereo, a pretty good spare tire thrown into the back, a twelve-mile-per-gallon original V8 engine, and enough power to tow Rush Limbaugh out of a Rib Shack—didn't have what anyone might label "power steering." It was a two-handed job just to keep the truck in the middle of the road most of the time. I was used to it, of course, but Meg hated it, and so wouldn't switch cars with me. I could have easily driven her Lexus.

"Why don't you buy another truck?" she said, when I suggested the switch.

"I just need it for a few weeks. If I bought it, I'd be stuck with it."

"Then rent one. For heaven's sakes, Hayden. You're a millionaire. Remember?"

"Yeah. Okay. I'll rent one."

But I hadn't. Not yet, anyway.

Meg dropped me off and headed to the mall and I found myself sitting in Kent's office, preparing to join him in his traditional afternoon bourbon.

Kent was well into his fifties and dressed, on this day as every day, in his tweed jacket, tie, and vest. His pipe was resting in the ashtray on the edge of his desk, and a slight drift of smoke rose from the bowl, although Kent was obviously letting it extinguish itself. He ran a hand through a shock of rather long salt-and-pepper hair, greeted me with a smile, and pushed a glass of his special blend across the desk at me while I sat.

"It's Friday," said Kent. "It's four o'clock. Time for a drink."

"Fridays at four? That's your new parameter?"

"Nah," he said. "I just thought I might entice you to join me since I've already poured."

I took a sip. "I don't require much enticing. You have news?"

"Yes, I do." He picked up a small sheaf of papers fastened together with a paper clip. "Killed by a small caliber bullet—9mm

52

to be exact. I'd say it was a handgun. Definitely at close range. The path of the bullet shows a slight upward trajectory."

"How close?" I asked.

"Two feet maximum. Probably less. There was some gunpowder stippling around the entrance wound. The water cleaned most of the residue off, but there were grains of powder that were actually imbedded in the skin."

"You have the bullet?"

Kent held up a small plastic bag containing the bullet retrieved from the victim, dangled it a moment, then pushed it across the desk. "Don't forget to sign the chain of evidence form before you leave," said Kent. He looked back down at his papers. "I took his fingerprints and sent them off, electronically, to the FBI data base. You'll hear something by Monday, I expect. That is, if they can match 'em."

"DNA?" I asked.

"That, too," answered Kent. "Although that will take substantially longer to find a match, even if his sample is in the system."

"What about the beard?" I asked.

Kent smiled. "Now we get to the good part. The beard is very good quality. Theatrical supply, I'd say. It's made of human hair and tied into a very fine mesh. It was applied with spirit gum." Kent flipped a page. "I will say this, though," he continued. "It was made specifically for your victim. It's not an 'off the shelf' model. The beard was fitted very exactly to his facial structure. His hair had been dyed, by the way. The natural color is much lighter. Not blonde exactly, but fairer by several shades."

I looked at Kent in surprise.

"There's more," he said, still smiling. "Caps on the teeth, cheek implants, and a new nose. The nose is a couple years old, judging by the scar tissue. The implants are older I think. I can't tell about the caps."

"So this guy had a new face," I said, pushing my glass toward Kent for a refill. "And a false beard."

"*And* he dyed his hair," Kent reminded me. "Sounds as though he didn't want to be recognized."

Chapter 9

St. Barnabas Episcopal Church had been rebuilt on the same footprint as the earlier building that had burned two years ago. It was a classic design, built in the shape of a cross.

The choir was in the back balcony that also housed the pipe organ. The steps to the choir loft were in the narthex, the entrance to the church. The transepts, or alcoves, formed the arms of the cross. The high altar was in the front in the sanctuary and a smaller Mary altar decorated the east transept. The sacristy, where the clergy and choir put on their vestments and where communion was prepared, was still behind the front wall with two invisible doors opening in the paneling behind the altar. St. Barnabas' nave seated about two hundred and fifty when the church was comfortably full.

It wasn't often that we had a Saturday choir rehearsal. We almost never had a Saturday choir rehearsal. The fact that we were having one on this particular Saturday was a testament to the choir's penchant for goofing off during Thanksgiving. The choir seemed to feel that the Thanksgiving break began on the Wednesday evening before Thanksgiving Day—they all were, in theory, cooking their big meals and couldn't possibly come to rehearsal—and lasted until the Sunday afternoon following Thanksgiving Day. Most years, the Sunday after Thanksgiving was, unfortunately, the First Sunday of Advent. Hence, I didn't ever schedule much fancy singing for the First Sunday of Advent. Sure, we could rehearse ahead of time. But I discovered, long ago, that the musical memory of an average church choir singer wasn't to be relied on.

"Have we ever seen this before?" asked Marjorie, my only female tenor, and the only one that had a low C. "You should give us this music ahead of time."

"We've been rehearsing it for four weeks," I said with a sigh. "We worked on it two weeks ago."

"I have never seen this music before," insisted Marjorie.

"Sure you have," said Steve from the bass section. "Remember? This is the one that has no time signatures and the dotted bar lines. You said it was driving you to drink."

Marjorie looked down at her score. "Hmm. Yes."

"You remember now?" asked Steve.

"Nope. I can just see where it would drive me to drink."

"Well, just sight-read it," said Mark Wells. "Lord knows, that's what I'll be doing."

"The instrumentalists will be here in a half hour," I said. "We'd better know it by then. Now,"—I gestured toward Edna, seated at the organ console—"I'd like to introduce you to our organist for the next six weeks. Or until I can play again."

"We wondered how you were going to manage," said Rebecca. "Or rather, how *we* were."

"This is Edna Terra-Pocks, an old friend of mine from college. She currently lives in Lenoir, but will be driving up for Wednesday night rehearsals and Sunday mornings."

Edna stood up at the organ and gave a smile and a small bow. She wasn't a great beauty by any means, but attractive in that well-put-together, very rich, middle-aged way. She was heavier than when I'd known her in college, but weren't we all? I remembered her as svelte. She couldn't be described as svelte now, but she still had a nice figure. Her dark brown hair was cut stylishly and fell about shoulder length. She was wearing a very expensive sweater, pearls and dark slacks. Old money. The picture of southern gentility. Her reading glasses dangled at the end of a gold chain and rested upon her, what could only be described as 'substantial,' chest.

"Are you married to Bill?" asked Mark. "Bill Pocks?"

"Yes, I am," said Edna, with a smile.

"I know Old Bill," said Mark. "We used to call him 'Chicken.'" He laughed. "Ol' Chicken Pocks! How about that? I haven't thought about him for years."

"What about our story?" asked Muffy LeMieux. She looked into her choir folder and came up with last week's opening hymn. She flipped the page over, held it up, and waved the previous install-ment at me. "The one about the under-dwarves of Kooloobati."

I shrugged with my one good arm. "I can't type. I don't know how I'm going to manage to finish it."

"You could dictate it to Meg, and she could type it for you," suggested Georgia.

"No way!" said Meg. "Not a chance."

"You could use that voice-recognition software," said Elaine. "You just talk into the microphone and the computer writes it down for you."

"I'll think about it," I said.

"But what about the under-dwarves?" said Muffy, a tear almost springing to her eye.

"They'll have to fend for themselves. We've got to look at this cantata."

●●●

"That went pretty well," said Meg as she drove us home from the rehearsal. "The instrumentalists were fabulous."

"I suppose," I groused. "I didn't much care for Edna's registration in the final movement."

"Then why didn't you say anything?" Meg sniffed. "You just don't like having to share the console."

"I don't mind sharing. I just don't want to have to be there for it."

"It's only for six weeks or so."

"Harumph!"

Chapter 10

Monday mornings were slow at the Slab. Saturdays were Pete's busiest days during December. Sundays were next, as the out-of-towners flocked into St. Germaine for the quaint, small-town atmosphere and the shopping.

"Well, how'd the service go?" asked Pete. "How was your first day as conductor of the choir?"

"Miserable," I said. "It's just not going to work. Where's Noylene? I need some coffee."

"Noylene's taking Mondays off," said Pete. "Not much happening on a Monday. Cynthia's back in the kitchen, but you can get your own coffee." He nodded at the coffee machine just behind the counter. Two pots of regular and half a pot of decaf were just waiting to be consumed.

"C'mon," I whined, flopping my cast piteously. "Look here. I've got a broken arm."

"Oh, fine," said Pete, getting up in exasperation. "I'll get your coffee."

"Might as well bring the pot," said Nancy, as the cowbell banged against the glass of the front door, announcing her entrance. She pulled off her heavy jacket and hung it on the rack of hooks by the door, then walked over to the table and sat down heavily across from me. "How was your substitute?" she asked.

"Not at all good," I said. "I can't do it, no matter what Meg says. The tempos were too slow on the hymns. The service music was too fast. Then, to top it all off, she played some eight minute, gawd-awful Advent prelude by Marcel Dupré. *Le monde dans l'attente du Sauveur*. It was too long, mind-numbingly boring, and all together unlistenable. It made my teeth hurt."

"I know I asked," said Nancy with a smirk, as Pete set a full coffee cup in front of her, "but I don't really care. I was just making conversation."

I snarled. "You'd better care. I'm your boss."

She took a sip and settled back. "Yeah? Well, I've got real news. We got a match on the prints that Kent sent to the FBI."

My mood brightened. "Hey, that's something. Care to enlighten me?"

Pete sat down and looked at Nancy. "Well?" he said.

Nancy lifted her hands in exasperation. "Police business, Pete. You ever hear of police business?"

"I'll shoot him if he tells anyone," I said. "Promise."

Nancy huffed. "Fine." She put her forearms on the table and leaned forward, excitement now evident in her voice. "Here's the thing. The feebs just called and said we've solved one of their big-deal cases."

"Really? The FBI?"

Pete's eyebrows went up. "Wow! Ten most wanted?"

Nancy shook her head. "Nah. Not that big. Just something they've been working on for a long time. The dead guy's name is Sal LaGrassa. Sal, short for Salvator. Apparently..." she paused for effect, "he's a professional killer."

Pete whistled. "A hit-man?"

"Big as life," said Nancy. "Well...not anymore. Anyway, the agent in charge, Ryan Jackson, wanted to know if we'd had any murders in town."

Pete snorted into his coffee. I chuckled as well. Murders? In St. Germaine? What were they thinking?

"I told him not lately," said Nancy, grinning back at us. "At least not any unsolved ones by a mysterious, unknown killer for hire."

"So who shot him?" asked Pete.

"That's the question, isn't it?" said Nancy. "Here's the interesting part. This guy was apparently part of a team—a man and a woman. At least, that's what the FBI thinks. They might have posed as husband and wife and lived together, but it's more probable that they lived totally apart and just got together for jobs."

"They think the woman killed him?" Pete said.

"Makes sense," I replied. "I think he knew whoever killed him. If he was a pro, he'd be hard to surprise."

Pete lowered his voice. "You think they were in town for a hit?"

I shook my head. "Nobody's dead that I know of. Nobody except for Old Man Frost, and he was eighty-something years old and died over a month ago."

"Maybe they lived around here," said Pete. "Or hid out. You know, in one of the little, nearby towns, or even up in the hollers."

"Yeah, maybe in one of the towns," agreed Nancy. "Not in the hollers. They'd need access to internet, phone service...a hundred things. That's what the agent told me. They're running a search for driver's licenses within a fifty mile radius—women, possibly single, aged twenty-five to fifty, who've lived in the area for less than five years. I doubt it will do any good."

"It's a place to start," I said. "Is the FBI taking this case over?"

"Nope. They're just happy he's accounted for. Agent Jackson would probably give a medal to whoever shot him. They're going to continue to look for the woman. He said if we find anything pertinent, he'd appreciate us giving him a call. I've got his number back at the office. Jackson's also e-mailing me Sal LaGrassa's dossier."

"That it?" I asked. Nancy was nothing if not thorough.

"I sent the slug over to ballistics in Raleigh. Just in case the feebs need it for a match."

"Nice work, Lieutenant Parsky," I said.

"But we still have a murder to solve," said Pete.

"We do, indeed," I replied.

"*If* she's still hanging around St. Germaine," said Nancy. She took another sip of coffee and added, "Which I doubt."

"Morning!" chirped Cynthia as she came out of the kitchen, wiping her hands on her apron. "How are you guys this morning?"

"Just great," I said sullenly. "I have a dead hit-man in the lake. I have a deacon who no one likes for the next six weeks. I have a broken arm and a substitute organist whose musical taste can be summed up in the 20th-century French literature and whose talent in determining what might be appropriate selections for the season consists chiefly of having an enormous bosom."

"Or maybe that's just sour grapes," said Nancy, hiding a smile behind her coffee cup.

"Nah," said Pete. "Hayden's right. I've seen her. She *does* have an enormous bosom."

"Be that as it may," said Cynthia, "I'm on Cloud Nine! This is going to be the best Christmas parade ever! We're even going to get a write-up in *Our State* magazine."

One thing that Cynthia Johnsson had wrangled in her two years as mayor of St. Germaine was one of the finest Christmas parades in the region. How? Simple. Money. Other people's money. Lots of it.

Mayor Johnsson had managed to hustle all kinds of funds, from local and county sponsorships, to a North Carolina State grant, to some federal government money set aside specifically to encourage the formation and furtherance of small town parades. Part one of Cynthia's idea was to encourage local and regional groups to be part of the parade by offering prizes. Prizes for the best high school marching band, the best musical ensemble that couldn't be classified as a marching band, the best overall float, the best float with an agricultural theme (prize sponsored by the Farm Bureau), the best children's entry, and so on. The second part of her plan was to actually offer an honorarium to those groups that might boost the parade's attendance and hence the visibility of St. Germaine. These invitations went to a nearby college band, the Grandfather Mountain bagpipe and drum corps, some of the *Horn in the West* (Watauga County's outdoor summer drama) cast in full regalia, Mr. Terwilliger's Marching Pigs (twelve full-grown pigs that could stay in reasonable formation while trotting to *The Dance of the Sugarplum Fairies* wearing Santa hats and white tutus), a guy named Jay from Tryon who happened to have an old Bullwinkle Moose balloon left over from the 1982 Macy's Thanksgiving Day parade, and various other high-profile acts. Those cynics who thought that you couldn't buy a marching band for an afternoon, and get 'em cheap, never met Cynthia.

The culmination of the parade, as far as the locals were concerned, was the judging. This happened in front of the reviewing stand, set up on the courthouse steps. Just like parades in bigger cities, each hopeful aspirant had the option of lingering for three minutes and performing for the three judges. It was an option that was embraced enthusiastically by the contestants, although the groups that were getting a guaranteed fee, and therefore were not eligible, usually marched on through. After three minutes, if the group hadn't finished, they were disqualified from any prizes. Hence, most performing groups had a two and a half minute routine. As far as the floats were concerned, they might slow a bit, so the judges could get a good, appreciative look, but they weren't allowed to actually stop unless there was some sort of performance involved.

Altogether, this made for a Christmas parade worthy of *Our State* magazine. In the old days, we were lucky to get three fire engines from Boone, two overweight Shriners on mopeds, and the Sand Creek Methodist Youth Group dressed up in Hebrew garb and hauled in on a trailer with a couple of hay bales and a forty-watt light bulb glowing in a manger. Now, the parade was nearing extravaganza proportions. How long Cynthia could keep it up no one knew, but for now, it was quite a show. Yes, quite a show indeed.

Since the Rotary Club and the Kiwanis Club switched sponsorship of the parade each year, Cynthia still had her hands full coordinating everything. Hopefully the Rotarians would take the reins this year and Cynthia would only have to concentrate on managing the downtown crowds. The parade would begin in the parking lot of the Piggly Wiggly, come down Maple Street toward town, make the corner in front of the Slab Café and head up the street to the reviewing stand. Then it would make another quarter turn around the square, pass Noylene's Beautifery, turn north on Main Street and head out of the downtown area for another mile before culminating at the end of the route at the doors of the St. Germaine Volunteer Fire Department.

Most of the crowd would gather downtown, but everyone involved would be performing all along the route. That's what their contract—yes, contract—stated. Cynthia wasn't giving an inch on this account. The parade would be first-class from start to finish. Every entrant vying for a prize paid an entrance fee and the prizes were hefty: $3000 for the best overall float, $2500 for the best band, $1000 for the best non-religious depiction of a Christmas tableau (a bone tossed to the Unitarians to prevent a lawsuit), and so on down the line. Some of the prizes were small gift certificates, others came with a six-foot-tall trophy, but make no mistake—this was something that St. Germaine had decided to take seriously.

"*Our State* magazine, huh?" said Pete. "I never even got those guys to give us a look. You must be doing something right."

Pete was always magnanimous toward Cynthia's mayorship, even though she'd beaten him in the hotly contested election. Pete thought he'd miss being mayor of St. Germaine, but, as it turned out, he didn't miss it at all, so magnanimity wasn't a problem.

"Well," said Cynthia, "I did have to promise the reporter that I'd be on a float and that he could get a picture for the magazine."

"Nothing strange about that," said Nancy. "Mayors do it all the time."

"In my belly dancing outfit," said Cynthia, looking up towards the ceiling at nothing in particular.

"I never had to do that when *I* was mayor," said Pete. "What else?"

"I told him I'd be dancing to *Jingle Bell Rock*."

•••

"Sunday's service wasn't that bad," said Meg over lunch. "Everyone liked it. And besides, you can always direct the hymns. That way they'll be the tempo you want."

"I can't pick the preludes and the postludes," I groused. "That Marcel Dupré piece was awful. And she noodles around during communion. That drives me crazy!"

"You noodle around during communion," said Meg.

61

"Yeah...well...that's different."

"And Deacon Mushrat did just fine."

"He didn't do *anything*," I said. "The bishop was right there beside him."

Meg crossed her arms and sat back in her chair. "I think it'll be a nice Christmas," she decided.

Chapter 11

"Dagnabbit!" I said, accidently banging the side of the typewriter with my cast. "I can't do it. I can't type one-handed."

"Then don't," said Meg calmly from the couch in front of the fire. She looked up from her book. "No one said you had to write another awful detective story. In fact, there are those of us in the choir who would relish the thought of six weeks devoid of bad fiction."

I grunted. "What am I going to do then? My muse needs a voice."

"How about concentrating on your children's books?" said Meg.

"What children's books? I don't have any children's books."

"The Sophie Slug series."

"Huh?"

"It's the perfect solution. You can follow up *Sophie Slug Goes to the Beach* with all kinds of adventures. *Sophie Slug visits Salt Lake City. Sophie Slug Visits the Salt Mines of Wieliczka.* You get the idea. And, since she only lasts for one sentence before she meets her demise, they'll be short and rather painless for us to read."

"Ah. And these are children's books," I said with a nod. "I like the idea."

"I only hope I haven't unleashed something very sinister," Meg said, going back to her reading.

It was worth a try. I typed one-handed.

```
Sophie almost wept aloud, upon her visit to Mozart's
birthplace, as she pondered the musical genius' life (so
like her own) and untimely death, but couldn't -- lacking
even a rudimentary set of vocal cords -- even when she
realized her error in coming to Salzburg (in English:
Salt Castle) too late to appreciate the irony when, being
a slug, she dissolved, non-metaphorically, into a puddle of
tears.
From: "Sophie Slug: Eine Kleine Slug-Musik"
```

I reached up from my chair and pulled the chain on the banker's light that shone down on my desk. It answered with a click. Raymond Chandler's typewriter grinned up at me from the shadows with its alphabet teeth.

•••

I had just put on a CD of Baroque Christmas concertos and fired up the laptop to check my e-mail when the doorbell rang.

"I'll get it," said Meg, as she uncurled from the leather sofa. "I've got to start supper anyway."

"Sounds great," I said, as the sound of the Torelli *Concerto de Noël* filled the house. I'd just opened the file that contained the beginnings of my next great work of literature when I heard a familiar voice.

"Where's that owl?!" hollered Moosey from the kitchen. He came dashing in a moment later, looking around in anticipation. "Where's Archimedes?"

"He's not here," I said, closing the laptop and setting it on the shelf. "He takes off when it gets dark and usually doesn't come back in until morning."

"Aw, man..." Moosey flopped onto the sofa in a disappointed heap. He was wearing the winter jacket Meg had given him for Christmas last year, but, even though Meg had gotten him a size larger than he needed, he'd grown so much over the past year, it looked as though he'd need another one in a few weeks. His mop of straw-colored hair was sticking out from beneath a lumberjack's cap, red-plaid with sheepskin earflaps. The wire-rimmed glasses sat slightly askew on his freckled nose and his red high-top tennis shoes now rested comfortably on the coffee table.

"Shoes off the table," I said. "If I can't do it, you can't either."

Moosey grinned and shifted his position, dropping his feet to the floor just as Meg and Ardine walked into the room.

"Ardine brought us a bottle of wine," Meg said, holding up a bottle of Shiraz.

"It was Bud's idea," mumbled Ardine. "He said to tell you not to drink any of the other bottles. Whatever that means."

Ardine was bone thin and hard. She'd had a tough life, no doubt, but now did a good business making and selling quilts. Her graying hair was tied back in a loose ponytail and she had on a wool overcoat that had seen many winters.

"He said you'd like this one just as well. Maybe better."

"Excellent!" I said.

"Hey, what's this?" Moosey, never one to sit still for more than a minute, had bounced over to my typewriter and was looking over my latest literary effort.

"That's my new children's book. *The Adventures of Sophie Slug.*"

"Hmm," said Moosey, reading over the page, his lips moving silently. He finished and looked up, a confused smile on his face. "I don't get it."

"You're not alone there," Meg said.

"This is very complicated and sophisticated humor, Moosey. It works on many levels."

Moosey looked at me, waiting for an explanation.

I sighed with exasperation. "Okay, Sophie is obviously on a trip to Mozart's birthplace, which, as we all know, is Salzburg, Austria. The first funny thing is that a slug is on a vacation in the first place. Then, the fact that she 'almost' wept aloud, but couldn't because she didn't possess any vocal cords, is the setup for the last bit of her dissolving in a puddle of tears."

Moosey looked at me blankly. I looked over at Ardine. Same expression.

"Because dissolving in a puddle of tears is a metaphor for crying," I continued. "And tears are salty. So when it's revealed that Sophie is a slug and dissolves non-metaphorically, it means that she really did dissolve—literally—because of her tears. Also, the fact that she empathizes with Mozart's genius is hilarious!"

Meg giggled. Moosey just stared.

"Salzburg," I explained, "literally means 'salt castle.' It's named for the salt mine on Mount Dürrnberg overlooking Hallein, just south of the city. Of course Sophie wouldn't know this, being a tourist slug and not speaking German."

Moosey blinked.

"And if you put salt on a slug, the slug dissolves. It's ironic, then, that Sophie Slug meets her demise in a city named after salt even though her own tears were the instrument of her death—tears that might just as well have killed her in Peoria, Illinois. Then, to top it off, there's the clever little tag: *Eine Kleine Slug-Musik*. It's a reference to a famous work by Mozart. So you see, Moosey, this story contains multiple layers of pathos and irony. It's a fable for our time."

"How could she get a ticket?" asked Moosey.

"Huh?" I said, confused.

"How could a slug get a plane ticket?" said Ardine. "I was wondering the same thing. It's a legitimate question."

Meg laughed out loud.

"You know," I said, "great writers and humorists aren't really appreciated until they're dead."

"There's a thought," said Ardine, a smile finally appearing on her worn face.

"I like Harry Potter better," said Moosey. "Not as many slugs."

"Are y'all gonna come up and get a Christmas tree this year?" asked Ardine. "We've still got some nice ten-foot-tall blue spruces left. I'll give you a real deal." Ardine was a seasonal employee at the Pine Valley Christmas Tree Farm.

"What kind of deal?" Meg asked, always on the lookout for a bargain.

"Forty-five bucks," said Ardine. "No one wants them ten-foot trees. They're two years too late in the harvesting. All we can do with 'em is chop 'em up for garlands and they're even mostly too big for that. Needles too far apart." She looked around the living room. "It'd go great in here, though."

"It would," agreed Meg. "We'll come up on Saturday morning and pick one out."

"Why so late?" asked Ardine. "Most folks around here get their tree up right after Thanksgiving."

"We like to leave ours up a little longer," Meg answered. "So we wait until a couple of weeks before Christmas to put it up."

"You know," I said, "the twelve days of Christmas and all that."

"Ten frogs a-leaping," sang Moosey, breaking into song and jumping over the ottoman to illustrate the verse. "Nine ladles prancing, eight days of milking, seven swiney swimmers, six something-something..." He went down on one knee and stuck his arms out like Al Jolson. "Five gooool-den riiings!..."

"That's the one," I said. "The very song. Here. Have a cookie." I tossed him a springerle from a basket on one of the end tables. Springerles are very hard Christmas cookies made from an old German recipe that uses quarry stone as the main ingredient. The upside is that they will last indefinitely, impervious to mold, insects, nuclear wars, and the ravages of time. The downside is, if you're not careful, you will break all your teeth trying to eat them. I liked springerles and ordered a tin of them every Christmas.

Moosey caught the cookie and immediately tried to take a bite. "Ow!" he said, then took it out of his mouth and looked at it in consternation.

"You've got to work at it," I told him. "Once you break through the outer shell, it's the most delicious cookie you'll ever eat." I didn't tell him that it was *all* outer shell.

"Tastes a little like licorice," said Moosey sitting down on the sofa and gnawing on the hardtack. "I like 'em."

He kicked his feet back and forth and sang to himself while trying to figure the best way to break the springerle code. He finally decided to lick it into submission. "Four clawing birds, three wenches, two turkledoves, and a parson up a psaltree."

Chapter 12

The first big snowfall of the year in St. Germaine is a beautiful thing, and this one was no exception. Getting snow the second week of December was about business-as-usual for us in recent years. Old-timers talk about getting blizzards in early November, but that hasn't happened for a while. Oh, every now and then a cold front will come through early in the season, but we don't really get geared up for a good, heavy snow until December.

Meg had driven me into Asheville the day before and I'd rented a new Toyota Tundra four-door pickup: four-wheel drive, automatic everything, a sound system with eight speakers, satellite radio, and more bells and whistles than you could shake a stick at. It rode like a dream, or so it seemed compared to a 1962 Chevy that saw its last new shock absorber when Nixon was president. More than that, I could make a turn with only one hand. My other hand rested on the steering wheel, encased in plaster, in a supporting role.

I drove slowly into town and was amazed, as I always am early on a sunny, cold morning following eight inches of powder, at the sparkling beauty of the square—the boughs of the fir trees weighed down with new snow, drifts resting against the gazebo in the middle of the park, the streets still pristine and unmarked except for the occasional footprints of other early risers. It was a picture that Norman Rockwell would have been proud to paint. It wouldn't last long, of course. As soon as traffic picked up and businesses opened, the snow on the streets would turn to sludge. But right now, it was a beautiful sight.

The Kiwanis Club had begun to put up their Christmas crèche, a project that would take most of the week. It was quite a structure, a full-sized stable with post and beam construction, and was being erected in its now-traditional location, the southernmost corner of Sterling Park, just across the street and down seventy yards from the front doors of St. Barnabas. The main posts had been set into the ground and the rest of the construction materials—beams, siding, thatching for the roof, and everything else—were stacked neatly in the vacant lot on the other side of Maple Street. Everything had been covered with tarps and looked, on this cold morning, like a mountain of snow. The Living Nativity program would begin a week from Wednesday and continue every night until the Sunday before Christmas. Five shows, each lasting forty-five minutes. The park would be packed. Our other big event, the Rotary Club's Christmas parade, was scheduled for this Saturday at two in the afternoon.

I parked my truck in front of the police station, went inside and was making a pot of coffee when the phone rang. It was Meg.

"Can you make a phone call over to England?"

"I guess so," I said. "What's up?"

"I just spoke to an Arthur Farrant. He's a vicar somewhere in Nantwich, wherever that is. He wants you to call him back."

"I don't know anyone named Arthur Farrant."

"I think Geoffrey put him in touch with you."

Geoffrey Chester was an old friend who worked at York Minster. He knew absolutely everyone. "Okay," I said, "I'll give him a call. What's the number?"

Meg read it to me. I wrote it down and sat at Nancy's desk, flipping idly through the week's reports until the coffee pot sputtered to a stop. Then I poured myself a mug and went into my office to make my overseas call.

•••

Gaylen Weatherall wasn't in the church office when I walked across the park to St. Barnabas about an hour later. Marilyn told me that, until Gaylen felt a little better, she wasn't planning to come in except for emergencies and Sunday mornings. She'd do her day-to-day business from her house.

"Would you like to see Deacon Mushrat?" she asked, her eyes darting to his open office door across the hall. "He's *always* here."

I declined the offer and decided that, on a beautiful morning like this, a walk up to the parsonage would be just the thing.

"I'm just going to go get my gun," I told Marilyn. "I'm getting in some target practice this afternoon. I'll drop in on Gaylen and see how she's doing."

I unlocked the side door of the church, entered the nave, and walked up the stairs to the choir loft. I slid behind the organ console, reached underneath the bench and felt for the box that my friend Michael Baum, of the Baum-Boltoph Organ Company, had built into the seat. I found the two hidden levers, released them both, and the drawer popped open. Then I took the Glock 9 mm pistol out of the box and slid it into my coat pocket.

•••

Gaylen answered the door when I rang the bell, looking pretty good, all things considered. Her makeup almost covered the two black circles under her eyes. Almost, but not quite. And the piece of tape that crossed her nose was flesh-colored. If you saw her from a ways back, she looked just fine. Or, as Raymond Chandler once wrote, "From thirty feet away she looked like a lot of class. From ten feet away she looked like something made up to be seen from thirty feet away." Her right hand was in a cast up to her elbow, and she held it tightly against her side.

"Glad to see you're up and about," I said.

"Uh-huh," Gaylen answered.

"C'mon. I know you can talk. Just use your lips."

"Yes, yes," she grumbled, her lips drawing away from her teeth in her effort to form words through a broken jaw that was wired shut. "I can talk. Slowly and softly. And it takes a lot of effort. Come on in."

I followed her into the living room, a comfortable room with an old sofa and two overstuffed arm chairs facing a gas fireplace. The fire was blazing. Heart-pine floors, original to the house, were tastefully covered by worn Persian carpets. The plaster walls had been freshly painted just before Gaylen had moved back and the pictures she'd chosen for the walls made the room both informal and inviting.

"Coffee?" asked Gaylen, through gritted teeth.

"I'll get it," I said, picking up Gaylen's empty mug from the side table. She sat down heavily in her arm chair, favoring her left side, and I saw a grimace before I disappeared into the kitchen to refill her cup and get one for myself. I was back a moment later with hers.

"Cream, no sugar," I said, as I handed her the cup.

"Thanks."

I headed back to the kitchen and hollered back over my shoulder. "Now that I've got this broken arm, I've got to make two trips to do everything."

Gaylen waited until I'd come back with my own coffee before replying. "I'm so sorry about the accident," she started. Tears sprang to her eyes. "I feel so terrible..."

"Don't worry about it," I said. "I'll be fine. You'll be fine. And good news! All the baby skunks survived."

Gaylen couldn't help but laugh. "Great. That's just great. All the skunks survived. The story of my life."

"How're the ribs?"

"They hurt, but they're getting better."

"That's good. So you'll be celebrating the Eucharist this Sunday?"

"That is the current plan," Gaylen said slowly, working very hard to enunciate her words. "Donald will be doing the sermon. I heard that your cantata was excellent last Sunday. I'm sorry I missed it."

"It was okay," I said. "I didn't care for the organist's registrations. And her prelude..."

Gaylen put up her hand and smiled. "We'll get through this. I'll be back to work full-time by Epiphany."

"That's why I'm here, actually," I said. "I have a proposal."

Gaylen's eyebrows went up in interest.

"I just had a phone call from a vicar in Nantwich," I said.

"Nantwich?"

"Northwestern England. Geoffrey Chester gave him my name and number. The church there has decided to schedule a tour of some religious treasures. Apparently, once the tour was announced, the vicar got a phone call identifying St. Barnabas as one of the wealthy churches on the east coast of the U.S."

"A dubious distinction," mumbled Gaylen. "I'm pretty sure our illustrious bishop flagged us."

"Be that as it may, this is quite an interesting proposition."

Gaylen settled back into the cushion and took a sip of coffee. "Okay, I'm all ears."

I reached into the pocket of my coat and pulled out a sheaf of papers. "I took notes," I admitted. "This is quite an amazing story." I unfolded the papers and began.

•••

"Arthur Farrant is the vicar of a small parish in Nantwich called St. Hywyn's. Like many of the parish churches in England, St. Hywyn's is trying desperately to raise money to repair the 16th-century building and keep the church going. It's in a very poor section of the town. The vicar says that the main mission of the parish is running a soup kitchen and providing clothing for the poor."

"You got verification?" Gaylen asked.

"I called Geoffrey and he gave me the number of a friend of his at St. Mary's in the same town. They both told me Farrant's on the up and up and does great work. He's even been featured in his local paper several times. But the British economy is as bad as ours and they're hurting for funds."

Gaylen nodded, but didn't say anything. She motioned for me to continue.

"So St. Hywyn's hired this fund-raising group. It was just a local firm and they didn't charge much, but they gave them some ideas on how to raise some money. One of the ideas was a throw-back to the Middle Ages."

"Don't tell me. They're going on a crusade."

"Nah. You're thinking of Billy Graham. This is even better. Relics."

"Relics?"

"Yep. January 6th is the Feast Day of St. Hywyn," I said.

"Same as the Feast of the Epiphany."

"Yep. Here's his story." I looked at the folded paper in my good hand to get my facts straight. "Some of this is just legend, of course. But still..."

"Let's hear it," said Gaylen.

"St. Hywyn," I began, "also called Owen or Ewen, was a disciple of St. Cadfan in the 5th century. He founded monasteries and churches in Wales and western England. No one knows how the little church in Nantwich became associated with this saint, but it may have been because of his feast day and what happened in 1164."

"My knowledge of medieval history being what it is, you'll have to elaborate."

"Really? You don't know what happened in 1164?"

Gaylen snarled.

I laughed. "In that year, Holy Roman Emperor Frederick Barbarossa gave the bones of the Three Kings to the cathedral at Cologne. According to the St. Hywyn parish legend, the bones were carried to Cologne in a caravan headed by a Welsh priest, coincidentally also named Ewen. The relics were enshrined and are in Germany to this day. But here's the rub. Ewen managed to get home to England with some of the relics hidden in his bags. He and they landed in the little monastery at Nantwich where the bones were stored for some seven hundred years. The reliquary where the bones are kept dates from the 1400s. Apparently it's quite a work of art, made of wood with silver and gold inlay. And these bones kept the monks flush for many, many years."

"You're saying that one of the Three Kings is in Nantwich?"

"That's the legend."

"One of the Three Kings that visited Bethlehem? The gold, frankincense, and myrrh Three Kings?"

"The very ones." I checked my notes. "The reliquary was hidden by the monks in 1536 when the monastery was shut down. It was rediscovered in 1892 and returned to the church where the monastery stood. It's been there ever since, along with Hywyn's staff, little known and rarely visited. Anyway, the vicar and the vestry thought that, if advertised correctly, sending the relics on a short tour of the eastern U.S. might generate several thousand pounds after expenses. The reliquary is to be displayed at several well-to-do churches. We'd have to make an offering to St. Hywyn's."

"Hmm. And the money would go to the feeding and clothing of the poor?"

"Well, that and the upkeep of the building. If that isn't done, there won't be any more feeding or clothing going on at all. Here's a picture of the reliquary."

I handed the last page of my notes to Gaylen, the page that I'd printed off the internet with a beautiful photograph of the Nantwich Reliquary. There had been a lot of information, once I'd Googled the subject, most of it put out by the publicity firm the church had hired.

Gaylen studied the photo, then pointed to the bottom of the page and said, "I see some links here to some auction sites. They're not selling it, are they?"

"Not that I know of. Farrant didn't mention that. But I suppose they would sell it if they had to."

"Hmm. How much will it cost us?"

"Four thousand bucks. And we get the reliquary the first week of January. It would be a great centerpiece for our Epiphany service. We can take up an offering for the mission work as well."

"Sounds reasonable. Just to be clear, you're saying that we're going to have the bones of one of the Three Kings on display for our Epiphany service?"

"Yep."

Gaylen managed a smile. "Well, why not?"

Chapter 13

The Slab Café was bustling for lunch, but with our reserved table status, Nancy and I calmly pushed our way through the line of would-be patrons and sat down to the angry glares of many out-of-towners.

"You know, dear," said one of the men to his wife, but loud enough for everyone in line to hear, "it's amazing that the police in these little burgs think they can just barge in wherever they want and get a table without waiting in line like civilized people."

Nancy stood back up, put her hand on the butt of her gun and gave him a hard look. "Patriot Act," she said.

The man mumbled something unintelligible and Nancy sat back down, followed by Pete a few seconds later.

"Don't scare the customers," he said.

Nancy pulled a sheaf of papers out of her inside overcoat pocket and put them on the table. "This is Sal LaGrassa's dossier. The hit-man. Remember?"

"Of course," I said. "Do I have to read the whole thing, or can you give me the highlights?"

"Highlights it is," said Nancy. "But first, some breakfast."

"Or lunch," suggested Pete. "It's eleven o'clock."

"Breakfast," said Nancy.

"Breakfast," I agreed.

"I'll order it in the kitchen," said Pete, getting to his feet. "But don't tell anything until I get back."

Nancy held her coffee cup aloft just long enough for Pauli Girl to spot her and come dancing over with a half-full carafe.

"Here you go, hon," she said, filling both our cups and Pete's as well. By the time we'd taken our first sips, Pete was back at the table.

"You're getting omelets," he announced. "And biscuits with gravy."

"Sounds fine to me," I said, then turned to Nancy. "Okay, what have you got on Sal LaGrassa?"

Nancy thumbed through her papers. "Born Salvator Francis LaGrassa. Forty-five years old. Six feet even, a hundred and ninety pounds. Wanted for questioning in sixteen murders-for-hire. He's also suspected in several major heists. Never arrested, never convicted, never even brought in for questioning. No siblings, no wife, no kids...no family at all, for that matter. His mother, apparently his only close relative, died in New York five years ago.

He's rumored to be one half of a team. The FBI suspects that the other person may be a woman."

"Can they close any of these cases?" I asked.

Nancy shook her head. "Nope. Ryan Jackson says they've got nothing substantial. No clear evidence at all. If they'd caught him, all they could do was question him and let him go."

"But they're pretty sure?" said Pete.

"Oh, they're sure, all right. He was a seriously bad guy. They just couldn't take him to trial."

"What else?" I asked.

"Says here he spent the last few years in Montana on a ranch that belongs to a dummy corporation on Grand Cayman. He was in Montana when the feebs lost track of him."

"That explains the clothes," I said. "Real cowboy stuff."

"He liked cars," said Nancy, now skimming the pages. "Owned a Maserati GranCabrio and an Audi R8 4.2. Also a Hummer. A big one."

Pete whistled. "Those ain't cheap."

Nancy continued skimming. "Several off-shore accounts that the FBI knew about. Probably more that they didn't. He bought a couple of original sketches by Gustav Klimt last year from Christie's. 10k apiece. But, at that same auction a painting disappeared. Something called *The Holy Family with the infant St. John the Baptist and two shepherds*. Oil and tempera on a panel. Circa 1500. Valued at between five and eight hundred thousand. The winning bid was three hundred two thousand, but when the buyer went to pick it up, the painting was gone. Mr. LaGrassa was a person of interest, but he was nowhere to be found. He also had an affinity for antiquities."

"Man!" said Pete.

"The thing is, there were many more expensive paintings at the auction."

"Opportunity?" I said. "Or maybe a buyer in hand."

"I'd say the latter," said Nancy.

"Okay," I said, "cars, art, real estate, bank accounts...what else?"

"Wine," said Nancy, with a big smile. "He really loved wine. Expensive wine."

"That's what he was doing at Old Man Frost's!" said Pete. "He was trying to buy your wine."

"He obviously knew what it was," I said. "And how much it was worth. I saw him trying to dial his cell phone in the middle of the auction, but he couldn't get any service out there."

"It caught him by surprise, I bet," said Nancy. "He didn't expect to see something like that show up at an auction in the middle of the Appalachian mountains."

"And he didn't have enough cash," said Pete. "And couldn't get it."

"Sounds right," said Nancy. "I doubt they would have taken an out-of-town check for more than ten grand."

"Still doesn't answer the most important thing," I said.

"What's that?" said Pete.

Pauli Girl appeared at the table with an arm-full of omelets, grits, baked apples, and a basket of biscuits. She set the plates down, one at a time, in front of each of us, the basket of biscuits in the middle of the table, a bowl of gravy beside it, re-filled all our coffee cups, and never spilled a drop. Then she smiled and whisked herself off to her next table.

"What's the most important thing?" asked Pete again, reaching for the bread.

"How 'bout it, Nancy?" I asked, smiling. "You know the most important thing?"

"Yep," she said. "Easy." She raised a forkful of steaming grits to her lips and gently blew across the top, cooling it enough to slide into her mouth. "Mmm," she said, closing her eyes for a moment. "I love grits!"

"The important thing..." insisted Pete.

Nancy looked at him. "Oh. Sorry. The important thing is, what was he doing in St. Germaine in the first place?"

•••

The choir loft was full for the first time since the dedication of our new church last May. Christmas always brought out the choir, it seemed. The bass section was populated by the regulars—Mark Wells, Bob Solomon, Fred May, Steve DeMoss, Phil Camp and Varmit LeMieux. Varmit didn't really sing. He was just there to keep an eye on his wife, Muffy, a redhead who would have made even Liberace consider playing for the other team. Muffy had a signature look, which included dark leggings and very tight angora sweaters in a variety of shades. Muffy dreamed of being a country singer and couldn't quite get the Loretta Lynn twang out of her rendition of *O Holy Night,* which she and Varmit lobbied for every Christmas Eve since they moved to town and joined the choir.

The tenors were anchored by Marjorie Plimpton and Randy Hatteberg. We had another tenor as well, Burt Coley, but he was employed by the Boone Police Department and took weekend duty whenever he could. He usually only showed up at Christmas and Easter. Marjorie was considering dropping to the bass section as soon as she drank her way into a low A.

Altos were plentiful at St. Barnabas. In fact, the Back Row Altos (BRAs) had formed their own militant feminist organization. In response, the Front Row Alto Union (FRAUs) had decided to band together into their own coalition, but they just didn't have the political clout that their back row counterparts had garnered. The BRA organization was "by invitation only." Very exclusive. Elaine Hixon had considered dropping out of the soprano section just to join, but she couldn't get in. Her application was rejected. "She's way too nice," said Martha Hatteberg, one of the dissenting voters.

Altogether we had ten altos on the roll and an equal number of sopranos. If everyone showed up, the choir loft was packed with twenty-eight singers. This rarely happened, but it happened tonight.

"What's this stuff about a slug?" said Marjorie, reading my latest masterpiece. "I hate slugs!"

"Me, too," agreed Muffy. "And what about the under-dwarves?"

"I only have one typing hand. I do what I can. Meg suggested I start a new children's book series starring Sophie Slug."

"Don't you try to pin this on me," said Meg. "I didn't write it, for heaven's sake."

"I kinda like it," said Rebecca, one of the BRAs. "It has a certain *je ne sais quoi.*"

"I don't get it," said Edna Terra-Pocks from the organ console. "Has this got something to do with choral music?"

"Nope," said Georgia. "I think it's about a slug."

"Right." I said. "So here's the plan. This Sunday we're singing the Redford *Rejoice in the Lord Alway* at the offertory and Thom Pavlechko's *Panis Angelicus* during communion."

"Not very Christmassy," said Edna. "What about *Silent Night*? I have a great arrangement!"

"We're still in Advent, Edna," I said.

Edna rolled her eyes and addressed the choir. "Well, this Sunday I've got a wonderful toccata for the prelude anyway. Y'all will love it! It's got so many notes, I have to wear my sports bra to play it!"

"Great," I sighed. "That's great. Anyway, we've got a lot to look at. Don't forget that we're singing the eleven o'clock service on Christmas Eve."

"How about Muffy singing *O Holy Night*?" called Varmit from the back row.

"Of course!" Edna called back good-naturedly. "What key would you like it in?"

I glared at Meg, but she suddenly pretended to be interested in a dynamic marking she'd previously missed.

"Key of D," said Muffy. "At least I think it's D. Which one has the high A?"

"That's D, all right," said Edna. "I can't wait to hear you!"

"I have an even higher high A than last year," bragged Muffy. "At least, that's what my vocal coach says."

Chapter 14

It wasn't emotion that made Sophie's lower lip tremble as she beheld the LDS Tabernacle on Temple Square, the seat of her faith and the final harbor of her pilgrimage, but as she felt her carefully-positioned Oprah wig begin to ooze off the side of her head and her eye-stalks droop like Tiger Woods' putter, it was the realization that, when her Uncle Alosquisious warned her against this odyssey saying she was "too tender" and that her "heart would melt," Uncle Al wasn't being at all figurative, but literal, since her destination had been Salt Lake City and she was, after all, a slug.

From: "Sophie Slug: A Mormon's Journey"

•••

"I rather like it," said Joyce, with a twinkling laugh. "It's got everything: drama, love, alliteration, poetry, religion, heartbreak, topical humor... and do I detect a hint of nutmeg?"

"That's just your *Weihnachtsgeist*," I said. "Your Christmas Spirit. We all smell nutmeg this time of year."

"How about an illustrator for your one-sentence books?" she asked.

"I'm pretty sure he doesn't need a good one," said Bev as she walked into the meeting room carrying a full mug of coffee in one hand and a carafe in the other. She set them both on the table. "I could do it. All he needs is someone who can draw a puddle with a couple of eyeballs floating in it. How hard can that be?"

"You're forgetting about the scenery," I said. "Salzburg Castle by night, the Alps, sea birds, ocean vistas, the Tabernacle. All very picturesque."

"Puddles," said Bev, pulling out a chair and settling behind her steaming cup. "Puddles and eyeballs. Where is everyone?"

"Gaylen's not coming to any worship meetings till after Christmas," I said. "I dropped by her house this morning and chatted with her. She gave me her proxy."

"I'll bet she did," said Bev.

Elaine and Marilyn walked into the meeting room with their empty coffee cups and wasted no time filling them. Elaine had brought me a cup as well and I gratefully took the last of the coffee from the carafe. Marilyn sat at the head of the table and readied her notebook for whatever notes she might need to make. Then she smiled demurely, cupped her coffee in both hands and silently sipped the hot beverage, peering at everyone from behind her round spectacles.

Kimberly Walnut and Donald Mushrat came in next, looking extremely guilty for two people who had nothing much to be guilty about. I'm a detective and trained to notice these things, but these two were as obvious as a tattoo on a Lutheran.

"You two look like you've been holding hands in the bathroom," said Bev.

Kimberly Walnut's face went beet-red and she sat down quickly, her hands fidgeting nervously in her lap. Deacon Mushrat found the other empty chair, but, except looking vaguely uncomfortable, didn't seem to be nearly as rattled as our Director of Christian Formation.

"Right," said Bev. "Let's get started."

"What about my prayer?" said Deacon Mushrat. "I'd like to open with a prayer."

"I expect you've got plenty to confess," mumbled Elaine.

"I'll do it," Bev said, clasping her hands on the table. "Bless the work of our hands, Dear Lord. Amen."

"I didn't even have time to bow my head," complained the deacon.

"Gotta be quick when Bev prays," said Elaine.

"Humph," grunted Deacon Mushrat, then asked, "Do we have anything special for this Sunday?"

"Nope," said Joyce. "Nothing special. It's a regular service. The Third Sunday of Advent. Gaylen will be back to celebrate the Eucharist. I'm sure we're all looking forward to her return."

Deacon Mushrat yawned.

"Don't forget the Christmas parade tomorrow," said Elaine. "Two o'clock. The youth group will be selling hot chocolate out on the steps. Proceeds go to the youth mission trip fund."

"Money changers in the temple," said the deacon with a sneer. "I may mention it in my sermon on Sunday."

"Oh, give it a rest," muttered Marilyn.

"What time are our Christmas Eve services?" Mushrat asked. "I presume I'll have to get my sermons ready."

"Five o'clock and eleven," said Bev. "The one at five is a family service. You'll have to tell the Christmas Story. No sermon."

"No sermon? On Christmas Eve?" Deacon Mushrat was incredulous.

"You can preach at the eleven o'clock service. Twelve minutes. There will be three hundred people here for communion. We'd like to get finished before one in the morning."

"I have to preach what the Holy Spirit leads me to preach," said Mushrat. "Twelve minutes or forty."

"Twelve," said Bev. "Practice in front of a mirror."

Deacon Mushrat sniffed. "We'll see," he said. "By the way, I had seven people come to my Wednesday night series on Malachi. We had an awesome prayer meeting for the leadership of St. Barnabas afterwards."

"How nice," said Elaine, sweetness oozing from every pore. "I would have come, but I had choir practice."

"Me, too," said Joyce, even though she didn't. She shot me a quick, apologetic look.

"And since I'm going to be here for six months," said the deacon, "I'd like to continue my Wednesday night Bible studies. In fact, when the new year starts, I'd like to begin leading my awesome, Biblical weight loss program."

"What?" said Joyce, not sure she'd heard correctly.

"Many people want to get in shape at the beginning of the new year," said Mushrat. "What better way to do it than through Biblically-based teaching? I call it *Jehobics: God's answer for losing weight and feeling great!*"

"What?" said Joyce again.

"We're going to take back the health and wealth the devil has stolen. We shouldn't make our members go to the 'world' to lose weight. They don't need Jenny Craig. They need Jesus! And we need to give them an awesome opportunity right here at St. Barnabas."

"So," I said. "*Jehobics*. Great idea, Donald. You're going to have to start it on the 13th, though. We're going to have our usual Epiphany service on January 6th and it's a Wednesday evening."

"Don't forget our 'Cocoon' program," said Kimberly Walnut. "Donald and I were just working on it. The kids will be here on Tuesday, the 5th."

"If Epiphany's on a Wednesday, we should have a church-wide supper," said Bev, still reeling from the *Jehobics* suggestion and trying to get back on track.

"Pot-luck," added Elaine. "I love a pot-luck supper."

"Absolutely. And as the highlight of the service—and I'm not kidding about this—we're going to have the bones of one of the Three Kings on display."

Everyone looked at me like I had just suggested hiring a praise band for Sunday mornings.

"The Three Kings, as in *We Three Kings of Orient Are*?" said Joyce.

"The very same—but just one of them."

"Someone has their bones?" asked Marilyn.

"Yep. They've been in Germany since the Middle Ages. They were originally kept in Constantinople, but moved to Milan in the fourth century. Then to Germany in 1164. In fact, the cathedral at Cologne was constructed to house the relics."

"You're kidding, of course," said Mushrat.

"No, really. Here's the deal..."

It took me another fifteen minutes to explain and answer questions, but when we were finished everyone was very excited. Everyone except the deacon.

"We should not condone the worship of bones," he said. "The Lord hath said, 'You shall not make for yourself an idol, whether in the form of anything that is in heaven above, or that is on the earth beneath, or that is in the water under the earth.' Exodus 18."

"Exodus 20, actually," I said.

The deacon sniffed.

"We're not worshipping them," said Joyce. "Sheesh!"

"It's a relic," Elaine said. "Possibly a relic of one of the Three Kings. It's...it's archeology."

"It's medieval idolatry," said Deacon Mushrat. "Simple people were told by corrupt monks and priests that, if they prayed to the bones and gave money to the monasteries, they'd receive a miracle and be healed. Even if they weren't sick, the monks would have them give their money to the church and pray to the bones in hopes of a better future and salvation."

"Gee," I said. "Sounds like there's a parallel here somewhere. Isn't that what televangelists do? Send in your thousand dollar seed-faith gift, I'll send you an anointed vial of oil, and you can ask for whatever you want."

"It is *nothing* like what televangelists do," said Mushrat, bristling. "Televangelists do the work of the Kingdom."

"I'm afraid I must agree with Donald..." started Kimberly Walnut, who'd been silent up to this point. "I've never even heard of Nantwich."

"Well, it doesn't matter," I said with a dismissive wave of my hand. "It's done. Gaylen already gave her okay and the contract's

81

been signed and faxed to England. Not only that, but I called Bishop O'Connell. He'd never heard of Nantwich either, but is happy to come to the service in full regalia. Put it on your calendars. Our Epiphany service on January 6th will follow a pot-luck dinner." I looked around the table. "That sound about right?"

"Yes," said Elaine. "That sounds about right."

Chapter 15

Saturday morning was cold and clear. It was a perfect day to find a Christmas tree, have lunch downtown and see the Christmas parade. Then home to decorate, drink hot mulled wine, and listen to a new recording I'd received from my classical CD subscription service featuring a Christmas oratorio by Gottfried August Homilius. I was anxious to listen to it, partly because Gottfried Homilius was a student of J.S. Bach, but mainly because I'd never heard of this particular oratorio. *The Joy of the Shepherds Concerning the Birth of Jesus*. The title sounded better in German.

Baxter jumped up into the bed of the new truck and found a seat before Meg or I had reached the doors. He looked at us over the tailgate with an anticipation that made us both laugh out loud. Meg was bundled up in a sweater, a heavy winter coat, gloves, Ugg boots, a red scarf and matching knit cap—all color coordinated to make her the most stylish Christmas tree hunter in the county. I happened to be wearing a pair of khaki canvas insulated overalls and an old jacket that I could manage to fit around my cast. I had a hat as well, one that covered my ears. Not stylish at all, but warm. Very warm. If past Christmases were any indication, Meg would be the one picking out the tree and I'd be standing idly in the wind for the next hour while she carefully inspected each prospect.

"See," said Meg. "I don't mind driving this truck a bit. It's just your old rattle-trap I don't like." She clicked on the stereo. I had a Burl Ives Christmas CD in the player and the strains of *Have a Holly Jolly Christmas* sounded forth from eight very expensive speakers.

"I've never heard Burl sound so lifelike," Meg said.

The drive up to Pine Valley Christmas Tree Farm was dazzling. Most of the snow we'd seen on Wednesday was still hanging on the boughs of the pine, spruce and fir trees, and the ice that glittered on the bare rock jutting from the cliffs reflected the sunlight like diamonds. We discovered, upon our arrival on this frigid morning, that we weren't the only ones to be hunting for our tree in mid-December.

Kimberly Walnut was exiting the parking lot as we drove in, a big tree tied and strapped to the top of her black Chevy Tahoe. She waved to us on her way out. Elaine and Billy Hixon were out talking to Ardine, and I recognized Dr. Hogmanay McTavish's old gold Cadillac and saw his familiar rotund form out on the lot sizing up some Fraser firs. Brother Hog, as he was known to his flock, was an ex-evangelist who had been lured off the tent revival circuit by the prospect of full-time ministry at New Fellowship Baptist Church. He never looked back. Bud trailed behind Brother Hog carrying a chainsaw, and following Bud was another, smaller person whom I couldn't quite make out. Ardine waved to us as we got out of the truck and crunched across the snow to the trailer that served as command central.

"Nice wheels," said Billy. "I almost got me one of those Tundras, but then I realized that it cost more than my house."

"It's a rental," I said. "I'll be back in Old Rattle-Trap before you know it."

"The blue spruces are on the lower lot," said Ardine. "Y'all go pick out the one you want, and I'll send Bud over as soon as he's back from helping Brother Hog. Billy can cut his own."

"I brought my own saw," said Billy. "I even brought Elaine so she could carry the tree back to the truck."

"Yuk yuk," said Elaine. "You're a riot. We'll see you guys at the parade?"

"We'll be there," said Meg. She pointed down the hill into the lower lot. "Ooo, there's a good one."

"Who's with Bud?" I asked, looking in the opposite direction, shading my eyes and squinting against the sun.

"Some girl he met called Elfie or something like that," said Ardine.

"Elphina?" asked Meg.

"That's it. Elphina. She told me it was her vampire name." Ardine frowned. "If you ask me, she could use a few good meals. That, and a smack."

I chuckled. "Well, tell Bud to watch his neck. We'll wait for him down on the lower lot. Tell him to take his time. We'll probably be a while."

•••

It took us most of the morning to pick out the perfect ten-foot spruce, have Bud and Elphina cut it down, tie it up, and put it in the back of the pickup with Baxter. We headed down the mountain to St. Germaine with plans to have lunch at the Ginger Cat. We drove into town, slipped into my reserved parking place, stashed Baxter in the police station and walked across Sterling Park to the restaurant. It was a quarter to two when we finished our flaming Christmas pudding (the chef's special) and walked back across the park to the judges' stand. Nancy was standing at the top of the courthouse steps and gave us a wave when she saw us. We climbed up and joined her.

The judges for this year's parade were already at their table and appeared to be taking their job very seriously, going over each applicant's entry sheet and busily making notes before the festivities commenced. The St. Germaine crowd had already gathered around the edges of the park, as well as up and down Main and Maple Streets. This year's head judge, Mr. Christopher Lloyd, looked up, smiled, and went back to his notes. His cohorts were Roderick Bateman, owner of Blueridge Furs, and Kimmy Jo Jameson, widow of Jimmy Jameson, the race car driver.

Kimmy Jo had gotten married again after Jimmy had been killed in a wreck, just after he'd won a race, but decided to keep her first married name since she was now in great demand as a speaker at women's church conferences. I didn't know her current husband, but word had it that he was a "couples minister" at a big, non-denominational church in Raleigh. Her book and video Bible study, *Victorious Secret—a Woman's Spiritual Guide to Purpose Driven Intimacy,* had risen to the top of the Christian bestseller list. Kimmy Jo was our celebrity judge, but was still considered to be a local gal by the folks in St. Germaine, seeing that her dear departed first husband had been buried, along with his race car, in Wormy Acres. Kimmy Jo had heard about *Our State* magazine covering the parade, and since she was about to come out with a line of Christian lingerie and faithwear, she was trying to get all the exposure she could. Mr. Christopher was still waiting for word on his HGTV show, so he hadn't quite risen to celebrity status. But he'd been offered the head judge position before Kimmy Jo came on board, and he wasn't about to give it up.

Across the park I could see the St. Barnabas Youth Group working the crowd in front of the church before the parade started, hawking hot chocolate for a dollar a cup. The Holy Grounds Coffee Shop was selling coffee and muffins right across the street, and since Biff and Kylie Moffit were both Kiwanians, the club had let them set up shop in the crèche that had been constructed for the Living Nativity. Parade vendors with balloons, horns, Santa hats, cotton candy, and who knew what else—or for that matter, where these vendors came from—were traipsing around the square doing a brisk business with kids who had badgered their parents out of a five dollar bill. The air was dry and cold, and the wind we'd endured up at the tree farm had quieted: perfect weather for a Christmas parade.

Pete and Cynthia appeared behind us while we were surveying the sight before us from the top step of the courthouse. As mayor, Cynthia supposed that she should make an appearance on the judging stand before making her way down to the Piggly Wiggly, changing into her belly-dancing outfit, and climbing onto her float.

"Merry Christmas!" said Cynthia. "Great day, huh?"

"Great," I agreed.

"Aren't you going to freeze?" asked Meg. "How're you going to shimmy in this weather?"

"I've got a flesh-colored body suit on under my clothes. And electric socks. If I keep wiggling, I should be all right."

"Well, that hardly seems fair," I said. "A body suit is cheating. We were hoping for an authentic, bare-midriff, middle-eastern rendition of *Jingle Bell Rock*."

"You'll get the Eskimo version, and like it," snapped Cynthia. "I don't know why I agreed to this in the first place."

"Publicity," Pete said. "There's no business like show business."

We heard the strains of the first marching band playing *Santa Claus Is Coming To Town* coming up Maple Street toward town, although we couldn't yet see it.

"That'll be Green Valley High School," said Cynthia. "They're first." She sighed heavily. "I'd better get going."

"How many bands this year?" asked Nancy.

"Nine, I think," said Cynthia. "If they all show up. I was down at the Pig earlier. We were still a couple of bands short."

"They'll be here," said Meg, looking around the town square at the lingering snow, the holiday decorations, and the bustling activity. "It's a beautiful day!"

•••

Moosey and Bernadette came scrambling up the steps of the courthouse, each of them carrying two cups of lidded hot chocolate, one in each hand.

"We thought you might like some chocolate," said Bernadette, handing one to Meg and another to Pete.

"Thank you very much," said Meg. She took the lid off the cup and took a sip. "It's delicious."

Moosey handed one of his cups to Nancy and the other to me.

"Thanks," said Nancy.

"Indeed," said Pete.

"Thanks, Moosey," I added.

Moosey waited until we'd all taken a sip, then said, "That'll be ten dollars."

"*Ten dollars?*" said Pete, almost choking.

"It's a dollar per cup," explained Bernadette. "Plus the delivery fee and gratuity."

"*Delivery fee?*" said Pete. "*Gratuity?*"

"Yessir," said Moosey. "Pauli Girl says that's usually twenty percent. She figured it up for us. "Four dollars for the hot chocolate. Four dollars for the delivery charge. Two dollars for the gratuity."

"Pretty steep," said Meg. "But never mind. It's well worth it." She handed me her cup and opened her purse to find a bill.

"Hang on," I said. "This is all going to the youth fund, right?"

"Well..." said Moosey. "The four dollars for the chocolate for sure. The delivery charge and the gratuity should go to the deliverers since me and Bernie thought of it." He shrugged his shoulders and gave us his lopsided grin. "Right?"

"Wrong," I said. "You two give all that money you've been collecting to Mrs. Sterling, you hear? And I'll find out if you don't."

Bernadette took Meg's ten dollar bill and huffed in disgust. "All that work for nothing," she said. Then she and Moosey turned and took the steps down to the street two at a time, then dashed across the pavement into the park well in front of the first band.

•••

Big Mel was a champion.

At the age of five, Melanie Louise Gedunken came off the cattle ranch her family owned in Texas and won her first beauty pageant by blowing away the competition in the talent department. She wasn't a beautiful child, not by any stretch of the imagination, but, in a certain muted light, wearing a wig and a lot of her mother's makeup (and before her permanent teeth came in,) she might have been taken as "cute." Still, she was head and shoulders above her competition. Literally. Hence her nickname, Big Mel. Melanie's talent—the one that cinched that early title of "Grand Supreme" in the American Royalty Tiny Tot Pageant—was tap-dancing. She took it very seriously, practicing until her mother begged her to stop breaking all the tiles in the kitchen.

At the age of seven, then five feet six inches tall and strong enough to throw and castrate a calf in three minutes flat, she took up the baton, and twirling became her passion. Throughout her formative years she won prize after prize in her age group at the National Baton Twirling Championships in the categories of Solo, Strut, Two-Baton, and Three-Baton. Big Mel graduated from high school (having reached her final height of six feet four) as the top-rated twirler in the nation, and her tap routines in the Dance-Twirl division garnered her a full scholarship to the University of South Carolina where she majored in Physical Education with a specialty in kinetics.

Big Mel married after graduation and moved to Boone (her husband Eric's home town) to open her own studio featuring tap, twirling, gymnastics, and her championship philosophy. Eric had long since left the union, but Big Mel wasn't interested in re-marrying. She poured her passion into inspiring children to walk (and tap) in her size fourteen shoes.

The trick, thought Big Mel, to making The Mud Creek Tapping Academy and Training Center a viable contender for the Grand Marshall's Prize in the St. Germaine Christmas Parade was to give the crowd what it wanted. The foundation of her float was a flatbed trailer, thirty feet long and eight and a half feet wide. She would have used her forty-eight foot trailer, but it was too long to make the turns downtown and thus against the rules. The beds of both special competition trailers were floored with planks of unfinished white oak to give the greatest percussive resonance and resilience to the tappers. Giant public address speakers, positioned in the back of the pickup truck pulling the float, could be heard as far away as Blowing Rock when Big Mel cranked up the volume.

She planned carefully. Her thirty foot trailer had two-hundred forty square feet of tapping area. If all the tappers stayed within their two square foot radius, Big Mel could put every one of her fifty tappers on the float, twelve of her best twirlers, a stable, a manger, several wooden sheep, and still have room for the grand finale she had planned for the judges. Big Mel had taken her exhibition to competition after competition and had a wall of trophies to show for it. Today would be no different.

•••

The temperature was hovering around thirty-five degrees when the Green Valley High School Marching Pioneers and dance team passed the reviewing stand. If the wind didn't kick up, I thought

Cynthia would be just fine in her body suit. Meg had her hands pushed deep into her pockets now that she'd finished her hot chocolate.

The band marched to a halt, turned and faced the judges and played their now signature *Santa Claus Is Coming To Town* with the dance team acting out "You better watch out, you better not cry," like the highly skilled thespians they obviously were. The band finished to applause, spun sharply a quarter turn to the left and marched on to a lively drum cadence. They'd play again once they exited the square. I looked around to try and pick out the reviewer for *Our State*, but then realized that I wouldn't know him even if I did spot him.

Following the first marching band were a couple of classic 1930s cars decorated to the nines with flashing Christmas lights and wreaths, then a stagecoach being drawn by four horses from the Jumpin' Jehosaphat Gem Mine in Newland. The Pipes and Drums from Grandfather Mountain turned the corner and let loose with a sound that was meant to strike terror in the hearts of the Highlanders' enemies. Instead, the ten pipers piping and the twelve drummers drumming were met by another round of applause from the crowd.

On and on came the floats: the Junior League of St. Germaine; the Praise Team from New Fellowship Baptist Church; the 4-H Club; the waitresses and mascot from the Bear and Brew; Ian Burch and Flori Cabbage and the other members of the Appalachian Rauschpfeife Consort, all dressed up in their snoods, jerkins and breeches. These floats were interspersed with smaller entries: the Shriners in their little cars, Mr. Terwilliger's Marching Pigs, the *Horn in the West* cast tossing out peppermints, and the Bullwinkle Moose giant balloon. Bullwinkle, unfortunately, had to make his way around the outside of the town square due to the overhead power lines, but we could see his colossal head poking around the steeple of St. Barnabas as he floated by on the next street. Every fifteen minutes or so another band would come marching through.

One sentimental favorite was the marching handbell choir from Lord's Chapel. They played a very nice rendition of—what else?—*Silver Bells,* arrayed in white robes, angel wings, and halos glowing with the power of LEDs. As the handbell choir finished their arrangement in front of the judges, complete with gentle choreography, we could just see Cynthia's float coming into view at the corner of the park. Behind her was Santa, the traditional culmination of any Christmas parade, high atop his sleigh and being pulled by a John Deere tractor. In front of Cynthia was the last band of the afternoon, a high school from Lenoir, and ahead of the band, taking the last corner before pulling up to the courthouse, was Big Mel.

The Mud Creek Tapping Academy and Training Center's float managed to tastefully combine the sacred and secular by placing the stable of Bethlehem squarely at the North Pole—not the literal North Pole, but the one that served as home to elves, directionally impaired penguins, Santa and Mrs. Claus, and the candy-cane forest. Wooden, cut-out sheep peeped out shyly from behind the red and white striped foliage.

Along the parade route Big Mel had her little tappers rap-tap-a-tapping to *Sleigh Ride,* while the twirlers free-styled through their three-minute routine. The fifty tap dancers, none of them taller than four feet and all dressed in little shepherd outfits, grasped the crooks in front of them in a two-handed Fred Astaire grip, and rowed with the rhythm of the shoes. Cute? This *defined* cute! There was a good-sized crowd actually walking on the sidewalk beside the float to watch the presentation again and again.

As the float turned the corner, the tappers were taking a breather, but Big Mel horse-whistled them to tapping position in short order. Big Mel was on the float, of course, dressed as the Virgin Mary and sitting in the stable beside the manger. Flanking her on either side were two wise men, their black tap-shoes sticking out from beneath their bejeweled robes. There was an angel praying on his knees in the hay-loft—a boy named Brian who had been studying at the Academy for several years. I recognized him from Bible School at St. Barnabas last summer—quite a little tumbler.

The float pulled up to the judges' stand. Big Mel smiled from beneath her blue veil as she eyed the prize. Big Mel was a champion.

Sleigh Ride was a fine Christmas tapping song as far as it went, but Big Mel knew that it would take something special to win. She'd already won this year's grand prize at the Fourth of July parade in Kingsport and the Veteran's Day parade in Galax, and she saw no sense in reinventing the wheel. Leroy Anderson's *Sleigh Ride* was okay for tapping the parade route, but for the competition she'd hung her star on another, more famous, composer.

The judges pulled out a new scoring sheet as the truck came to a stop, positioning the float directly in front of the courthouse. The two kings wasted no time in jumping down from the flatbed and pulling a set of hidden steps from underneath the trailer. The twirlers, dressed in angelic, gold-sequined spandex, poured quickly down the steps and took their place in front of the stage as the opening notes of *Stars and Stripes Forever* bellowed forth from the giant speakers in the back of the pickup.

Meg's mouth dropped open. Pete's eyes grew wide. Nancy gulped. I just stood there, unable to look away.

Fifty tap-dancing shepherds waited out the four-measure introduction, then attacked the oak stage like the little stars they'd been trained to be. Big Mel had shortened the march by cutting the beginning section and splicing the introduction straight onto the most famous part of John Philip Sousa's magnum opus: the trio, the part that every child knows as "Be kind to your web-footed friends, for that duck may be somebody's mother." The speakers blared, the kids tapped their well-rehearsed routine, the twirlers twirled, and the two wise men, who had gotten back into the stable, were spinning a couple of flags that were emblazoned with "Merry Christmas" on one side and Mud Creek Academy's logo on the other.

Baby Jesus, up till now hidden by a thin layer of hay, sat up in the manger and waved. The stunned judges waved back. Mary sat there serenely, treasured up all these things and pondered them in her heart.

She pondered them until the repeat: the part where the music slows, trombones and tubas come in with the countermelody, and the piccolos take off into the stratosphere for the big finish.

Yes, Big Mel was a champion. She'd won the Two-Baton National Title in 1983. She'd won the Three-Baton Title in '85. She didn't twirl three anymore, but two batons were her bread and butter. When she heard the trombones come in, she jumped up, threw off her veil, dropped her white robe, grabbed her top hat from behind the manger and tapped to the front of the stage in her black tie and tails with matching hot-pants. Standing almost seven feet tall in her top hat, with size fourteen tap shoes that sounded like machine guns, she dwarfed her co-stars. The two wise men took a beat to reach down and retrieve Mel's batons from where they were hidden in the hay, torch them with a couple of fireplace lighters, and, as the wicks on the ends burst into flames, tossed them to Big Mel. She caught them, still spinning, and whipped them into an artistic blur of flame and smoke.

This was the cue for Brian, the angelic host in the hayloft, to push the button and ignite the fireworks. Four pyrotechnic fountains erupted from the roof of the stable. Red, white, and blue fire shot up into the air, accompanied immediately by a number of Roman candles and something the fireworks company had dubbed *The Battle of Vicksburg*. The crowd cheered as Brian turned to face them and accept his accolades, but then he appeared to stumble, arms waving frantically, and he tumbled out of the loft and plummeted toward the floor of the flatbed trailer. The crowd gasped and Kimmy Jo Jameson leapt to her feet and screamed in terror.

The flailing Brian dropped like a rock just behind the manger, but our fears came to naught as the little acrobat landed squarely on the hidden trampoline and bounced back up into the air, executing a neat somersault just above the head of Big Mel. The only casualty seemed to be Brian's halo which flew off his head and into the crowd of shepherds.

The spectators roared their approval. The tiny tappers heard the crowd and redoubled their tapping efforts, their feet firing like little cap guns. The trombones boomed, the piccolos shrieked, the angelic twirlers spun their batons in a blur of holiday exultation. Brian bounced higher, doing a piked front somersault, followed immediately by a cat twist and a double back flip. The wise men spun their flags like airplane propellers and Big Mel tapped and twirled for all she was worth.

And Big Mel was a champion.

She threw her first fire baton ten feet in the air, spun around once, twice, still twirling the other, and caught the falling baton without dropping a step. The crowd gasped. Another fireworks fountain went off with a *whoosh*. The driver of the truck turned the music up a notch as the march headed toward its final cadences.

The clatter of the tappers was unimaginable, one hundred heels and toes slapping white oak with a rhythmic precision that was astonishing. Faster and faster went the batons of the twirlers; higher and higher bounced Brian. Roman candles exploded and blazed into the afternoon sky. Big Mel threw her fire batons up into the air, one after the other, in rapid succession. Ten feet into the air, twenty. The music slowed slightly for the penultimate chords. Then, just as all the performers were preparing for the big finish, the unexpected happened.

Big Mel, fueled with adrenaline, sent one of her aerials soaring dangerously high. This wasn't a problem for Mel; she was well used to catching flaming batons from dizzying heights. It *was* a problem for the St. Germaine Electric Co-op. The overhead wires that prevented Bullwinkle the Moose from making his trip around the downtown square seemed to reach out and pluck Big Mel's baton from the air. Still spinning, it circled the live wire twice and spun off in an altogether different direction, stopping only when it banged, flaming end first, into a nearby transformer sitting atop an electric power pole. The explosion and resulting cascade of sparks that rained down from the ruined transformer blended right in with the fireworks finale, now reaching its zenith on the roof of the stable. In a few moments, the final chords of John Philip Sousa's masterpiece sounded, the pyrotechnics sputtered to a halt, and the performers finished, breathless, standing in expectation of thunderous applause. Unfortunately, most of the crowd was too busy watching the blaze that had started in the stable when the hay caught on fire to clap.

In the dimming, late-afternoon shadows, we watched in silence as the two kings used their emergency fire extinguishers to put out the flames, while at the same time, all the electric lights in the square, first the outside decorations, then the lights in the shops, blinked twice and went out.

•••

"Wow!" said Nancy.

"I've never seen anything like it," said Meg.

Pete nodded but was speechless.

"Well, someone had better call the electric company," I said. "Nancy, you want to do it?"

"Already dialing." Nancy had all the emergency numbers for the town in her cell. Efficient.

The parade continued on its route and folks who had been inside, for some reason or other, began to emerge from the powerless buildings to see what was going on. I looked across the street to the library and saw Rebecca Watts and Diana Terry come out of the front doors and look around. The same thing was happening in every doorway of every shop around the square.

After the band marched by, Cynthia's float was next. Her belly dancing to *Jingle Bell Rock*, although both seasonal and scintillating, was rather a letdown after Big Mel's extravaganza. A number of camera flashes went off, though, and I suspected that Cynthia's shimmying mayoral snapshot would be adorning *Our State* magazine. Her float didn't stop in front of the judging stand and neither did Santa's, and in a few minutes the parade was on its way out of town, a chorus of children, including Moosey and Bernadette, dancing in its wake.

"Hayden!" Rebecca called as the crowd on the street began to disperse. "C'mere, will you?"

"Be right back," I said to Meg, then hurried down the steps of the courthouse, across the street and up to the library doors.

"What's happened?" asked Diana. "I was inside using the computer and all the electricity went out."

"I checked the breakers," said Rebecca. "They seem to be okay." She looked around the square. "It seems as though the power is off everywhere…"

"Big Mel blew up one of the transformers."

"How'd she do that?" asked Diana.

"Fire baton," I said, like it was the most reasonable explanation in the world.

"Oh," said Diana with a confused look. "Fire baton. That explains it."

Rebecca rolled her eyes. "Sheesh. How long till the power comes back on?"

"I expect that the power company will need to replace the transformer. I'd give them a few hours, anyway."

"I'm locking up and taking the rest of the afternoon off," declared Rebecca. "I've got to open back up tonight for a book club meeting. I hope the power's back on by then. We're Skyping Jan Karon."

"I was in the middle of an email," said Diana, her irritation evident. "The whole computer just shut down."

"Yeah," I said with a shrug. "Nothing we can do about it."

"It's always *something*," said Diana.

Chapter 16

"I forgot to tell you," called Meg from the library. "Your Christmas beer came yesterday. I put it in the garage fridge."

"Excellent! Thanks."

I'd been sitting at the typewriter, resolved to generate some first-rate detective fiction, or at least some first-class second-rate fiction. Failing that, I was determined at least to enjoy the process. I trekked to the garage and opened the door to the old refrigerator. Looking up at me, a twinkle in their eyes, were twelve bottles of *Samichlaus*—Swiss-German for *Santa Claus*. Only brewed once a year on the feast day of St. Nicholas, this beer is the strongest in the world. Few occasions call for such a strong brew, but, the way things were going, I figured that the stresses and strains of this festive season justified an encounter with Santa Claus in his most powerful incarnation. I carried it into the kitchen, popped open a bottle, filled a frosted mug, and carried it back into the living room.

She stood there in front of my desk like one of those long-legged birds you see in Florida that stands on one of them and gobbles frogs, except she was standing on both of them and wasn't gobbling frogs, so I knew right away she was trouble, which those birds usually aren't, unless you're a frog or maybe a very ugly adolescent male with really bad acne, bulging eyes and a greenish complexion, so she wasn't actually like one of them after all. I lit up a stogy and remembered I didn't like those birds.

"What's the problem, Polly?" I asked, thinking about a parrot I had once that I also didn't like.

"My name's Annie," she said. "Annie Key. I'm a singer. It's my Life Coach Accompanist. I think she's trying to ruin me."

I gave her the old "once-over," the "up-and-down," the "eye-frisk," the "peeper-perusal," the "yo-yo ya-ya," and I liked what I saw.

"Life Coach Accompanist?" I asked.

"I thought you'd given up the noir detective genre for a few weeks," said Meg, reading over my shoulder and then uttering a heart-felt sigh. "I was so happy."

I adjusted my fedora and chomped down on my unlit *Romeo y Julieta* Cuban cigar. "Couldn't do it. Sophie Slug was okay, but she had no real ethos. No magnetism. No charisma."

"She's a slug."

"Exactly. She keeps melting."

Meg shook her head in mock-disgust. "Well, our company will be here in a few minutes to help with the tree. Don't get too involved." She bent down over the back of the chair and gave me a kiss on the cheek opposite the cigar. "How's that beer, by the way?"

"Stout. Stout and delicious. Just the thing for a cold Saturday night after the greatest Christmas parade in history."

"Save me some." Meg disappeared into the kitchen.

I took another sip and looked down at the page. I not only had to type one-handed, but one-fingered, since it was now hunt-and-peck. But hunt-and-peck I would.

"Life Coach Accompanist?" I asked again, because Meg had interrupted and I'd lost my train of thought.

"It's the 'in' thing," said Annie Key, twirling a delicate digit through her blonde curls. "They play for you when you sing. Then they tell you how to run your life. They give you advice."

"Sounds like every voice teacher I've ever met," I said. "But I've never heard of a Life Coach Accompanist. What's the skinny on a deal like that?"

She shook her head and I could have sworn I heard a rattle. "I don't know what you mean."

"How much do they charge?" I asked.

"Three hundred twenty-five dollars an hour. But it's easy. You just give them your credit card number."

A light bulb blinked over my head. I remembered I hadn't paid the electric bill and then an even brighter, although metaphorical, light bulb blinked and I had an idea. A brilliant, hundred-watt idea.

Life Coach Accompanists were charging three hundred twenty-five semolians an hour. I was getting two Cs a day, and that was when the fish were running. It didn't take a genius to do the math, especially with a fancy calculator like the one I had sitting on my desk, thanks to a little game I invented called "You Bet Your Calculator" that I talked the bishops into playing when I invited them over

96

for casino night, them and their calculators.

By day, I was an L.D., Liturgical Detective duly licensed by the Diocese of North Carolina and dedicated to the prospect of early retirement. But by night... I had a phone, advice, and a Rolodex full of more suckers than the all-you-can-eat Wednesday night octopus buffet at the Red Lobster.

"You want my advice, Toots?" I asked. "And would you take it, if I gave it?"

"Of course. That's why I'm here."

"You need a new Life Coach Accompanist."

•••

"Oh, *no!*" said Meg. She was on the phone in the kitchen. "That's *terrible*. What does the doctor say?"

I picked up my beer, clicked off the banker's light over the typewriter and headed for the kitchen to get whatever bad news was looming, then decided that Baxter might need to romp outside for a few minutes, at least enough of a romp to let Meg finish her phone conversation.

We snuck out the front door and Baxter tore off into the field after a phantom herd of deer, barking his head off, then returned in short order, his tongue hanging out, and a very satisfied look on his face. I scratched him behind his ears and followed him in the kitchen door.

"What's up?" I asked, dreading the answer. I set my oversized bottle of *Samichlaus* on the counter, only half empty. I sensed I'd be finishing it up pretty quickly.

"It's Gaylen. She was walking down the basement stairs when the lights went out all over town. She fell down the last three and the emergency room doctor thinks one of her broken ribs might have punctured a lung. Luckily she had her cell with her. That was Georgia calling from the hospital."

"Should we go over?"

Meg shook her head. "Georgia said not to. Gaylen will be okay, but she's staying the night at least."

"That's a relief," I said, "but this does not bode well for St. Barnabas."

•••

97

"That's it, then," said Dave, standing up and brushing his hands on the front of his sweater to get rid of any loose needles. "Looks good to me."

"It's leaning to the left," said Cynthia. "And it needs to be turned a quarter-turn to the right, so that bald spot is against the wall."

"Yes, exactly!" agreed Meg.

Dave and Nancy had come over to help Meg put up the Christmas tree. Pete and Cynthia had come over to watch and give directions. Ruby, Meg's mother, was happy to join in the festivities as well.

Dave sighed, got back on his knees, and grabbed the tree stand, so he could help Nancy spin the tree.

"There," said Meg. "Perfect."

"Whew! I'm exhausted," said Pete, watching from my overstuffed, leather club chair. "What's for supper?"

"Chili and jalapeño cornbread," I said. "And a nice Christmas beer, if you'd like."

"I'd rather try some of that fancy wine you bought," said Ruby.

"No," muttered Meg. "Absolutely not. Not ever. Never, in fact." She looked around the room, a blank look on her face. "Fancy wine? What fancy wine?"

"Okay, okay," said Ruby, raising her hands in surrender. "Anything but beer, though."

"Cheap chablis?" Meg asked.

"Wonderful," said Ruby.

"I'll have the beer," said Cynthia. She'd changed out of her belly dancing outfit, much to my disappointment.

"Ditto," said Nancy.

"Yes, please," agreed Dave. "Beer."

"We'll put the decorations up after we eat, then," decided Meg. "Dave, you and Nancy are in charge of the lights. That's usually Hayden's job, but he is incapacitated."

"I still have one good drinking hand," I said. "And I can probably point to stuff."

"Well, point your way to the kitchen," said Ruby.

•••

"Well," said Meg, "I, for one, am glad that Big Mel won the float contest. I mean, how could anyone have topped that?"

"There are those that would argue," said Nancy. "You can't put out all the lights in town and walk away with three thousand dollars."

"Nothing in the rules about that," said Pete.

"Not to change the subject or anything, but how's the investigation going?" asked Cynthia. "This cornbread is great, by the way!"

"Thanks," said Meg. "The secret is to use creamed corn. That way it doesn't get dry."

"The investigation is going just fine," I said. "And I affirm the cornbread as well."

"We've got nothing," said Nancy glumly.

"Nothin'," agreed Dave, his mouth half full of chili.

"Aw, c'mon," I said. "We know the guy's name. We know he was a killer-for-hire. We know he was shot with a 9mm handgun at close range."

"It's not much," said Nancy.

"Umm," agreed Dave, still eating.

"We know he has a partner. We're almost sure it's a woman, we think she lives in the area, and that she's the one who killed him. She might have moved here within the last five years."

"Slim," said Nancy. "Very slim."

Dave nodded.

"We know he was trying to buy some very expensive wine at a foreclosure auction. What we don't know is why he was there in the first place."

"Or who killed him," said Nancy.

"Well, it seems like you know quite a lot," said Ruby.

"But not the important stuff," said Pete.

I looked across the table at him, blowing gently on a spoonful of too-hot chili.

"Really," I said. "How about this? His partner's white, in her late thirties, five feet eight inches tall, slim, athletic and attractive, although she probably wears oversized and unflattering clothes. She has brown hair, unless it's been dyed and she wears it either short or tied back. She drives a late model SUV four-by-four. Probably black. She has a checking account at a local bank, but it doesn't have more than two thousand dollars in it. Her off-shore accounts are where she stashes all her money. She buys almost everything locally with cash."

"What?" said Meg in astonishment. "*What?*"

Pete laughed. Nancy looked up from her meal, a startled look on her face, and Dave choked on half a piece of cornbread.

"Pretty good, eh?" I said with a grin. "I saw it on *Criminal Minds*. Those FBI profilers are *so* clever."

"Yeah?" said Nancy. "Explain, please."

"Kent said that Sal LaGrassa was shot at close range and that the bullet had a slightly upward trajectory. Sal was six feet even, so Kent and I did the math and came up with five foot eight for the shooter. Sal was forty-five years old, and it's reasonable to assume that, if he's romantically and professionally linked with this woman and she's in the same business as he is, she would be in her thirties or early forties. He might have had a girlfriend that was a teenager or in her twenties, but it wouldn't be prudent to have her for a partner. Plus, she's good. She's experienced. She got the drop on him and put a slug right between his eyes before he could say 'Blow me down a rat-hole.' Still, he'd go for a slightly younger partner. Vanity and all that. He'd see himself as the senior member of the team. She wouldn't."

"Blow me down a rat-hole?" said Cynthia.

"She's attractive, because Sal was attractive: well-built, athletic, trim. He's a player—cars, art, wine, property—so he's not going to be romantically involved with someone who's frumpy. Also, being fit kind of goes with the job. Sal wasn't a lightweight. He weighed one hundred ninety pounds and she managed to carry or drag him quite some distance."

"Huh," said Nancy, turning this information over in her head.

"Also, seventy-three percent of white females have some shade of brown hair. Pretty good odds, wouldn't you say? There were no aberrant hairs on the clothes or on the body even though she lugged it down the hill and tossed it in the lake. Odds are she's very careful about leaving any DNA and pretty pragmatic as far as her appearance is concerned. Hence, short hair, or hair pulled back most of the time. If she only pulled her hair back when she was getting ready to kill someone, it would certainly be a giveaway to her partner."

"A *dead* giveaway," said Ruby.

"What if she actually shot him down by the lake?" asked Cynthia. "She wouldn't have had to carry him. Just roll him in."

"Didn't happen," I said. "Meeting him down at the shore of a deserted lake would have thrown up so many red flags to the victim that he would certainly have known something was up. Plus the fact that she couldn't have known who might be visiting one of the graves. He wouldn't have allowed himself to be marched down at gunpoint. Remember, he was a buttonman, too, and he would have made a move to escape long before ending up in the lake." I rubbed a hand over my chin. "Nope. He never saw this one coming."

"Buttonman?" said Cynthia. "What's a buttonman?"

"A dropper," said Meg pointing her finger at Cynthia and bringing her thumb down ominously. "Hatchetman, trigger, gun, torpedo."

"Wow," said Nancy with more than a little sarcasm. "You really know the lingo."

"I've been reading up," said Meg. *"Sophie Slug Versus the Maltese Falcon."*

"The falcon would win," observed Pete. "You see, a bird always beats a slug unless the slug is some sort of mutant, nuclear slug."

Cynthia looked at Pete as though he had lost his mind. "What on *earth* are you talking about?"

"I'm just saying..."

"Hang on a minute," said Dave, who had stopped eating. "Why is she white? The shooter, I mean. Not the slug."

"If she's a person of color, and she's trying *not* to be noticed, she certainly wouldn't be living here. She'd be down on the coast of South Carolina." I shrugged. "Somewhere in Georgia. Maybe Chicago. Miami. She'll have a job, and live comfortably but not extravagantly. Her checking account will have enough in it to make a rent payment or two, but she probably doesn't write checks unless she has to. Cash is easier and untraceable."

"Yep," agreed Pete.

"She drives a late model SUV because she needs four-wheel drive up here in the mountains and she's not going to be driving a pickup. She'll be in a soccer-mom vehicle: a Jeep Cherokee or a Ford Expedition or something like that. Mid-sized. She has to carry bodies, remember. It'll be newish, but not new. She doesn't want to attract attention, but at the same time, she doesn't want it breaking down. Also, she has plenty of money, so price isn't an object. She probably gets a late-model car every few years. She buys them out of state and pays cash."

"Okay," said Nancy. "Why is the car black?"

I smiled. "Let's say you're a female professional killer living in a small town. You look good and have a lot of money and expensive tastes, but you need to go unnoticed, so you wear dowdy clothes, not much makeup. You have to keep a low profile, but you still have your self-respect. You're driving a generic soccer-mom SUV. So what color is it?"

"It's black," said Nancy without hesitation.

"Black," said Meg.

"Black," said Ruby.

"Black,"said Dave.

"Black," agreed Cynthia.

"I don't know," Pete said thoughtfully. "Maybe teal."

Chapter 17

On Saturday, as soon as she'd gotten off the phone with Bishop O'Connell, Bev had called Father Tim and explained our dilemma. He'd agreed to come over at eight a.m. and bless the communion elements for the eleven o'clock service. Deacon Mushrat would then hand them out as a "reserved sacrament," and all would be well. At least, until next week.

I arrived at St. Barnabas at ten o'clock to meet with Edna Terra-Pocks and Mushrat and go through the service, making sure there would be no surprises.

Fifteen minutes (and two cups of coffee) later, Edna and I went up to the choir loft to go through the anthems with the choir. The early arrivers were poring over my latest masterpiece.

"At last!" said Marjorie. "No more Sally Slug. This is more like it."

"*Sophie* Slug," said Meg sadly. "Her name was Sophie. And this isn't more like it. This is less like it than ever."

"I'll miss Sophie," said Rebecca. "She had some real potential."

"Maybe I'll bring her back as an ancillary character," I said. "You can't keep a good slug down. How did your Skyping with Jan Karon go, by the way?"

"It was fine. I had to run Deacon Mushrat out of the library, though. He was using the computer to type his sermon. He said the church hadn't ordered his computer yet, and all the other computers at the church were either locked up or required a password."

"Oh, brother," said Meg, rolling her eyes.

"We have wireless, so anyone can bring their laptop in if they want," Rebecca explained, "but we only have one computer that's connected up to the internet as well as a printer. And when the power came back on, there were a couple of people waiting to use it. Mushrat got to it first and was on it for an hour and wouldn't get off. He got very belligerent when I told him we were closing so we could have an author Skype."

"How many were there for the Skype?" asked Bev.

"Maybe thirty or so," said Rebecca. "It was a good turnout and Jan Karon was just great!"

The rest of the choir had found their seats and their voices and so, under brilliant direction, we attacked the offertory anthem—"attack" being the operative word.

"Really, choir," I said. "We don't need to sing this as though we're going to war. *Rejoice in the Lord Alway.* It's the Epistle text. Let your moderation be known unto all men."

"Could Edna accompany us?" asked Phil. "I can't ever find my notes in measure...um...well, dang, now I can't even find the measure."

"Sure I will!" said Edna.

"No, she won't," I said, giving the choir my sweetest, or as Meg later described it, "scariest" smile. "She'll be playing on the Mendelssohn anthem though, so you can all find your notes then."

•••

The service began at eleven o'clock and the church was almost full. Edna Terra-Pocks began the Third Sunday of Advent with a toccata and fugue on *Tempus Adest Floridum*. We all recognized the tune immediately as *Good King Wenceslas*. It was a good piece, maybe a little too Christmassy in my opinion, but certainly within the compass of the season. I'd still grump about it. It was my duty. Edna had been right. She *did* need to wear her sports bra to play it. Toward the end of the fugue, I thought for a moment she might knock herself unconscious.

We sang the first hymn, *Comfort, Comfort Ye My People*, too slowly of course, and launched into the service with a will. We heard all the readings for the day and then Deacon Mushrat got up to give his sermon.

"I know we've heard the readings from this *lectionary*," he started, almost spitting the word onto the floor in disgust, "but the Holy Spirit has convicted me to preach on another subject."

Meg and Bev both looked at me nervously.

"Hear now the awesome Word of the Lord," said Mushrat. "From the Book of Malachi."

"What's he doing?" whispered Edna.

"I'm sure we're going to get a sermon on tithing," Elaine whispered back. "He's been chomping at the bit all week."

"'I the LORD do not change,'" began the deacon. "'So you, O descendants of Jacob, are not destroyed. Ever since the time of your forefathers you have turned away from my decrees and have not kept them. Return to me, and I will return to you,' says the LORD Almighty. "But you ask, 'How are we to return?'

"'Will a man rob God? Yet you rob me. But you ask, 'How do we rob you?'"

Bev had her head in her hands. Meg's eyes were starting to glaze over.

"'In tithes and offerings,'" read Mushrat. He looked up and pointed a finger out at the congregation. "'You are under a curse,'" he hissed. "'The whole nation of you because you are robbing me. Bring the whole tithe into the storehouse, that there may be food in my house. It is imperative, therefore, that you attend the offering and barter the purchase if your property is to be preserved.'"

"What on earth?" said Marjorie, loud enough for everyone in the congregation to hear. "This ain't right." Some titters came from below the balcony. It did not deter Mushrat.

"'Test me in this,'" says the LORD Almighty, 'and see if I will not throw open the floodgates of heaven and pour out so much blessing that you will not have room enough for it. The mark is set. Twenty thousand is the price. I will prevent pests from devouring your crops, and the vines in your fields will not cast their fruit,' says the LORD Almighty."

"The Word of the Lord," he said with a flourish, picking up his notes and shaking them at us.

"Thanks be to God," muttered the congregation.

•••

Elaine was right. We did get a sermon on tithing. A *forty-minute* sermon on tithing. Now, a forty-minute sermon is fine if you're in a church that thrives on forty-minute sermons. The Episcopal denomination is not one of those. Let's face it. We have a lot to do: prayers, scripture readings, hymns, processions, psalms, service music, creeds, standing up and sitting down, taking communion. Even *with* a twelve-minute sermon, we were accustomed to getting out of church at 12:15.

At 11:35, about fifteen minutes into Deacon Mushrat's sermon, his pontificating seemed to be generating a lot of yawns. At 11:45, people were starting to fidget and look at their watches. At five after twelve, three families got up and left. This did not bother Deacon Mushrat in the least. By the time his sermon was finished, it had become clear, to the choir at least, that the deacon must go.

When the service ended at 12:45, no one stayed for coffee, no one congregated in the fellowship hall to chat. Those Episcopalians emptied out of the church like they were Lutheran and there was an all-you-can-eat tuna casserole buffet at the Holiday Inn.

•••

"My," said Meg as she drove us home. "*That* was special."

"Wasn't it?"

"I especially like how he invited everyone to come to his Wednesday night Bible study. Who does he think is going to attend?"

I sighed. "Muffy said she was going. Not that it's a big loss to the soprano section, but it sort of irks me that he's now poaching choir members."

"Maybe you should tell her she can't sing *O Holy Night* on Christmas Eve if she misses rehearsal," Meg suggested.

"That would suggest to her that she *can* sing it if she *doesn't* miss rehearsal."

"Oh. Right. It doesn't matter anyway, because you cancelled choir this Wednesday. Living Nativity. Remember?"

"I remember. Still," I said whimsically, "Muffy does fill out the soprano section. I mean, she *really* fills it out. It's those angora sweaters—now in holiday colors."

Meg punched me in the cast and immediately regretted it. "Ouch," she said, shaking her fingers.

"Both hands on the wheel, please." I smiled at her. "It serves you right. You shouldn't punch a cripple this close to Christmas."

Chapter 18

"Hiya, Chief," said Dave, when I came through the police station door on Monday morning. "How's the good bishop doing?"

"She's back home and doing okay," I said. "She'll be back by Christmas Eve. Where's Nancy?"

"Out doing police stuff," said Dave.

"Ah. Police stuff."

"Yep. I asked her to stop by the Piggly Wiggly on her way in and get us a dozen donuts."

"That's police stuff, all right," I agreed. "Anything happening we need to check up on?"

"Nope. I've got about three reports to finish up. Then I'm going home."

"You're on for Wednesday, right? Living Nativity duty. Nancy's on duty Thursday and Saturday. I've got Friday and Sunday."

Dave nodded. "Nancy said she'd help me out on Wednesday, so we'll both be there. I might have to shoot that camel and I'm not really comfortable with that. Nancy says she wouldn't mind."

Chapter 19

Annie. Annie Key -- singer, looker, and potential cash cow.

"Why'd you come to me?" I asked. "Who gave you my name?"

"Pedro did," she whispered, moving across the desk like a piece of Guernsey flotsam. "Pedro LaFleur."

Her breasts pressed against me like spent sausage casings while the moonlight played on her thighs like two tennis players engaged in mortal combat to the death.

"My credit card has been declined," she sobbed. "My LCA maxed it out, and now she won't answer my calls!"

Suddenly Annie had lost her bovine luster.

I struck a match and lit a stogy. "So what do you want from me, sister?"

"Won't you help me? Won't YOU be my new Life Coach Accompanist?"

"Listen, Bossie. I'm a shamus, a gumshoe, get it? Sure, I can tickle the ivories and give advice, but it ain't my bread and butter. Besides, your credit card has been declined."

"Won't you do it out of love?" Her eyelashes flapped like clothes-lined underwear in a stiff breeze, not banging noisily against the pole like those stiff cotton briefs that are usually on sale at Walmart, three for five dollars, but fluttering gently like the $69.95 J Peterman imported knee-boxers made of grasshopper silk and hand-stitched by the seamstresses of Kooloobati.

"I might," I said, adjusting my knee-boxers.

"Pedro said you were the best."

"Yeah. What was the name of your last LCA?"

"Sophie. Sophie Slugh."

The kiss that was halfway out of my mouth crawled back inside like a startled mushrat.

"What's wrong?" asked Annie, a pucker still dangling from her lips like a blister on an overcooked bratwurst. "You've gone all verschlunken."

I didn't answer. Sophie Slugh, alias Sophie Slug, alias Sophia Limacé. My archenemy. Ten years ago I'd thrown her off Reichenbach Falls into the salt mines of Kooloobati. Now she was back.

•••

I didn't plan to go to church. A Wednesday night off during December was something to be savored, but I was backed against the counter by Bev Greene as soon as I walked into the Slab for a cup of coffee early in the afternoon.

"You've got to go to Deacon Mushrat's Bible study tonight," she said.

"No, I don't."

"Gaylen wants you to," said Bev.

"You're fibbing," I said.

Her shoulders slumped. "Yes, I am," she admitted. "I can't go. I told Gaylen I'd keep an eye on him, but I've got to pick up the donkey at Connie Ray's farm and take him back after the show. It's my Kiwanis Club assignment. It was either that or be the innkeeper's wife, and I don't look good in burlap."

"You'd look great in burlap," I said. "It could be the fashion move of the season."

"C'mon," she wheedled. "You owe me. What about that time I didn't tell Meg that I saw you..."

"Don't finish that sentence," I said. I thought for a moment, then decided. "Okay, I'll go, but I'm not staying for the whole thing. I'll go and listen for just a bit. Then I'm heading home."

•••

At six o'clock I was up in the choir loft, sitting in the dark on the back row, waiting for Mushrat to begin. There were about twenty people in the pews. The deacon had decided that, since there wasn't any choir practice, he'd go ahead and use the church instead of his usual Sunday School classroom, and had gallantly run Edna Terra-Pocks off the console and out of the loft, even though it had taken her an hour to drive into town just so she could practice. Edna was storming out just as I walked up. She was *not* happy.

I looked out over the church and tried to recognize folks from the back. It wasn't that difficult since I'd watched most of them walk in. Varmit and Muffy LeMieux were sitting near the front. Kimberly Walnut was by herself, up on a kneeler, looking as though she was praying fervently. Ruby Farthing, Meg's mother, was sitting with Wynette Winslow and Mattie Lou Entriken. She was keeping them company. Kylie Moffit, the owner of the Holy Grounds Coffee Shop, was sitting with Shea Maxwell. Flori Cabbage was there. Diana Terry. Karen Dougherty, the town doc. I saw Benny Dawkins, our thurifer, who, I had heard, had just returned yesterday from his European tour. He was sitting toward the back and chatting across the aisle with Frank Harwood. Gwen Jackson...

Donald Mushrat came into the church through the sacristy door, took a moment to adjust the lights, then walked up to the pulpit. He was wearing his white alb and his purple deacon's stole. Since he was beginning on time, I quit trying to identify the participants. I wouldn't be here that long. Just a few minutes to fulfill my obligation and then off to the Bear and Brew for a quick beer before heading home.

"Good evening. Thank you for coming to this awesome Advent study on the Book of Malachi. And since you all are agreeing with me in faith, I'm going to share something else with you this evening. Something I think we should all be aware of."

"What's that?" asked Kimberly Walnut.

"There's a jail in our community. I've come across some correspondence and I don't think any of you are aware of the spiritual consequences that this implies."

I perked up. Jails were *my* jurisdiction. But what on earth was he talking about?

He continued. "Cicero said it best. But before we start, I'd like us to stand and sing the first and seventh verses of *O Come, O Come Emmanuel*, as I light the Advent wreath. It's hymn number 56."

I frowned. There were three keys to the lock-box in the pulpit that housed the control for the winch that lowered the giant wreath. Bev had one, Gaylen had one, and Billy Hixon had one. I couldn't see any one of the three handing it over to Deacon Mushrat for his Bible study.

The congregation stood and Mushrat started the hymn with Muffy leading the assemblage and Flori Cabbage, who had brought her flute, accompanying. The deacon held down the toggle switch and the wreath lowered to its prescribed height.

O Come, O Come, Emmanuel,
And ransom captive Israel,
That mourns in lonely exile here
Until the Son of God appear.
Rejoice! Rejoice! Emmanuel
Shall come to thee, O Israel!

As the congregation sang, Deacon Mushrat snapped his fireplace lighter and lit two purple candles and the rose one, three of the four candles on the wreath. Then he went back to the pulpit and held the toggle to raise the wreath back into position.

Oh, come, Desire of nations, bind
In one the hearts of all mankind;

Mushrat suddenly looked startled. His eyes grew wide and he dropped his hymnal. It clattered into the back of the pulpit. The congregation was still looking down at their music and continued singing.

Bid thou our sad divisions cease,
And be thyself our King of Peace.

The deacon walked slowly from behind the pulpit and toward the congregation, a horrified look on his face. His eyes were fixed on the back doors and his lips were moving, but not in time with the music.

Rejoice! Rejoice! Emmanuel
Shall come to thee, O Israel!

Mushrat stood on the top step of the chancel, hands clutched in front of him as if in prayer. He dropped to his knees and suddenly there was a horrific squealing that caused everyone in the congregation to drop their hymnals and clap their hands over their ears. The wrenching sound was followed seconds later with what could only be described as a car wreck—steel on steel, two immovable objects hitting head on—followed by a loud bang. Mushrat never even looked up as the cable holding the Advent wreath snapped.

•••

I raced down the stairs as the screams echoed through the church.

"Back up, give me some room!" I hollered as I ran up the aisle.

"I called 911," said Gwen, as I barreled past her.

By the time I'd gotten to Mushrat, Frank, Benny and Varmit had lifted the wreath off of the deacon and rolled it to the side. Dr. Dougherty was kneeling by his side. The crowd backed up and gave me enough room to get next to the doctor. Mushrat was lying on his side in a fetal position. I knelt down beside him, looked at him closely, then looked at Karen who was trying to find a pulse. She looked back at me and shook her head.

"He's probably just stunned," said Muffy. "Or maybe knocked out. I was watching the wreath. It didn't hit him square on. In fact, his head went right through that opening." She pointed to the large gap in between two of the candles. "Can't you do some CPR or something?"

"I'm sorry," I said. "He's gone."

"His neck is broken," said Karen. "There's no pulse."

"I'll wait here for the paramedics. You all please go wait in the fellowship hall. And Gwen? I think Nancy and Dave are across the street policing the Living Nativity. Would you go and get them, please?"

Gwen nodded and ran down the aisle toward the front doors.

"Everyone else, please go wait for me in the fellowship hall now."

"What about CPR?" one of the voices insisted. A woman. "You've got to at least try!"

"It won't help him," Dr. Dougherty said sadly. "I'm so sorry."

Chapter 20

Nancy and Dave raced into the church, followed closely by Gwen Jackson.

"Sorry it took so long," said Gwen, trying to catch her breath. "I couldn't get the dead-bolt open."

"What on earth happened?" asked Nancy, quickly appraising the scene. "My God! The wreath fell on him?"

Dave was speechless.

"It fell on him, all right," I said, "but he's been shot."

I rolled the deacon over, lifted his purple stole, and revealed a spreading crimson stain in the center of his chest.

"I'll fill you in, but first you and Dave go on into the fellowship hall, take everyone's name and phone number, and get their statements. If there's someone you don't know, bring him back in here, but I'm pretty sure everyone's local. Then send 'em home. We'll call them tomorrow. I'll be in to help as soon as I secure this mess."

"Will do," said Nancy. "Did you see it happen?"

"Yeah. Hurry up now. I'll be in shortly."

•••

The EMTs arrived, but, as Karen had indicated, there was nothing they could do. I ordered them to leave everything as it was, go watch the Living Nativity, get a cup of coffee, and come back in an hour or so. I wanted Dave and Nancy to look at the crime scene with me. I entered the fellowship hall thirty minutes after Nancy and Dave had begun questioning the shaken members of the Malachi Bible study.

"Everyone saw the same thing," said Dave.

"I saw it, too," I said. "Still, due diligence, and all that. How many statements do you have left?"

Dave looked around the room. "We're about half-finished. It doesn't take long. They were singing a hymn, they heard the winch screech, the cable snapped, the wreath fell on Donald Mushrat. Except some of these folks say Moo-shrat."

"Same guy," I said. "I can't take notes, but I'll help you finish up. Then we'll go back into the church."

•••

Nancy, Dave and I stood at the front of the church, directly in front of Deacon Mushrat's body. The Advent wreath, having been lifted off him, now leaned on the steps, the broken rose candle nearest the altar.

"Everyone had the same story," said Nancy. "You're a trained detective, so to speak. Did you see anything different?"

"Well, I was looking right at Mushrat," I said. "I wasn't singing. He lowered the wreath, lit the candles and was raising it back up. He had his hymnal in his left hand. His right hand had to have been on the toggle switch."

"Yeah," said Dave.

"Then, about halfway through the second verse he looked spooked. Confused. He stopped singing and dropped his hymnal. That's what happened to the switch. The hymnal landed on the toggle and the winch just kept turning until the cable snapped."

"I thought there was a safety brake on that thing," said Nancy.

"Sure," I said. "That wreath will come down very slowly, but not if it's not attached to anything. No one figured that someone would run the winch up until the cable snapped. That's a lot of pressure. See there." I pointed up and both Dave and Nancy's gaze followed my finger. "The winch pulled the connecting mechanism right through the ceiling. There's a hole the size of a dinner plate up there."

"Hmm," said Nancy. "Go back to before the cable broke."

"Yeah," I said. "So Mushrat is looking confused. He's staring at the back wall."

"Up where you are?" asked Nancy. "In the balcony?"

I thought for a moment. "Nope. Downstairs."

"So he's looking at the back wall downstairs? Where the doors are?"

"Yeah." I tried to replay the scene in my head. "The back wall for sure, but he could have been staring at the doors."

"How about this, then?" said Dave. "The killer comes in during the service, the deacon recognizes him..."

"Or her," said Nancy.

"Or her," agreed Dave. "Then the killer shoots him, he drops his hymnal on the toggle and staggers to the steps where the cable breaks and the wreath falls on him, finishing him off."

"Sounds right," I said.

"Silencer?" asked Nancy.

"Yeah," I said. "I didn't hear a gunshot."

"Noise suppressors make rifles unwieldy," Nancy said. "I'm betting handgun. Easier to hide, easier to carry."

"I'd say it was a 9mm," I said. "That's a small hole in Mr. Mushrat. If this isn't the work of our Lake Tannenbaum shooter, I'll eat Raymond Chandler's hat."

"It was a good shot," said Nancy, appraising the distance, "but certainly not terribly difficult. The shooter didn't go for a head shot. Now that would have been something from seventy-five yards. Especially with a silencer."

"Someone might have seen the shooter come in or leave," I said. "Sterling Park was packed."

"You want to interview everyone in the park?"

"No," I said. "We'll put out a call and ask for witnesses to come forward. But, you know, I'll be surprised if anyone saw anything."

"I agree."

"Let's check the rest of the church," I said. "Look for a casing..." I shrugged. "Anything. This gal's good, but maybe we'll get lucky."

Chapter 21

Meg joined us for breakfast since she was currently "on vacation." As she explained it, during the few weeks leading up to Christmas the investment business slowed to a crawl. Then between Christmas and December 31st there was a flurry of activity as her clients tried to take advantage of as many tax breaks as they could before the end of the year. She didn't *have* to work, being married to a millionaire, but she enjoyed her job and since she was extremely good at it, was chiefly tasked with keeping our fortune intact.

It was a gloomy Thursday morning, the day after the tragedy and ten days before Christmas, that found us at our table in the back of the Slab Café. I'd already had a busy a.m., having met Kent Murphee at the morgue in Boone and returned with the medical examiner's official report on the murder.

Noylene, now approaching beach-ball proportions, was still doing her best to keep up with the needs of the customers. Pete had moved the tables slightly farther apart in deference to her expectancy and had taken a couple of two-toppers off the floor and put them in the storeroom.

"Y'all gotta pardon my butt," she said, as she waddled by with the coffee pot. "It always gets like this when I'm pregnant." She filled Meg's cup first, then squeezed around the table replenishing the rest: Pete's, Cynthia's, Nancy's, Dave's, and finally, mine.

"How about I just bring out some French toast?"

"Great," said Pete. He rubbed his hands together. "Just wait till you guys try this. It's a new recipe. Straight from the Food Network."

"I can't wait," said Meg. "I love French toast."

We sat in awkward silence for a moment as Noylene headed for the kitchen. The Slab was unusually quiet, although most of the chairs were occupied. People were talking in hushed voices.

"It's the shock of it all," said Meg quietly. "It has everyone on edge."

"You know," said Cynthia, "I did a little research. Statistically, over the last five years, a person is more likely to get murdered in St. Germaine than in Chicago. We have the highest *per capita* murder rate in North Carolina."

"Hey!" said Pete, brightening. "Maybe we could work that into our new town motto."

"Everyone has already heard about Mushrat being shot," said Dave. "I don't know how it got around so fast."

"Wasn't me," said Cynthia.

"I suspect it was one of the EMTs," I said. "I didn't tell them to keep quiet about it. Joe's living in St. Germaine now, so he might have spilled the beans. Once the cat is out of the bag, you can't stop the small town grapevine."

"That's probably it," agreed Pete.

"Also, I had to go over to Gaylen's last night and tell her what happened. She might have told someone."

"Well, she's been over at the church since nine o'clock this morning doing grief counseling," said Meg. "And here's the strange thing. Most of the folks coming in weren't even at the church last night. Apparently there are a lot of people who are overcome with grief, even though they couldn't stand the man when he was alive. Emily Douglas hauled the twins out of school and brought them, and I haven't seen Garth or Garrett in church since last summer. I doubt they ever even met Deacon Mushrat."

"This thing has everyone shaken," I said. "People feel like they have to do something, even if they didn't like him. I expect his funeral service will be packed." I changed the subject. "I saw Billy and his crew at St. Barnabas when I drove out early this morning."

"Are they going to hang the wreath back up?" asked Dave.

"Not a chance," I said. "They'll probably haul it away and stash it somewhere. You know, since they aren't going to be using it, I wouldn't mind having it for the cabin. I could have it wired with bulbs..."

"You will *not!*" exclaimed Meg. "That wreath killed someone."

"Well, technically it did," I said. "But according to Kent, Mushrat's ticker had already stopped even though he was still staggering around. The bullet was a nine, just like we thought. It hit him just to the right of the sternum and tumbled through his heart. He might have been alive when the wreath hit him, but there was no chance he was going to survive."

"You have the round?" asked Nancy.

"Yeah," I said and pulled a sealed, polypropylene bag out of my pocket. "Here you go."

Nancy took the clear bag and held it up against the light coming through the front plate glass window. She studied the bullet for a moment.

"Nine mil all right. Not too much damage. We can compare the rifling to the other round, but I'll bet it's a match."

"Maybe," I said, "but from what I've read about these professional killers, they use a gun once, then dump it."

116

"Yeah," agreed Nancy. "I read that, too."

"But why kill Deacon Mushrat in the church?" asked Meg. "How much easier would it have been to wait until he got home, then go in and shoot him?"

"I've been asking myself the same question," I said. "And I think the answer lies in what Mushrat said right before he was killed."

Everyone at the table looked at me in expectation just as Noylene toddled up with empty plates and handed them all around.

"I'm bringing a platter of toast out in a sec," she said, then grimaced, grabbed her belly with both hands, and started puffing.

"Noylene," asked Cynthia, "are you in labor?"

"Just a little," growled Noylene through gritted teeth. "I'll be okay in a minute. Mind if I sit down?"

Dave, Pete and I all jumped to our feet. Dave's chair was the closest and Noylene plopped down heavily. "Pete said that if I could just take the first shift, he'd have someone else in here at noon."

"How far apart?" asked Meg.

"How far *what* apart?" said Pete.

Cynthia's eyes flashed. "Contractions, you idiot," she said. "You're making this poor woman wait tables *while she's in labor?*"

Pete raised his hands in supplication. "*What?*" He pointed an accusing finger at Cynthia. "*You* said you couldn't work this morning."

Cynthia was incredulous. "I had a meeting at eight!"

"Noylene said the baby probably wouldn't come till this afternoon," Pete explained.

"How far apart?" asked Meg again, wiping a bead of sweat off of Noylene's forehead with her napkin.

"Maybe five minutes," puffed Noylene. "For the last couple of hours."

Nancy stood up decisively. "We've got to get you to the hospital," she said. "My car's out front. Who wants to go?"

"I'm coming," said Meg, helping Noylene to her feet.

"Me, too," said Cynthia, joining the trio of women.

"I'll stay here and wait for news," I said. "And Pete's got to stay and take care of the customers."

Pete eagerly nodded his agreement.

"I'll stay, too," said Dave. "Someone's got to guard the French toast."

•••

117

Dave and I finished almost all the breakfast while Pete was on the phone with Pauli Girl begging her to come in and sub for Noylene. It didn't seem to either of us that he was having much luck. I took my leave of the Slab and headed across the park toward the church, consigning Pete to the mercy of his customers. Dave sauntered back to the station, just in case there was a stray donut left over from the week before.

I met up with Gaylen as I walked into the office suite. Marilyn was at her desk on the phone, making an appointment for the Right Reverend Dr. Weatherall to counsel yet another bereaved parishioner.

"This whole thing is somehow your fault," said Gaylen. Her jaw was still wired shut, but I could understand her much more easily now, her articulation labored and precise. "No. I'm just kidding, even though this is nothing to be kidding about. Bishop O'Connell wants a meeting to know why his deacon was killed."

"I wish I knew for sure," I said. "I'm thinking that his deacon was killed because he made someone very angry. Either that, or Mushrat found out something he had no business finding out."

"Well, I hope you solve this case in a hurry. I told Marilyn I'd do some grief counseling, but most of these people are not grieving. They just want some answers. I can't blame them." Gaylen held up her hands in dismay. "How could God allow this? Why was the deacon killed inside the church? Shouldn't we cancel Christmas services? And, of course, there's all the speculation about who committed the murder."

"All good questions," I said. "I have another one. How did Donald Mushrat get the key to the toggle switch box? You had one, Billy had one, and Bev had one. Three keys. As far as I know, that's all there were."

"I can answer that one," said Gaylen. "He got the master key to the building from out of Marilyn's desk, used it to unlock my office, then came in and stole it."

"Wow," I said. "That's pretty brazen."

"Yes," said Gaylen. "If he hadn't been killed, he would have been fired pretty darn quick, bishop or no bishop."

"I presume Marilyn won't be keeping the master key in her desk any longer."

"No, she won't," said Gaylen. "That was my fault. We thought it'd be safe in the back of the bottom drawer under some Sunday School literature. That way, if we needed it for some reason, we'd be able to get it. Anyway, we moved the key to a magnetic box and stuck it behind the copy machine."

She paused for a moment to rest her facial muscles before continuing.

"Apparently, Mr. Mushrat rifled through all the drawers in Marilyn's desk one evening when he had nothing else to do. Then, after he found the key, he headed for my office. I have to assume he went through all my files. Luckily, my computer has a password or who knows what else he would have been into."

"This puts a whole new slant on things," I said. "Maybe the killer found out that the deacon had been privy to your files."

"I don't see how. I didn't even realize it until this morning. The key hung on a cord right beside the door to the bathroom. Once I noticed that the key was missing, I started looking around and found several files out of place, papers out of order, that sort of thing. And you..." She pointed a stern finger at me. "You can't say anything about this to anyone."

"I won't. But I may come back to you with some more questions."

"I know." Gaylen sighed. "At least I'm feeling a little better. And I'll be in church on Sunday morning, of course."

"If someone comes in and confesses, you'll let me know, right?"

Gaylen eyebrows went up. "No."

I laughed. "By the way, Noylene's down at the hospital. The little Fabergé-Dupont heir is imminent."

"That's good news, anyway." Gaylen smiled, probably for the first time this morning. "A flame is extinguished, a new light comes into the world. The circle of life."

"Amen, sister."

•••

It was one o'clock before I heard from Meg.

"Well, Noylene was in labor for about two hours after we checked in," she said.

"Is that a long time?"

"Not so long," said Meg. "Pretty quick, actually, although she'd been having contractions since five this morning."

"So everything is good?"

"Everything's fine." Meg was silent for a long moment. "Well?" she said.

"Well, what?"

119

"Oh, *really!*" I could almost see Meg's eyes roll in exasperation. "Don't you want to know what it is?"

"I presume it's a baby," I answered.

"You're not one bit funny. It's a boy, for your information. Eight pounds, eleven ounces."

"That's great. What's the little biscuit's name? And who's the proud papa?"

"I actually helped Noylene fill out the birth certificate," said Meg. "So I guess it's all public record now."

"Yep. Spill it."

"His name is Rahab Archibald Fabergé-Dupont. Noylene thought it sounded exotic."

"Rahab is a girl's name," I said. "She was a prostitute in the Old Testament. Did you point that out to Noylene?"

"No, I did not. And neither will you."

"It's gonna be tough," I said. "But I shall try to remain silent on the subject. So who's the father?"

"The father of record is Hogmanay McDonald McTavish."

"Brother Hog?!"

"One and the same," said Meg. Another silence. "There's one more thing..."

"Yes?"

"This baby..."

I got a nervous feeling in the pit of my stomach.

"What?"

"He's just fine!" said Meg brightly, hearing the anxiety in my voice. "But he was born with a...a slight..."

My heart sank.

"That is...he has a rather conspicuous..."

I closed my eyes, waiting for the worst.

"Tail."

Chapter 22

"So," said Pete. "A tail, eh?" He leaned against the counter that separated Nancy's and Dave's desks from the waiting area in the police station. "Could I have one of those donuts?"

"They're from yesterday," I said. "Help yourself." I slid the box across the counter. "Who's watching the store?"

"I finally talked Pauli Girl into taking the full-time job. Until Noylene comes back, anyway. She was divvying her shifts up between the Slab and the Bear and Brew, but I've got her now."

"What was the final offer? If I know Pauli Girl McCollough, she drove a hard bargain."

Pete huffed a heavy sigh. "Minimum wage plus tips, plus meals, and a gas allowance."

"Let's hope Noylene doesn't find out."

Pete looked panicked. "You all are sworn to secrecy!" he said. "*I mean it!* Aren't you bound by some kind of policeman's oath or something?"

"Nah," said Nancy.

"Get back to the tail," said Dave. "And pass me that chocolate one with the sprinkles."

Pete pushed the donut box back across the counter.

"Well, a tail's not very common, that's for sure," Nancy said, "but the obstetrician says it happens. He called it a caudal appendage. The doctors usually take care of it right away, but apparently Noylene wants to think about it before snipping it off."

"Huh?" I said. "What's there to think about?"

"How long is it?" Dave asked, seemingly fascinated by the prospect of someone having their own tail.

"Maybe three or four inches," answered Nancy.

"Wow," said Dave, nodding. "It'll probably grow though, right? Is it a prehensile tail? I mean, will the baby be able to use it to carry his bottle around and stuff?"

"I doubt it," said Pete. "Although that would be very cool. Who's the proud daddy, by the way?"

I grinned. "That would be our friend, Brother Hog."

Pete laughed. "No kidding?!"

Nancy was smiling, too. "It's on the birth certificate," she said.

"Back to this tail thing," said Dave. "Is it curly? Like a pig's?"

"Shut up, Dave," said Nancy, with a dismissive wave. "It's

nothing. They'll whack it off and the baby will be just like any other web-footed child running around town."

"He's got webbed feet?!"

"Shut up, Dave," Pete said.

•••

"As I was saying, before I was so rudely interrupted by Noylene's unexpected natal occurrence," I said, "I think that Donald Mushrat's *schwanengesang* may have something to do with his demise."

"Schwanenge-what?" said Dave.

"His swan song. His final words. His last articulation."

"You never said anything about that," said Nancy. "Neither did anyone else. He said something?"

"I suspect no one really thought about it. I know I didn't. At least not until later. It wasn't part of the critical event *per se.* We all remembered the singing of the hymn, Mushrat lighting the candles, the screeching and the wreath coming down, but just before that, he came out and welcomed us all to his Bible study. Then he said he was going to tell us something about a jail in our community."

"We don't have a jail," said Nancy. "The closest one is the county jail in Boone."

"It's baffling," I agreed. "The county jail could be considered in our community, I suppose, but he also said that he'd read some correspondence. Then something about spiritual consequences and mentioned Cicero."

"Cicero?" said Pete. "The Roman philosopher?"

"Yep. He said 'Cicero said it best,' but never gave the quotation. The whole thing didn't really make any sense."

"So how is this a clue?" asked Pete, reaching for another donut.

"I was talking with Gaylen this morning and she said that Mushrat had been going through her files." I glanced over at Pete. "This is confidential, by the way." Pete grunted and nodded, half a cruller momentarily obstructing his utterances.

"Ah," said Dave. "I see where this is going. Maybe he read a letter that implicated someone in the parish."

"And he was going to spill the beans," added Pete.

"I think so," I said.

Pete shrugged and shook his head. "Nah. What would a killer write to a priest? A confession? I doubt it."

"Can't you just ask Gaylen?" asked Dave.

"Well, I could, but it wouldn't do any good. She can't and won't say."

"We may be looking at this all wrong," said Nancy. "What if the two killings are totally unrelated? What if the shooting in the church was done by someone with a different motive entirely?"

"Stranger things have happened," I said.

"Especially in *this* town," muttered Pete.

"You need to compare those two bullets," Dave said. "That should tell us."

"Maybe," I said. "Maybe not. If the killer's a pro, she probably would have dumped the first gun anyway. But I think Nancy's got a valid theory. Let's keep it in mind. More importantly, I think I can narrow our list of suspects down to ten or so. Remember, the deacon was about to divulge something that the killer didn't want known."

Nancy looked puzzled for a moment. "Hang on," she said. "I just thought of something. How would the shooter, who was coming in from the outside, know that Mushrat was going to spill the...?" She stopped as realization crept across her face.

"You see what I'm saying?" I asked.

"Yep. The shooter was already inside."

"Someone hiding in the back?" asked Dave. "Maybe she ran out as soon as she shot him."

I shook my head. "Nope. When Gwen Jackson ran out to find you two at the Living Nativity, she couldn't get the dead-bolt open. Remember? If the killer had gone out that way, the dead-bolt would have been thrown."

"So that means that the shooter..." Pete paused to take a bite of his third donut, this one creme-filled with a generous dusting of powdered sugar and nuts. A few crumbs dropped on his chin and he brushed them off with the back of his hand.

"Was in the congregation," he finished.

•••

"They're a match," said Nancy, coming back into the station and waving two clear plastic evidence bags in my direction. "I went over to Kent's and used the good microscope. He wants to know if the St. Germaine Police Department will be making the traditional Christmas donation of a case of Maker's Mark bourbon to the Watauga County Medical Examiner's Office."

"Yep," I said. "A little graft never hurts."

"Anyway," continued Nancy, "Same exact gun. She didn't toss it."

"There's something else," I said. "I just can't put my finger on it."

Chapter 23

"Let's go over the statements," I said. "All the folks we interviewed the night of the shooting."

Nancy found the file folder on her desk and opened it up.

"All the statements are almost identical," she said. "No one mentions anything about a jail."

"We won't worry about that right now. Let's just put a list together."

Nancy nodded and handed the folder to me. "You read them off. I'll write them down."

"Okay," I said. "Number one, Ruby Farthing."

"Meg's mom," said Dave. "I don't think she did it."

"Of course not," I said. "Write her down, anyway."

I turned the page and continued reading. "Darla Kildair, Mattie Lou Entriken, Iona Hoskins, Gwen Jackson."

Nancy typed each name into her word processor.

"Kylie Moffit, Muffy LeMieux, Varmit LeMieux, Benny Dawkins, Flori Cabbage, Karen Dougherty." I paused for a moment while Nancy caught up, then continued, flipping pages and reading the names at the top of each statement.

"Benny Dawkins, Shea Maxwell, Frank Harwood, Kimberly Walnut. Got 'em?"

"Got 'em," said Nancy.

"Roweena Purvis, Cleamon Downs, Wendy Bolling, Annette Passaglio, Lucille Murdock, Katherine Barr, Wynette Winslow, Sammy Royce."

Nancy looked up from the screen. "That's it?"

"That's it," I said.

Nancy took a moment to count the names on the list. "Twenty-three. That sound right?"

"Yep. Some of these names we can go ahead and cross off."

"Meg's mother?" asked Dave.

I laughed. "Yeah. Scratch Ruby off. Also, since we're looking for a woman, take off the men."

"How about Wynette and Mattie Lou?" asked Nancy.

"Take 'em off." Wynette and Mattie Lou were both pushing eighty and had been members of St. Barnabas since the '40s. "Lucille and Iona Hoskins, too. They're both pretty mean, but I don't think they have the skill set to shoot a deacon in the chest from fifty feet away."

"That leaves us with twelve."

"Take Karen and Gwen off the list," I said. "Wait a second. Hang on. Leave Gwen on there. She fits the profile pretty well. Take Karen off, though. And Annette Passaglio."

"Katherine Barr?" asked Nancy. "She's a blonde."

"Can't discount a blonde," I said, grinning. "I just pointed out that the odds were good that it was a brunette."

"How about Wendy Bolling? She's old, she drives an old VW bug, and she wears glasses like the bottoms of Coke bottles." Nancy shook her head. "I don't think she's the one."

"I agree. Go ahead and take her off the list. Roweena Purvis, too. Roweena's had Parkinson's disease for the past three years."

"Kimberly Walnut?"

"She and Mushrat had something going on," I said. "Last week they came into the worship meeting together, both of them looking guiltier than Adam and Eve in the fruit department."

"Like they were having an affair?" asked Dave.

"Exactly like that," I said. "It sort of seemed as if they might have been tussling with each other right before the meeting, probably in her office. Bev remarked on it and Kimberly Walnut blushed like a teenager. She was certainly flustered."

"Well," said Dave. "Counting Kimberly Walnut and Gwen Jackson, we're down to eight."

I looked at the list: Darla Kildair, Gwen Jackson, Kylie Moffit, Muffy LeMieux, Flori Cabbage, Shea Maxwell, Kimberly Walnut, and Katherine Barr.

"You have any favorites?" asked Nancy.

"Let's see. Shea Maxwell has two little kids. I've known Katherine Barr since I was six. Her parents and mine were friends back in Raleigh. I've known Gwen for about fifteen years, but Gwen fits the profile. She has a four-wheel drive pick-up for making her vet house calls. I've seen her shoot and she's good. She's strong, fit, and single."

"What color is her pickup?" asked Dave.

"Light green," said Nancy.

"Well, it can't be her then," said Dave.

"Well, I don't think it's her, but not because of that," I said. "Call it a hunch. I've seen Gwen shed tears over a dog she had to put down. I don't think she's a killer."

"How about Darla?" asked Dave.

"Darla cuts hair at Noylene's Beautifery. I don't know her very well. It could be her, but she's really tiny. She'd have needed help to carry Sal LaGrassa's body down the hill."

Nancy looked at me, waiting for a final answer.

"I don't know much about Kylie Moffit," I decided. "Same with Flori Cabbage. They're both new in town. Let's look closely at them."

"And Kimberly Walnut," said Nancy.

"Yep."

"How about Muffy?" asked Dave. "I'd like to keep an eye on her."

"Yeah. Muffy, too," I said. "Redheads can be a tad volatile, or so I've been told. If she's the one, that character she's playing would make a heck of a cover, wouldn't it?"

Chapter 24

It was late in the afternoon when Nancy found me in Sterling Park, waiting for Meg and pondering the case. The next day was the winter solstice, and this time of year the sun dropped behind the mountains at about five o'clock. The Christmas lights around the square had come on an hour earlier and, as the sunlight faded, downtown St. Germaine began to glow with electric holiday cheer. I'd found a comfortable bench, purchased a large cup of joe from the Holy Grounds Coffee Shop and was absently watching the crew of Kiwanians clean up the Christmas crèche for the evening show.

The harder I thought about it, the more convinced I was that I was missing a piece of the puzzle: something I'd heard that wasn't quite right. I hoped it would come to me in a flash of insight, but that hadn't happened yet.

"I have some interesting news," said Nancy, sitting down beside me.

"Do tell."

"Well, the ballistics report came back on the bullet that killed Sal LaGrassa."

"I thought it was the wreath that actually killed him."

"Potato, potahto," said Kent. "Dead is dead. The rifling on the two bullets matched. They were both fired from the same gun."

"Huh. What else?"

"Ryan Jackson just called."

"The FBI guy? What did he want?"

"He wanted to know..." Nancy paused.

I took a sip of coffee. I saw Meg coming across the park and waved at her.

"Wanted to know what?" I said.

"He wanted to know why Sal LaGrassa was killed by a bullet from *your* gun."

"What?!"

"Your 9mm Glock 17," said Nancy. "You remember...we all sent in a spent round for identification. Procedure and all that."

"Yeah?"

"Well, the slug was in the system. It came from your gun."

I stood and drained the Styrofoam cup, digesting this information along with the dregs of the coffee. Meg walked up a moment later and gave me a kiss.

"What's up?" she said. "You look positively flamboozled."

127

"It seems as though my gun was the one that shot Mushrat and Sal LaGrassa."

"Surely not," said Meg. "Who says so?"

"The FBI."

Meg's eyes widened. "Oh," was all she could manage.

"Let's go check it out," said Nancy. "It's under the organ bench, right?"

"No, it's not," I said. "I took it out from under there a week and a half ago, the day I got the new truck. I wanted to shoot some rounds out at the house. It's still locked under the back seat of the Tundra."

•••

"So is it yours?" asked Nancy.

Meg looked on as I inspected the handgun.

"It's mine." I handed it to Nancy and tapped on the butt of the gun. "I had my name etched right here on the back of the grip."

"You were up in the loft when Mushrat was shot," said Meg. "And your gun was locked in the truck."

"Yep."

"But your gun was the gun that killed him."

"It sure looks like it," I said.

"Well, how did *that* happen?" asked Meg.

"I wish I knew," I said. "But it looks as though someone is setting me up."

"I have an idea," said Nancy. "Let's keep this quiet. No need to make this public knowledge."

"For now," I agreed.

Chapter 25

"Let's go, Toots," I said, grabbing Annie's hand. "We need to go find Pedro."

Sophie Slugh and I had a history. I met her when she was just a wee snaif, peddling pump organs for Peter Pooter's Portable Penny Pumpers. But Pooter's Penny Pumpers went plooie and Peter Pooter became a pensive pauper.

Sophie Slugh, on the other hand, turned to crime. She was as slimy as pearl onions in clam sauce and left a trail of despair and mucus wherever she went. Although she never had the spine for it, she had a rap sheet that included a-salt, i-stalking, and mollusktation. Sure, I had some fun with her -- me and all the other boys in Miss Galloway's Garden Glee Club -- but once the bottle stopped spinning and we got into her genes, we discovered a hermaphrodite gastropod whose idea of afterglow consisted of chomping off whatever got stuck in the mix. I got away easy. Stumpy Johnson never sang baritone again.

Our paths had crossed since then, but I'd kept my nose and my shoes clean, and the last time I saw Sophie, she was dribbling down the side of Reichenbach Falls, the tiny teeth of her radula gnashing in anger. I didn't give her a second thought. A few months in the salt mines would do her good. As my Aunt Terraria used to say "Easy come, escargot."

"Pedro's at The Lettuce Patch," said Annie. "He told me to tell you."

"I'll bet he did," I said.

Her kiss grabbed my lips like an aroused sea barnacle. "Baby," I said. "You're my kinda gal."

•••

"It seems to me," said Edna Terra-Pocks, "that I should get some sort of life-insurance policy or something. People don't last very long in this church."

"Oh, most of them do," said Elaine. "I've been here for years."

"It's true," agreed Fred. "I don't think you have to worry. If you weren't killed after that first prelude, you'll probably make it through Christmas."

"Who's celebrating communion this morning?" Rebecca asked.

"Gaylen's here," I said. "She said the sermon's going to be short, though, so we're doing two anthems. One after the Epistle reading and one at the offertory."

Marjorie walked into the choir loft and shook her photocopied hymn at me. On the back of the page was my latest effort. "I would like this slug story better if it had some Christmas stuff in it," she complained.

"Like what?" asked Georgia, coming in behind her. "Shepherds? Angels? Reindeer?"

"Reindeer," decided Marjorie, plopping down in her chair.

"You know," said Mark Wells, "I think there should be something in science called the 'reindeer effect.' Just once I'd like to turn on CNN and hear a newscaster say 'Gentlemen, what we have here is a terrifying example of the reindeer effect.'"

"I'm not sure how a reindeer would fit into the plot," said Elaine, reading over my glorious prose.

"I'm not sure how *anything* fits into the plot," sighed Meg.

"*Sing Lullaby*," I announced. "By Richard Shephard. Get it out. Then we'll go over Parker Ramsay's *Magnificat*. You already know it, so don't pretend that you've never seen it before. And don't forget choir rehearsal this Wednesday."

"Are we singing the *Mouldy Cheese Madrigal* on Christmas Eve?" asked Muffy.

"I suppose so," I said.

"Before or after I sing *O Holy Night*?"

"Umm..."

"We practiced it before you came up," said Edna. "I think it sounds just great."

•••

"Have you seen Benny?" I asked Bev as the choir was getting ready to go downstairs for the processional hymn. "I need to ask him something."

"He's gone again," Bev said. "He had a gig at All Souls' in Asheville. They're giving him the entire prelude. That place is going to be smokin'!"

"I'll be glad to get him back," I said. "Not that Addie isn't doing a great job."

Benny Dawkins, our thurifer, hadn't been to a Sunday service at St. B's for months. Oh, we had incense, but the pot was being wielded by Benny's protégé, a little eight-year-old girl named Addie Buss. Addie, although she showed flashes of brilliance for one so young, didn't have the polished showmanship of a true master. Not yet. But Addie was good. She'd already mastered some of Benny's easier signature moves with the incense pot: *Walk the Dog, Around the World,* and the *Double Reverse Swan.* Now she was beginning to step out and improvise with routines reminiscent of the Chicago legend, Wilson "the Firefly" Gillette. We all knew that it wouldn't be long before she was giving Benny a run for his money.

Benny Dawkins had won the International Thurifer Competition in Spain last year and, having demolished his archrival Basil Pringle-Tarrington and receiving the highest score ever recorded in the event, decided to retire and travel the circuit. He'd been touring Europe most of the fall, playing all the major cathedrals. Benny was apologetic, of course, for missing the Advent and Christmas season, but vowed to be back for the Feast of the Epiphany.

The lay reader on this, the Sunday before Christmas, was Joe Perry, an English professor with a glorious speaking voice. The Old Testament lesson was from the Book of Micah.

"But you, O Bethlehem of Ephrathah, who are one of the least of the tribes of Judah, from you shall come forth for me one who is to rule in Israel, whose origin is from of old, from ancient days."

It may have been Joe's voice that triggered the memory, or perhaps it was the fact that I enjoyed listening to Joe read and hence was actually paying attention. All of a sudden, I realized what had been lurking just behind the frontal lobe of my brain, occasionally peeking out to taunt my medulla oblongata. Or maybe my hippocampus? I'd have to ask Karen about that.

•••

"Shall we go out to lunch?" asked Meg. I met her in the fellowship hall where the St. Barnabas coffee hour was in full swing, but not before I'd made a quick stop in the church office.

"I'm hungry," I admitted, "but I can't yet. I've got to go and check something. I could use your help."

"Sure. What are we checking?"

"Deacon Mushrat's last sermon."

"He never got to the sermon. He was killed during the hymn," said Meg.

"Not Wednesday." I held up a CD. "Last Sunday. I have a recording of the whole service. I think I know what we're listening for."

"How about if we get some sandwiches?" suggested Meg. "Then we can work in your office."

•••

Meg and I sat in the police station and unwrapped the two Reuben sandwiches we'd purloined from the Slab. Corned beef and sauerkraut on rye bread, Russian dressing and Swiss cheese—the perfect combination of ingredients, in my humble opinion.

I put the CD in the stereo and hit the play button. Our service recordings didn't have any tracks—they were one continuous sound file, so I held down the fast-forward button and zipped ahead to the sermon.

"The Holy Spirit has convicted me to preach on another subject," said the voice of Deacon Mushrat. "Hear now the awesome Word of the Lord from the Book of Malachi."

"Is this it?" asked Meg.

"This is it," I said. "Listen now." I took a big bite of my Reuben.

"I the LORD do not change, so you, O descendants of Jacob, are not destroyed."

"What am I listening to?" asked Meg. Her bites were more delicate, but she was catching up.

"The lesson," I answered, swallowing quickly to avoid the don't-talk-with-your-mouth-full glare. "I'll tell you when."

Mushrat went on with his lesson. "Bring the whole tithe into the storehouse," he intoned, "that there may be food in my house. It is imperative, therefore, that you attend the offering and barter the purchase if your property is to be preserved."

"There!" I said. "Right there!" I pushed the pause button on the CD player.

Meg shrugged. "I don't get it."

"I didn't either, but Marjorie caught it right away. We thought she was just irked at Mushrat for ignoring the lectionary but she heard what we all missed."

Meg looked hopelessly confused. "What'd we miss?"

"You know, most of us just tune out the scripture lessons. I must have heard that scripture in church a hundred times growing up. Every time a stewardship campaign would kick off, we'd get a sermon on tithing."

"Okay," said Meg. "But I still don't understand."

I went over to the bookshelf, found a Bible and handed it to her. "Malachi 3:10 and 11."

Meg looked it up, read it to herself and looked up at me blankly.

"Follow along," I said, backing the track up about thirty seconds.

"Bring the whole tithe into the storehouse that there may be food in my house. It is imperative therefore that you attend the offering and barter the purchase if your property is to be preserved."

I paused the CD again.

Meg's eyes grew wide. *"That's* not verse ten!"

"No, it's not."

"Play the rest!"

I pushed the play button again. Donald Mushrat's voice came out over the speakers.

"'Test me in this, says the LORD Almighty, and see if I will not throw open the floodgates of heaven and pour out so much blessing that you will not have room enough for it. The mark is set. Twenty thousand is the price. I will prevent pests from devouring your crops, and the vines in your fields will not cast their fruit,' says the LORD Almighty."

Meg was now busy taking notes on one of Nancy's legal pads. "Play it one more time," she said. "I want to make sure I have it word for word."

I played it again. Meg compared Mushrat's words to the text in Malachi, furiously scribbling when the two didn't correspond.

"One more time, please," Meg said.

I obliged.

"Got it?" I asked.

"Got it! Mushrat said, 'It is imperative therefore that you attend the offering and barter the purchase if your property is to be preserved.' Then he said, 'The mark is set. Twenty thousand is the price.' None of that is in Malachi. But if he was reading from the Bible, why would he put that into the lesson?"

"He wasn't reading from the Bible, remember? He was reading from his notes. He kept shaking them at the congregation."

"Oh, ho," said Meg. "A clue!"

"A clue indeed. Mushrat wasn't the sort to add his own spin to the scriptures. He copied those sentences into the Malachi reading by mistake."

Chapter 26

"When's the funeral?" asked Georgia.

I was in Eden Books doing some Christmas shopping: a new graphic novel called *Crogan's March* for Moosey, a Dan Brown thriller for Dave, and about a hundred other assorted titles that I'd ordered throughout the year, thinking that I'd save a bunch of time at Christmas. Now I was looking at spending a whole day wrapping a hundred-plus books with one good hand.

"No funeral for us," I said. "It's Christmas. Donald Mushrat's body will be shipped back to Winston-Salem from whence he came, where he will be buried with full ecclesiastical honors."

"Ecclesiastical honors, eh?" said Georgia. "And what might those be?"

"Hmm. Twenty-one acolyte salute and a donkey-drawn hearse. Hey, would you mind wrapping those books for me?"

"I already did," said Georgia. "I started as soon as I heard you'd broken your arm. They're all wrapped and numbered. Here's the list with the corresponding titles so you don't give the wrong books to the wrong folks. Why don't you decide who gets what, and I'll put the tags on for you."

"Wow! Thanks!"

"See anything else you'd like? You still have a couple of days left."

"Lemme look."

"Take your time. Hey, I heard about the Epiphany service. Is the king still coming?"

"That sounds like the title of a bad Christmas cantata. But, yes, the king is coming."

"Which king is it?"

"We don't really know. You see, here's the deal..."

"I hope it's Balthasar. I love Balthasar. He's the cool king—hip, tough, black. He's like the Denzel Washington of dead kings."

I had to agree.

•••

Pizza was the specialty of the house at the Bear and Brew. They had a number of signature dishes, but Nancy and I preferred the "Black Bear Attack" pizza with the stuffed garlic crust. Dave didn't care what we ordered. He was just happy to be included.

We divided the pitcher of Barn Burner Red, a local brew, and I filled Nancy and Dave in on what Meg and I had discovered the night before.

"So you think Mushrat was killed because he read some stuff that wasn't in the Bible?" asked Dave.

"Not exactly," I said. "I think that Mushrat got into something he wasn't supposed to. He copied it into his sermon by mistake, and whoever it belonged to found out about it."

I pulled a piece of paper from my inside jacket pocket and read it aloud.

"'It is imperative, therefore, that you attend the offering and barter the purchase if your property is to be preserved.' That's the first sentence that Mushrat read that isn't included in the scripture. Later on he said, 'The mark is set. Twenty thousand is the price.'"

"Okay," said Nancy. "Let's start at the beginning." She took a new legal pad out of her briefcase, then took a pen out of the breast pocket of her uniform and wrote across the top of the page.

"Let's go back to the auction," I said.

"The auction?" Dave said.

"We have two dead bodies," I said. "Salvator LaGrassa and Donald Mushrat. What do they have in common?"

"Nothing," said Nancy.

"Sure they do. They were both shot by the same gun and therefore by the same person."

"*Your* gun," whispered Dave.

"My gun," I agreed. "The gun that was locked under the back seat in the pickup."

"It was locked up for the second shooting," observed Nancy. "Not the first."

"Right. And the first time we saw Sal LaGrassa, he was bidding on wine at the auction at Old Man Frost's."

Nancy reached across the table, took hold of my scribbled notes and read them again.

"It is imperative, therefore, that you attend the offering and barter the purchase if your property is to be preserved," she read. She looked up at me. "Someone's talking about the auction."

"I believe so," I said. "That's why LaGrassa was at the auction in the first place. There was no reason for him to be there otherwise. And, if he had stumbled across the auction, as we originally surmised, there certainly was no reason for him to show up with thousands of dollars in cash."

"So something happened at the auction that caused LaGrassa to get killed?" asked Dave.

"Yep. I bought the wine. The wine that he wanted."

"You think there's something in the wine?" asked Nancy. "He was a killer, you know. Maybe the wine is poisoned?"

"I don't think so," I said. "Meg and I drank four of the bottles. Random bottles. If it had *all* been poisoned, we'd be dead. If a few bottles contain poison, what's the point in that? LaGrassa was a professional killer. He's not going to use poisoned wine. He'll shoot you in the head. No, I'm thinking that LaGrassa's interest was strictly monetary."

"Ten thousand dollars isn't that much money," said Dave. "Not in the big scheme of things."

"That's what I bought the wine for. That's not what it's worth. Bud told me that I could sell it for maybe a quarter million."

"What?!" exclaimed Nancy, then lowered her voice. *"A quarter million dollars?"*

"Yeah," I said. "In a couple of years when it reaches maturity. Bud and I will sell it then. But here's the thing. The sentence says 'It is imperative that you barter the purchase if *your* property is to be preserved.' *Your* property. That implies that the wine was LaGrassa's property in the first place. Or at least that he thought it was."

"Huh," said Nancy. She refilled her beer glass from the pitcher on the table. "Old Man Frost's place was foreclosed on, wasn't it?"

Yeah," I said. "The bank came in and slapped padlocks on everything in sight. What if LaGrassa was storing the wine at the Frost farm and it got locked up before he could get it?"

"But why wouldn't he have it stored at his own house?" asked Dave.

"Hang on," said Nancy, pulling out her iPhone. "I read something about this. He lived in Montana, right?"

"Yeah," I said.

The Black Bear Attack pizza arrived at our table, delivered by our waiter, a skinny, college-aged kid who identified himself as Jared.

"Y'all want another pitcher?" he asked, as he set plates down in front of each of us.

"Yes, please," said Nancy, still tapping information into her iPhone.

Dave and I took a moment to savor the first couple of bites, then Nancy held up her phone and announced her internet discovery.

"In Montana, residents have to apply for a 'connoisseur's license' before he or she can have wine shipped over the state line. You have to be registered and have a valid and up-to-date license. And apparently the state of Montana and the postal service take this very seriously. I'm pretty sure Sal LaGrassa wasn't about to register with the government for a connoisseur's license."

"And he wouldn't have wanted to chance shipping a quarter million dollars' worth of wine," said Dave. "What if it had been discovered? Even by mistake? It would have been confiscated."

Nancy nodded and put a slice of pizza on her plate.

"Well," I said, "we know that this LaGrassa guy was a big-time thief as well as a killer. So, let's just say that he stole this wine..."

"Him or his partner," added Dave. "Or maybe both of them."

Nancy pointed her finger in agreement. "And she was storing it for him until he could get over to this side of the country to get it."

"He'd have to drive it back to Montana," said Dave.

"Probably," I said. "So LaGrassa shows up at the auction with four thousand dollars after getting a message that his property is going to be auctioned off. He might have even had more than that. What we *do* know is that he didn't have ten thousand because that's when he stopped bidding. Whatever the figure was, he thought that he had plenty. More than enough, in fact."

"But then Bud spotted the wine," said Nancy, smiling. "And he knew it for what it was."

"And I just happened to be there," I said. "And, by golly, Sal was outbid."

"He must have been furious," said Dave, finishing off his second slice and taking a third.

"What about the second sentence in Mushrat's reading?" asked Nancy. "The mark is set. Twenty thousand is the price."

"Sounds like a hit to me," I said.

"Yeah," agreed Nancy. "Me, too."

"So Deacon Mushrat stumbled onto a hit and inadvertently announced it in his Bible reading?" asked Dave.

"It appears so," I said.

"How would he have gotten that information?" said Nancy.

"I'm betting it was an email," I said. "Gaylen told me he was going through her files. He didn't have much compunction about sticking his nose where it didn't belong. Right click, left click. What if he pasted part of an email he didn't even know he'd copied into his sermon notes? Notes that included the scripture lesson?"

"What about his computer at the church?" asked Nancy. "Why don't we get a warrant and go through it?"

"He didn't have one yet. He did have a friend on the staff, though. She might have let him use her computer to type his notes."

Nancy and Dave both looked at me.

"And Kimberly Walnut drives a black Chevy Tahoe."

Chapter 27

"I'd really like to get on her computer without her knowing about it," I said.

"Well, Judge Adams gave us the warrant. You want me to call Panty Patterson?"

"Yeah. Let's give him a call. We need to do this after hours. See if he can come over tonight. Maybe around eleven o'clock."

"They're up all hours anyway," said Nancy.

Panty Patterson was one of the Patterson brothers. He and his brother Dale ran the crematorium outside of town. Meg's mother, Ruby, had owned the enterprise for a brief period, after inheriting it from Thelma Wingler and before selling the whole shebang to Panty.

Panty was an albino. He had a high forehead and very small, piggy features. He always dressed in clean overalls, white, collared shirts buttoned all the way up, and Wolverine steel-toed work boots. He'd also just completed his doctorate in computer science at Georgia Tech. Dale, his brother, was not as fortunate, having barely completed the second grade. Panty took care of Dale. Dale took care of the bodies in the crematorium.

"You know," said Nancy, "we still have a few questions that need answering."

"Yeah, I know."

"Questions like, how did *your* gun kill Donald Mushrat and Sal LaGrassa when it was locked in your truck? And, what did Mushrat say on Wednesday night that caused whoever shot him to risk plugging him during the service right in front of you, God, and everybody?"

"Two good questions," I agreed. "Here's another. 'The mark is set. Twenty thousand is the price.' It sounds like a contract to me. Who's it on?"

"Oh, crap!" exclaimed Nancy. "I forgot about that."

"I expect that, if LaGrassa's partner is still in the game, that hit is still scheduled."

"Maybe it's somebody in California. Or Australia. Nothing to do with us."

"Let's hope so."

•••

Panty Patterson drove up to the back door of St. Barnabas Church at eleven o'clock sharp. Most of the electric Christmas decorations downtown had been shut off and, except for a small crowd at the Bear and Brew, the square was all but deserted. Nancy and I were waiting for him under a security light, and I unlocked the church as he exited his old Cadillac and rumbled up the steps to meet us.

"Hi, Chief," he said. "Merry Christmas!"

"Merry Christmas to you," I said. "Thanks for helping us with this."

"We have the warrant right here," said Nancy, fishing around in her coat pocket.

"Don't worry about it," said Panty. "You're the one that needs it. Not me."

We entered the church and made our way down the hall to the suite of offices. I reached behind the copy machine, found the magnetic box, retrieved the master key, and unlocked Kimberly Walnut's door. Her computer was a Dell PC, about a year old.

"Vista," Panty sneered as he sat down in the chair and pushed the on button. "This won't take long."

The computer hummed to life and a couple of welcome screens came and went.

"I think the computer's password protected," I said. "At least mine is."

Panty's fat fingers flew over the keys for about seven seconds.

"Okay. We're in," he said. "What are we looking for?"

"Wow," I said. "That's it?"

"Vista," said Panty, as if the one word explained everything.

"We need all her email," said Nancy. "Everything on the St. Barnabas server, plus her Gmail and any Yahoo accounts. Let's copy her hard drive, too. Also, we need a list of every web-site this computer has accessed in the past month and all the passwords, if any. And don't leave any tracks. Can you do that?"

"Yep." Panty's fingers danced across the keys. "This'll take me about a half-hour," he said. "How do y'all want the information?"

Nancy produced a small black and red box and a couple of wires from her pocket and laid them on the desk. Panty nodded absently and turned his concentration back to his task.

"That little box will hold all that?" I said.

"It's a plug and play, USB 37 terabyte encrypted hard drive," said Nancy.

"I see," I said, not seeing at all. "So the answer would be 'yes?'"

Panty snorted but didn't look up.

"This box will hold all the information stored on every personal computer in Watauga county," she said.

"Really?"

"Pretty close," agreed Panty.

"Too bad you can't play the organ," said Nancy, looking wistfully at my broken arm. "I wouldn't mind listening to some Christmas music while we wait."

•••

"It's going to take me a few hours to go through all this," said Nancy, dropping the hard drive back into her pocket. "Even using a data search. But if Donald Mushrat was playing on her computer, I'll find out."

Chapter 28

"Kimberly Walnut owns a black 2003 Chevy Tahoe. Four-wheel drive," said Dave.

"That'd be about right," I said. "She parks it in back of the church."

"Flori Cabbage drives a Jeep Grand Wagoneer, but it's an '89. Dark blue with wood trim on the doors. Kylie Moffit has a dark gray Nissan Murano. It's all-wheel drive, rather than a 4x4, but I wouldn't rule it out."

"Neither would I."

"Muffy drives a Beemer."

"It's not Muffy," I said.

"Can I still keep an eye on her?" asked Dave.

"Sure," I said with a smile. "Knock yourself out."

"Hey! What if Sal LaGrassa was gay. Maybe his partner is a man."

I thought for a moment, trying to come up with a reason this theory wouldn't work. I couldn't.

"Can't discount it," I said, "but the FBI is pretty sure it's a woman. I think we have to go with their assessment for the time being."

Nancy came into the station, took a donut out of the box on the counter and plopped down in her chair.

"Nothing," she said. "Mushrat was not using that computer."

"You're sure?" I asked.

"I'm sure. I *will* tell you that Kimberly Walnut has been spending quite a lot of time on eHarmony.com."

"The dating site?" I asked.

"Yep. She's hot and heavy with an insurance salesman from Knoxville. You should see some of their emails!"

"No, thanks," I said. "Any evidence that she and Mushrat were dancing the horizontal tango?"

"Nope," said Nancy. "They never exchanged any emails, as far as I could tell. Of course, that doesn't mean that they weren't involved. Just that Mushrat didn't send her any emails."

"Okay, then," I said, "if Mushrat wasn't using Kimberly Walnut's computer, whose was he using?"

Nancy and I looked at each other, as the realization hit us both at the same time.

"The library," we said, in unison.

Rebecca Watts and Diana Terry were behind the circulation desk filing books when Nancy and I entered through the double glass doors.

"We need to see the library computer," I said.

"Sure," said Rebecca. "Which one?"

"The public one that's hooked up to the printer and the internet," I answered.

"It's right there," said Diana, pointing to an old Hewlett Packard sitting on a small table against the wall. "But I'm afraid it won't do you any good. I haven't gotten it up and running yet."

"What do you mean?" asked Nancy.

"Someone tried to use it yesterday afternoon, and the system wouldn't come up. There's something wrong with it."

"Maybe it's just old," I suggested.

"Could be," said Diana. "It was working yesterday morning. Then, nothing. I was going to reload all the software, but I haven't gotten around to it yet."

"Can we take it with us?" asked Nancy. "Maybe Panty can get something off of it."

Diana looked at Rebecca, who returned a shrug.

"Sure," Rebecca said.

"Bring it back when you're finished, though," said Diana. "That's the only internet service some of our older patrons have. They like to check their email."

"Who was the last person on the computer?" I asked. "Before it stopped working?"

Diana looked at Rebecca, squinched her eyes and thought for a moment. "Well, it was Allison O'Steen who complained about it. Before her..."

Rebecca snapped her fingers at Diana. "I remember. Oh, *you* know...that woman...I can't think of her name..."

Diana looked at her blankly.

Rebecca turned to me. "You know...ol' what's-her-name. She's your friend. The one who's been playing the organ. Edna something."

"Edna Terra-Pocks," I said.

"That's her," said Rebecca. "I remember 'cause she had her black Range Rover parked illegally out front."

"What are the chances of finding anything on that computer?" I asked Nancy.

"I don't know," said Nancy. "But even if she wiped the hard drive, there will be something left. I'll take it out to Panty. He's good. Really good." She thought for a moment. "Was Edna in the building when Mushrat was shot?"

"Maybe," I said. "I saw her coming down the stairs as I went up. She'd driven in from Lenoir to practice, but Mushrat had just run her out so he could conduct his Bible study."

"And was your gun still under the organ bench when she started playing at St. Barnabas?" asked Nancy. "You know, after the accident?"

"Yep."

"I have an idea," said Nancy, smiling.

"Me, too," I said.

Chapter 29

It was snowing again. According to the Weather Channel we were in for a white Christmas. Meg was in the bedroom wrapping presents, Baxter was lying on the rug in front of the fire, Archimedes the owl was perched on the head of my stuffed buffalo preening his feathers, and I was hunkered down in front of my typewriter, flexing my brain muscles like Arnold Schwarzenegger at a cabinet meeting.

I was being set up like duck pins. I could feel it. Annie Key was no more a singer than I was Hillary Clinton's rent-boy. Sophie Slugh was a squishy piece of work, but what were the chances that she'd oozed her way past the killer gas-slugs, evaded the under-dwarves, and escaped the salt mines of Kooloobati? Slim, I decided. Virginia Slim.

Then there was Pedro. Pedro LaFleur was a hard case, a countertenor with high Cs to burn, and my righthand man. I knew Pedro. He ate his veal cutlet so rare he had to taunt it like a rodeo clown to get it to come from behind the baked potato. He wouldn't be caught dead at the Lettuce Patch, a vegan eatery with more sprouts than Rosie O'Donnell's upper lip.

Things were coming together like...like...

"Dagnabbit!" I grumbled. "I've run out of similes."

"That's nice, dear," said Meg. She peeked out of the bedroom door. "Would you like an early Christmas present?" she asked coyly. "I'm all out of wrapping paper and I don't want to go back to the store to get some."

"You bet I would," I answered, happy to take a break. "I only hope it's what I think it is." I took off my hat and dropped it on top of the typewriter.

"It's not," said Meg, coming out of the bedroom. "Nice try, though." She had a large box in her hands. "Here, let me open it for you."

She tore the tape on the bottom of the box, tipped it, and a large book slid out onto the desk.

"Nice!" I said. It was an art book, one I hadn't seen before. I immediately recognized the painting on the dust jacket, a depiction of an Old Testament story titled "Judith Beheading Holofernes," although until I read the cover, I didn't remember who painted it. *The Female Hero in Italian Baroque Art—the work of Artemisia Gentileschi.*

"It's a first edition," said Meg. "Signed by the author."

"Beautiful!" I said. "Thank you!"

"Well, I thought the gruesomeness of the subject matter would be right up your alley," said Meg. "All that Biblical gore."

"Excellent!" I said, as I flipped one page after another, quickly scanning and admiring the plates that I'd spend some serious time studying after supper. "I love early Christmas presents! I thought I'd have to spend all evening at the typewriter with Soph..." I stopped talking and stared at the book.

Meg looked at me, a question forming on her face. "What's wrong?"

I pointed to the painting on the page. It was titled *Jael and Sisera* and dated 1620. The work depicted the climax of the story in the Book of Judges. Sisera, a general whose army has been routed by the Israelites, takes refuge in the house of his friend Heber the Kenite. Heber's wife, Jael, tells him that he's safe there, but when he falls asleep, she nails his head to the ground with a tent peg. This was the scene I was looking at, rendered in beautiful, rich Baroque brush strokes.

"So?" said Meg.

"You know the story?"

"Sure."

"Donald Mushrat wasn't talking about a jail. He was talking about a 'Jael.' In Hebrew, it's pronounced with a 'Y', but I doubt that Mushrat knew that. And with his North Carolina accent..."

"Ja-el," said Meg. "So Cicero was..."

"Not Cicero at all," I said. "*Sisera.* Jael and Sisera. 'We have a Jael in our community. I've come across some correspondence and I don't think any of you are aware of the spiritual consequences that this implies.' Mushrat found out that there was a killer. He knew it was a woman. He read her emails."

"Did he know who it was?" asked Meg.

I thought for a moment. "No, I don't think so. He would have seen her sitting in the congregation. But she didn't know how much he'd found out. She didn't know how many emails he'd read. She couldn't take a chance."

"So she shot him," said Meg.

"So she shot him."

145

"Okay," said Meg. "I'll buy it. But how did he get her emails?"

"I don't know."

"Do you know who it is?"

"Not for sure, but we're closing in."

"Oh, you'll figure it out," said Meg. She walked over and gave me a kiss. "I have something else for you. Another early Christmas present. You want it?"

I didn't have to be asked twice.

Chapter 30

"When's Noylene coming back in?" asked Dave.

"The baby's not even a week old," said Nancy.

"Yeah. I know. But I really want to see the little fella."

"You just want to see his tail," said Nancy. "But that's not going to happen. He wears this thing called a 'diaper.'"

"Maybe he'll need changing," Dave said hopefully.

Our table at the Slab Café had been easy to get since Nancy had started stringing yellow "Police Line—Do Not Cross" tape across it.

"What can I get all y'all?" asked Pauli Girl, sidling up to Dave and giving him a wink.

"Um...how about an omelette," said Dave. "Hash browns and some whole wheat toast."

"Will do, Sugar," said Pauli Girl. She looked at Nancy and me.

"Flapjacks," said Nancy. "Short stack."

"I'll have a couple of country ham biscuits," I said. "And some grits."

"Gotcha," said Pauli Girl, writing quickly. She tore the ticket off the pad and headed for the kitchen.

"And some more coffee," Nancy called after her. Pauli Girl waved at Nancy over her shoulder.

"What's the news on the computer?" I asked.

"News?" said Nancy. "Here's the news. There was no hard drive in that computer. It was gone."

"Gone?" I said.

"Taken out. Removed. Stolen. Gone. A big hole where the hard drive should have been."

"How long would that have taken?" Dave asked. "To disassemble the computer and pop out the hard drive?"

"'Pop out' being the operative words," said Nancy, shaking her head in dismay. "These things are almost disposable. Panty and I tried it a couple of times with one of his spare drives. The fastest time we had was one minute forty seconds. The slowest was three minutes and that was because we dropped the screwdriver behind the table and couldn't find it."

"So, nothing on the computer?" I said, knowing the answer.

"Nope."

"Well," said Dave glumly. "What's next?"

"We need to shoot the Glock," I said. "And check the rifling on the bullet."

"*Your* Glock?" asked Dave.

Pete walked out of the kitchen wiping his hands on a greasy towel. He tossed it behind the counter, pulled out a chair and sat down at the table.

"What's up?" he said.

"Police line. Do not cross," said Nancy, pointing at the plastic yellow banner.

"Yeah, yeah. So what's up?"

"Nancy was just going to show us how long it takes to change the barrel on a Glock 17," I said.

"I have a Glock 19," said Nancy, unsnapping her holster and putting the gun on the table. "It's the compact model—a little smaller, but it breaks down the same." She dropped the magazine, pulled back the slide, looked in, and then stuck her finger into the opening to make sure there wasn't a round in the chamber.

"A Glock has fifty percent fewer parts than other handguns of this caliber. This one, for instance, has only thirty-three parts."

"Is the safety on?" said a man at the next table. The gun was pointing vaguely in his direction and he looked very nervous.

"Actually, there are three safeties," said Nancy. "But none you can see. There's a trigger safety, a firing pin safety, and a drop safety. It's the safest pistol on the market. The only way a Glock handgun will fire is for the trigger to be pulled fully to the rear. It won't go off by itself." She sniffed. "Anyway, it's not loaded."

"Okay," said Pete nervously. "I'm sure we all feel very safe."

"Watch this," said Nancy. She located the locking tabs on both sides of the frame and pulled down on them while tugging on the slide. The slide dropped off into her hand. She lifted out the recoil spring, removed the barrel, held it up for us to see, and then reversed the process.

"That's it," she said, clicking the slide back into place. "Barrel removed and replaced in well under a minute. And I didn't even need a tool."

"So what's the point of all this?" asked Pete.

"Well," I said, "we just wanted to know how long changing a barrel might take. Plus, we have a gun we have to re-test."

"Ah," said Dave, comprehension dawning on his face.

Cynthia came out of the kitchen. "Pete! We could use a little help back here!"

Pete huffed and got to his feet. The cowbell on the front door announced another patron and Brother Hog walked into the restaurant.

"Brother Hog!" called all the regulars.

148

The Rev. Hogmanay McTavish waved dejectedly and made his way over to an empty stool at the counter.

"I hear congratulations are in order," Pete said. "Let me get you some breakfast. On the house."

"Thanks," said Brother Hog.

"Have you visited the little nipper?" I asked.

Hog shook his head in the affirmative. "Oh, yes."

"Have you seen his tail?" asked Dave.

"Shut up, Dave," whispered Nancy.

"Noylene doesn't want the doctors to snip that little rascal's rudder," Hog said. "But I'm afraid I'm going to have to insist. As the father, I'm sure I have at least *some* rights."

"What's her rationale?" Pete said. Cynthia gave him a withering look. "If I may ask?" he quickly added.

"She says that maybe little Rahab..." Hog fixed an unblinking eye on us. "You *know* that's a girl's name, right?"

We all nodded.

"She says that maybe little Rahab should keep his tail until he reaches an age where he can decide for himself whether or not he wants to keep it. I say that we know what's best for the child and should point him in the way that he should go."

"Ah," Pete said. "Sort of like infant baptism."

Hog pondered this for a moment then rejected the notion. "No," he said. "Nothing like it at all."

Pete laughed.

"So," I said. "Are you getting married again? Are you going to make an honest woman out of Noylene Fabergé-Dupont?"

"I asked her. She hasn't said one way t'wor the other."

"How does New Fellowship Baptist Church feel about all this?" asked Cynthia. "Did the congregation make a big stink?"

"They're not happy," admitted Hog. "In fact, I've taken a leave of absence until after the New Year. I may have to go back into the tent revival business."

"Well, you were awfully good at it," I said. "You could preach a badger into a turtle hole."

"None better," agreed Pete.

"Binny Hen the Scripture Chicken was top notch," said Dave.

"Souls were saved," added Nancy. "People baptized."

"Picnics on the grounds," I said. "Music, games, fun..."

"And a good time was had by all," Noylene said, standing in the doorway with a bundle in her arms. "Hog," she added sternly. "We gotta talk."

Chapter 31

"Things are heating up in the world of Sophie Slugh," observed Marty Hatteberg. Members of the choir who happened to show up to rehearsal on time were treated to my latest treatise on the adventures of Sophie and the under-dwarves. The rest of the group would have to wait. But perhaps that was their plan from the beginning.

"I still don't care for slugs," said Marjorie, tossing the page over her shoulder in disgust. "Anyway, I have an announcement. I'm thinking about starting a blog."

"What?" said Steve DeMoss. "Do you even know what a blog is?"

"Sure. You get on the computer and you type in stuff for people to read. Then they give you their credit card numbers."

"And you have something that people want to read?" said Phil. "I mean besides how to make bathtub gin?"

"An important skill back in the day," Marjorie said. "But I used to be quite a soprano, you know. I thought I'd share my techniques on voice production. You know, some anecdotes, followed by singing advice. Then people will pay to read it and I'll be a millionaire. I found out about all this on the interweb down at the library."

"You were a soprano?" Meg said. "When was that?"

"In the forties, dear. We had quite the choir in the forties."

"But you're a tenor," I said. "The lowest tenor we have, in fact. Most sopranos at least keep some semblance of their range over the years."

"That's just the way God made me," said Marjorie, taking a sip from the flask that she kept under her choir chair. We never asked what was in the flask. None of us really wanted to know.

"My first blog-thingy article is going to be called *Smoking Your Way to a High B*."

Guffaws erupted from the choir.

"No, really," said Marjorie. "Sometimes sopranos don't like to give away their singing techniques, but I've been singing in the church choir for eighty-seven years and I know a thing or two."

More laughter.

She took another sip. "Back in WWII, we sopranos here at St. Barnabas were very competitive. I remember one girl who had a solo with a high A in it. On Christmas Eve she squawked that note like a goose getting sucked into a jet engine. Oh, how we all laughed at her!" Marjorie closed her eyes and smiled, fondly remembering those glory days.

"We taunted her all the way into Lent," she added matter-of-factly. "She eventually had a nervous breakdown and had to quit the choir just before Palm Sunday. We really had a lot of fun back then! Anyway, I've decided that it's time I told my story."

Marjorie leaned forward in her chair. "The secret of my success..." she glanced around the choir and lowered her voice, "has always been a couple of stogies in the bathroom before the church service!"

"Hey," said Mark Wells, "mine, too! I wondered who that was smoking cheroots in the ladies' room."

"Take out the *Mouldy Cheese Madrigal*," I announced. "Shephard's *Mass of the Nativity,* and the Holst *Christmas Day.* Also Carson Cooman's *In the Beginning.*"

"When does Muffy sing *O Holy Night?*" asked Varmit.

I glared at Meg who'd suddenly decided that Gustav Holst's use of the half-diminished seventh chord was very intriguing.

"You can sing it during the pre-game show," I said with a sigh. "We'll start singing at 10:30. We'll have music for a half hour. The service starts at eleven o'clock."

•••

Rehearsal wrapped up after an hour and a half and the choir members made their way down the stairs and through the nave chattering merrily. Christmas was almost upon us. Even the pall of Deacon Mushrat's demise didn't keep us down for long.

Edna sat at the organ, setting a few stops and going over her music for Christmas Eve.

"Edna," I said. "I've got a question for you."

"Yes?"

"Did you use the computer at the library on Monday afternoon?"

Edna looked confused. "Yes," she said hesitantly. "I believe it was Monday. Yes, it was," she decided. "Monday. I came up to practice but had left my copy of the Olivier Messiaen piece I was going to play for communion at home. I downloaded a PDF off the internet." She gave me a suspicious look. "Why?"

I was horrified. "Messiaen? Christmas Eve? During communion?"

"Sure," said Edna. "I'm playing *Dieu Parmi Nous.*"

I heard myself make a small, pathetic sound.

Edna patted me on the cheek. "Don't worry, honey. I'll play all the right notes."

That's what I was afraid of. I shook my head to clear the thoughts of a Messiaenic Christmas Eve. "Anyway, someone took the hard drive out of the library computer," I said, looking for a reaction. There was none. "I told Rebecca I'd ask around."

"It was working fine when I used it," Edna said. "That was around three in the afternoon."

She told a convincing story. I don't know if I believed her.

Chapter 32

Christmas Eve. I was walking across the park toward a row of shops I hadn't been in for a while. Since last Christmas Eve, in fact. The snow was just beginning to gather against the hard corners of the gazebo as the wind lifted the large, wet flakes and chased them across the frozen ground. My right hand was stuck deep into the pocket of my old coat; my left hand, partially encased in its plaster cast, was bundled against the chill by a woolen boot sock. Cynthia came bouncing out of a boutique called "Sassafras" with her six-year-old niece Penny in tow. She saw me and gave me a wave. Cynthia was positively glowing.

"I just love Christmastime," Cynthia said when I walked up. Both her hands were dripping with shopping bags. "Isn't this the *best*?"

"Very festive," I agreed.

"Have you finished your Christmas shopping?" asked Cynthia. "Penny was all done, but she's helping me with a few last-minute gifts."

"Well, not exactly," I said. "I did get some books and a few choice bottles of wine, but I don't really do my shopping until Christmas Eve."

"Really?" said Penny, looking as haughty as a six-year-old possibly could. "How pedestrian."

"*Penny!*" said Cynthia, then looked at me apologetically.

"It's an old German custom," I said, making up yet another old German custom. "Very bad luck. If you do your shopping before Christmas Eve, the Krampus knows what you're up to and will come to your house instead of Santa Claus."

"The Krampus? I've never heard of the Krampus." Penny looked mildly concerned but crossed her arms defiantly. "And I've heard of almost everything."

"Well, after all, you *are* six," I said. "I'm just saying that *some* people believe that if you've already gotten your presents, and you weren't a good girl all year, the Krampus will come to your house on Christmas Eve and change your presents for switches."

"Oh, I've been pretty good," decided Penny, but chewing nervously on the side of her lip.

"And the very bad children..." I looked up and down the busy street. "The *very* bad children not only get switches, they get all their old toys taken away as well."

Penny's eyes grew a little wider.

"And the *extra-bad* children, the children that aren't respectful of their elders and also police chiefs, they get whisked away to the coal mines where Black Peter makes them work until they've learned to behave."

"Hayden!" said Cynthia.

"But," I said, bending over to Penny's height, raising a finger and tapping the side of my nose. "But, if you've waited until Christmas Eve to do all your shopping, the Krampus doesn't have time to figure out what's what. He skips right over you."

"I don't believe you," decided Penny.

"We'll see," I said.

Cynthia glared, but gave me a secret smile.

"Humph," said Penny as she walked away. "Krampus, indeed!"

•••

"Merry Christmas!" said Mr. Schrecker, smiling as I walked into his jewelry shop. "I have your purchase right here. They did a wonderful job in New York."

He reached under the counter, took out a small, velvet-covered box, set it in front of me, and opened the lid. Inside was Meg's great-grandmother's cameo necklace, reset in gold filigree and surrounded by diamonds. A new chain had been handmade to match, replacing the original, long since lost. When I'd gotten the piece from Ruby last summer, it had been badly chipped and the setting almost destroyed. Now the cameo had been restored and looked almost perfect. Almost—which is exactly what I told Mr. Schrecker. Almost perfect. I didn't want it to look brand new. I needn't have worried. The New York jewelers were artists. The necklace was exactly right.

"Beautiful!" I said.

"I'm sure Meg will love it," said Mr. Schrecker. "Shall I wrap it up?"

"Please."

"Oh, just one more thing," said the jeweler, taking another box from under the counter. "I liked the necklace so much, that I took the liberty of having a pair of earrings made to match." He held up his hands apologetically. "Now, I know you didn't order them, and if you don't want them, I'm sure someone else in town will be happy to take them off my hands..."

He opened the second box. The matching earrings—diamonds

dangling in the same gold filigree that held the cameo—winked up at me from the black velvet cushion.

"You sly dog," I said with a grin. "You're making me look better and better."

Mr. Schrecker smiled right back. "Now, about Meg's birthday..."

•••

"It's not a match," said Nancy. "The bullet I fired from your Glock doesn't match the other two."

"So someone switched the barrels," I said.

"Sure did," said Nancy. "And whoever it was switched them before the first murder. Before Sal LaGrassa was shot."

"But probably after the shooter had decided that Sal LaGrassa had to go."

"So she could pin it on you?" said Nancy.

"At the very least, to throw a monkey wrench into the investigation. Especially if the FBI got involved. Luckily, they didn't."

"Yep," said Nancy.

"By the way, Merry Christmas! Here's your present." I handed Nancy an envelope.

A smile split Nancy's face. "Thanks, boss. What is it, a couple of lottery tickets?" She tore open the end of the envelope, pulled out a sheet of paper and took a moment to read it. Then she gasped, threw her arms around my neck and gave me a kiss right on the lips.

"Lieutenant Parsky!" I said, not able to hide my smile.

"When is this for?" Nancy asked, excitedly rereading the sheet of paper.

"You leave the fifteenth of January. Two plane tickets and paid vacations to Belize. The resort is all-inclusive, so you can have a blast for ten days. I expect you back tanned and well-rested."

"I'll need a new bathing suit," said Nancy. "And who on earth do I take with me?"

"Take whoever you want," I said. "You have a couple weeks to decide. Meg said I should make it a vacation for two. She said you'd have more fun if you took someone with you."

"Well," said Nancy, now at a loss for words. "Umm. Thanks."

"Back to the case at hand," I said. "Who knew that the gun was under the organ bench?"

Nancy snorted. "Who didn't?"

"Yeah," I agreed. "I guess. So, let's go back to the auction, this time tossing out the possibility of coincidences."

"Okay," said Nancy.

"Let's say that we were right, and that the wine was Sal LaGrassa's to start with."

"By hook or by crook," said Nancy. "He probably stole it."

"Probably. LaGrassa got an email from his contact, or partner, or whoever, saying that his wine was going to be auctioned and that he'd better get back here to bid on it if he wanted it."

"Right. The email that Donald Mushrat pasted into the Malachi reading."

"His partner couldn't do it, or didn't want to, because that's not her persona in the town and she's keeping a low profile. Someone buying three expensive cases of wine would attract some local interest to say the least."

"Especially if she spent a few thousand dollars," agreed Nancy.

"She might have gotten it for a couple of hundred dollars and gone unnoticed, but you never know what's going to happen at an auction."

"I'm with you so far."

"So Sal LaGrassa loses the bid and he's pretty hot. A quarter million bucks—gone. He's mad as hell at his partner. The question is, what would have been LaGrassa's next move, having lost that bid, keeping in mind that he's a thief and a killer for hire?"

Nancy took a deep breath. "He would have found out exactly who you are and where you live. He'd have gone out to your house, shot you, shot Meg, taken the wine back, as well as whatever else he could find that was easy to carry, and burned down your cabin."

"Pretty harsh, but that's what I was thinking, too," I said.

"It would have been like shooting fish in a barrel," said Nancy.

"Hey! I am not without certain skills, you know."

"Think about it," said Nancy. "Sal shows up at your cabin. You know he was the guy who was bidding against you at the auction. He obviously wanted the wine. You figure he came over to make you an offer, probably for quite a bit more than you paid for it."

"Hmm," I said.

"You invite him in to hear what he has to say and blam!"

"Blam?"

"Blam," said Nancy, pointing a finger gun at me and dropping her thumb.

"Exactly," I said. "So why didn't he do just that?"

Nancy thought for a second. "No reason except one. His partner shot him."

"In the forehead," I said. "And he never saw it coming. Caught him completely by surprise. Next question. Why did she shoot him?"

"He threatened her?" said Nancy.

"No doubt. But I expect he'd threatened her before. If his plan of action was to get his wine back, she shouldn't have been afraid for her life."

"Ah," said Nancy. "But she was afraid for *yours*."

"Maybe. But I'm the heat. The fuzz. The man."

"The fuzz?" said Nancy with a smile. "You're the fuzz?"

"You bet. Extremely fuzzy. But there's another answer."

"Meg," said Nancy.

"Meg," I said. "She's friends with Meg." I paused and thought for a moment. "That's probably not the whole story. And let's not tell Meg about any of this just yet."

"Agreed," said Nancy. "And if it's any consolation, rest assured that I would have avenged both of your horrific deaths."

"That's very kind."

•••

The *Mouldy Cheese Madrigal* has an interesting history. I'd vowed, early in my St. Barnabas career, never to perform any anthem in church that attempted to rhyme any word with "Jesus." This avowal came after we'd been forced to sing (at the behest of a Philistine bishop) an installation anthem by an unnamed composer that began, "Here's to Jesus, the one who frees us." The composer went on to attempt many other such rhymes in the course of the verses, including: "release us," "sees us," "tease us" and, of course, my personal favorite, "squeeze us." It was then that I'd sworn my oath. The choir dubbed the dictum the "Jesus-Squeezus" rule and it had been in play ever since.

Except on Christmas Eve.

Many years after that bishop had gone on to greener pastures, I amused myself one Christmas by penning a holiday madrigal. Eric Routley, an authority with keen insight, wit, grace and style, always held that a good English carol contained a reference to a mouldy cheese. Taking his advice to heart, my madrigal contains the following lines spoken by the shepherds:

What offering can we bring
to give this little king?
A coat of fur to warm him,
And a little lamb to charm him.
Some milk and mouldy cheeses,
We give to the Holy Jesus.
Fa la la la la la.

Rhyming "Holy Jesus" with "mouldy cheeses" was a stroke of genius. Generally, the "fa la la's," were followed by "ha ha ha's"—at least in *our* choir. But even so, the *Mouldy Cheese Madrigal* had become a Christmas Eve standard.

We finished it up with hardly a snicker; evidence, in my mind at least, that anything too stupid to be said can easily be sung. We sang some carols and listened to Edna Terra-Pocks rattle around some French Noëls that made my ears bleed. Then Muffy got up to sing her big solo. Varmit was on the back row, beaming.

"She's got it memorized," he said proudly to Bob Solomon, who was sitting beside him in the bass section.

"We *all* do," said Bob.

The church was only half full at 10:45. On Christmas Eve, people wandered in from their parties, dinners, and celebrations anywhere from half past ten until the service started at eleven o'clock. It was an informal time; some people chatted, some sat and listened to the music, some spent their time in silence, reflecting on the miracle of the birth of Jesus Christ. It was relaxed; it was special; it was the way we celebrated the Nativity.

This being our custom, there was naturally some talking downstairs in the church when Muffy stood to sing. Varmit frowned.

"Why don't they shut up?" he said to no one in particular.

"This is the pre-game show," said Fred. "We're just here to provide some background music. Folks will listen if they want."

"That ain't right!" insisted Varmit, but Edna Terra-Pocks had started her introduction.

"Hang on," Varmit whispered across the choir at Muffy. "Don't start yet. They ain't listening!"

Muffy glanced back at him, a confused look taking the place of her confident performer's countenance. She was standing at the front of the balcony, her hands clasped in front of her. She had no music, having memorized all three verses at the behest of Edna. She turned back to the congregation, unsure of the best course of action.

Edna finished the four measure introduction and indicated to Muffy that she should start singing.

"Don't do it," hissed Varmit.

Muffy made up her mind in an instant, but her concentration was lacking.

"O holy cooowww," she sang.

"Hahahahaha!" roared Marjorie, unable to contain herself.

"Dammit!" said Muffy loudly, stamping her pretty foot and crossing her arms in front of her in a fit of pique. "We gotta start over!"

Edna, unsure of what to do, kept playing, although she'd begun to hiccup in an effort to keep her own amusement in check.

Muffy was furious. *We gotta start over!* she called to Edna again, this time louder, since she supposed that Edna hadn't heard her the first time. Edna, finally unable to continue, stopped playing, managed to turn off the stops, and put her head down on the keyboard, her shoulders racked with laughter interspersed by hiccups.

"Okay," whispered Varmit. "Everyone's listening now."

"Varmit," Muffy growled through clenched teeth, "I'm gonna kick your kiester from here back to Virginia!"

"Hahahaha!" howled Marjorie. "This is even better than waiting for that high A!"

Most of the rest of the choir had fallen out of their chairs and were rolling on the floor of the loft holding their sides. Although they were doing their best to stifle their mirth, their snorts and gasps of merriment were, pretty much, being echoed in the congregation below.

It took me about thirty seconds to wade through the bodies to the front of the loft and restore order.

"Okay," I said, wiping tears from my eyes. "That was a very special Christmas gift, and one we won't soon forget." I looked over at Muffy, who was still furious. "You want another shot at it?" I asked.

The anger on Muffy's face dissipated in an instant and she brightened immediately. "Sure! Sure I do!"

I pointed at Edna, who'd managed to compose herself, and she began the introduction again.

"O Holy Naaht," sang Muffy, with more than a hint of Loretta Lynn. "The stars are brightly shahning..."

Chapter 33

Christmas was over and things were getting back to normal in St. Germaine, at least as normal as we ever managed. There was still snow on the ground and the holiday lights were still up, but the crowds that flocked to our little village for shopping and that down-home atmosphere had dissipated considerably.

"Okay," I said, reaching across the table and stabbing a bite of Nancy's egg-and-cheese breakfast casserole. "Another question arises. Why was the wine at the Frost farm in the first place? Hiram Frost lived by himself."

"Good point," said Dave, also eyeing Nancy's breakfast. "Can I try a bite of that, too?"

"No," said Nancy, moving her plate closer and guarding it with her forearm. "Order your own." She turned her attention to the question at hand. "I've been thinking about that and I have no idea."

"Me, neither," said Dave.

"You know," she added, "quite frankly, ever since we decided that she saved Meg's and your life..." She shrugged. "I'm just not that interested in hunting her down."

"Yeah," I said. "But she shot the Mushrat. We've gotta get her."

"It's our sworn duty," said Dave.

"Did you ever tell Meg?" Nancy asked. "That we think it's one of her friends, I mean?"

I shook my head. "Not yet."

"More coffee?" said Pauli Girl, suddenly appearing beside Dave.

"Yes, please," said Dave. Nancy and I just pushed our cups across the red and white checkered, vinyl tablecloth.

"We have to solve this thing before you leave on vacation," I told Nancy. "Otherwise, you can't go."

Nancy smiled. "Whatever," she replied, but I didn't think she was taking the threat seriously.

Chapter 34

The Lettuce Patch was an icebox -- it had to be to keep its clientele from desiccating and permanently becoming part of the moss-covered carpet. The tables were covered with dead leaves, fungus and decaying vegetables. Trails of slime crisscrossed the walls and floor like angry argyle wallpaper. I caught the unholy stench of osmosis. Yep. I knew it. This was a slug-bar. And they were everywhere.

Annie Key gave me a hard shove from behind and I slid into the room, my feet slipping and sliding like the lead penguin at the Ice Capades.

I saw Pedro LaFleur lying in a mushroom patch behind a table in the corner, all trussed up with a couple of extra long bamboo shoots. I pulled my heater and let the Maitre D'Limpet have it right in the pneumostome. Once, twice. He didn't flinch, just blurgled a horrible, muculent laugh.

"Won't work, pard," Pedro said sadly. "The bullets get sucked right in. I unloaded a whole clip at the cigarette girl and she slurped 'em like they was oysters. And don't bother aiming for their brains. They're too small to hit."

I nodded and put the gat back in my sock. "What do you dirty snails want?" I said.

All the slugs ground their tooth-like denticles angrily and wheezed in umbrage. If I knew one thing about slugs, I knew that they hated to be called snails.

"Isn't it obvious?" said Annie Key. She spun on her foot, pulled off her wig, and spit the false teeth out of her mouth. It was her. It was Sophie. Sophie Slugh.

•••

Gaylen Weatherall was presiding over the worship meeting, a meeting I agreed to attend, even though I'd done enough meetings at St. Barnabas in the last month to carry my meeting obligation deep into Lent.

"I'd like to thank you all," Gaylen said, "for your work in my absence. I know it's been a very trying time."

Gaylen's jaw was still wired shut and would be for another couple of weeks, but her arm was out of its sling, evidence that she wasn't having too much trouble with her shoulder. Her ribs (according to Meg) were healing nicely and her two black eyes were unnoticeable under a light concealer. Her nose still had a bump in the bridge, but that might be there forever, or at least until she decided that the plastic surgeon should get a crack at it. Her right hand was in a cast, but the fiberglass ended at her wrist, unlike my own cast that traveled up way past my elbow.

"Now, we have a couple of big events coming up," she said. "Kimberly?"

Kimberly Walnut picked up a sheaf of photocopied papers and started passing them around the table.

"This is some information on our 'Cocoon' lock-in for the kids," she explained. "This is a curriculum that I've written. I'm hoping to get it published later this year. As you can see," she pointed to a chart on the second page, "the children come at five o'clock on Tuesday afternoon. We'll have an activity, then dinner, then a prayer time, then a children's vespers service..."

"How long does this Cocoon thing last?" asked Joyce Cooper, flipping through the pages.

"It lasts from five o'clock on Tuesday until lunchtime on Wednesday," said Kimberly Walnut. "The last thing we have before lunch is our big communion service."

"So they come in like worms," I said. "They're transformed and leave like butterflies."

"Caterpillars," said Kimberly Walnut. "They come in like caterpillars. Not worms." She tapped on her documents and said, very slowly to make sure we understood, "*It's in the curriculum.*"

"I am a worm and no man," said Elaine. "I remember that from Bible drills."

"Caterpillar," snapped Kimberly Walnut.

"Maybe the kids could learn all the 'worm' scriptures, " I said. "You know, God prepared a worm in the Book of Jonah. It smote a gourd, as I recall. Maybe the kids could decorate gourds. Also, the worm dieth not, and the fire is not quenched."

"Caterpillars!"

"Now, children," said Gaylen.

"Don't the kids have school?" asked Joyce.

Kimberly shook her head. "Wednesday is a teacher in-service day. It's the perfect time. This gives the children something to look forward to right after Christmas, and the parents who work won't have to be scrambling around trying to arrange day care."

"Well, they'll still have to if we toss the kids out at lunchtime," Joyce said.

"Oh, no," said Kimberly. "The program ends at lunch, but we'll be happy to keep them until 3:30 if they need to stay."

"Very nice plan," said Gaylen, giving Kimberly Walnut a smile. "And, of course, I'll be here to help out. But I'm not staying the night."

Kimberly Walnut promptly forgot about worms and beamed.

"Where are the kids going to sleep?" asked Bev.

"We're going to use the fellowship hall. Everyone will bring sleeping bags. I'll be on a cot, but the children will just sleep on the floor."

"You have meals all figured out?" asked Gaylen.

Kimberly nodded vigorously.

"Chaperones?"

"Oh, yes. One adult for every five children. That's what the curriculum calls for."

"And how many children are signed up?" asked Elaine.

"Twelve," said Kimberly Walnut.

"So, three adults," said Elaine.

"Yes," said Kimberly Walnut. "Well, no. Two for sure. But maybe three.

"And who are the two for sures?" asked Gaylen.

"Well," said Kimberly Walnut, "me and Emily Douglas. Then Diana Terry said she'd try to make it after supper. You remember Diana? She helped out at Bible School last summer. I don't know for sure if Diana's coming, but we can do it with two if we have to."

"I'm sure you'll be just fine," said Gaylen. "Now, then...our Epiphany service." She looked over at me. "What's the status on the bones?"

"The bones of one of the Three Kings will be at St. Barnabas at the beginning of next week. They're coming here straight from the National Cathedral. Arthur Farrant and another priest are driving the relics down here on Monday morning."

"How exciting!" said Elaine. "Is the bishop still planning on attending?"

"Yes," said Gaylen. "Although, when I asked him if he was the one who gave our name to the church in Nantwich, he denied it. It doesn't matter, of course. I'm glad they found us."

"Are we getting any publicity on this?" Bev asked.

"Oh, yes," said Gaylen. "An article in *The Watauga Democrat, The Tattler,* of course, and I'm pretty sure *Our State* magazine is sending their reporter back up. Word has it that Mayor Cynthia made the cover this month."

"I'm sure she'll be thrilled," I said.

Chapter 35

"What do we have?" I asked. "Or rather, *whom* do we have?"

Nancy looked at her list.

"Kylie Moffit. New to town. Married to Biff Moffit. She drives a dark-gray 2008 Nissan Murano. Dark hair tied back, fit, looks strong."

I conjured up a mental image of Kylie and her husband.

"Flori Cabbage. She's been in St. Germaine less than a year. She may be Ian Burch's girlfriend, although it's hard to tell. They're together all the time, but there are no PDAs—public displays of affection. She drives an '89 Jeep Grand Wagoneer, dark blue with wood trim. It's tough to tell her body type. She wears those bulky sweaters and full skirts."

"Nah," I said. "I don't think so."

"Any particular reason why?"

"I've heard her play a rauschpfeife," I said. "Also a bladderpipe, a crumhorn, and a pretty good cornemuse. I find it inconceivable that anyone who has spent time mastering the intricacies of a cornemuse would bother to kill people for a living. She could torture them much more easily simply by playing it."

Nancy laughed. "That's your reasoning?"

"That, and she couldn't have shot Mushrat. She was playing the flute when he was killed."

"And when did you remember that?" Nancy asked.

"When I listened to the recording of the service, which I happened to find yesterday. The new sound system that the church has records everything to a hard drive. It creates a new file each time you turn it on. Then the sound file stays on the drive until you burn it onto a CD. After that, it's automatically deleted. We never bothered to check and see if Mushrat was recording his Bible study. I went in to make a copy of the Christmas Eve service, checked the hard drive, and there it was."

"Anything else on that recording?" asked Dave.

"Nothing we didn't hear before."

"Did you hear the gunshot?" asked Nancy.

"Nope," I said. "Nothing. Who else?"

"Edna Terra-Pocks," said Nancy, running her finger down the page. "Fifty, rich as Croesus, drives a black 2010 Range Rover."

"I don't think she did it," I said. "She wasn't even in the picture when Sal LaGrassa was killed. St. Barnabas hadn't hired her yet."

"I don't think she did it, either," said Dave. "Doesn't feel right."

Nancy rolled her eyes. "Doesn't feel right? Oh, puhleease." She looked back down at her notes. "Kimberly Walnut. She drives a black 2003 Chevy Tahoe. She had something going on with Donald Mushrat. Maybe it was a simple game of liturgical slap and tickle in the vestibule. Maybe they'd just decided to ally-up against you."

"Me?" I said.

Nancy smiled. "You do tend to give Kimberly Walnut a hard time. Or so I've heard. Then again, it could be something else entirely."

"If Kimberly Walnut's the one, and she killed Mushrat because he read her emails at the library, she certainly wouldn't have pretended to like him," I said. "She would have ignored him."

"Unless she was trying to find out exactly what he knew," said Nancy. "And once he started spouting off in the Bible study, she had to shut him up. She didn't know if he was going to name her as the killer or not."

"True," I agreed.

"What I don't get," said Dave, "is why the killer used the computer at the library. Surely she can afford her own internet connection."

"Of course she can," said Nancy. "But the library's far safer. IP addresses are easy to track. At the library, she could simply log in on a web account, answer her emails, log out when she was finished, and no one would be the wiser."

Dave thought about this for a moment, then said, "Well, how did Deacon Mushrat get into her email?"

"Obviously," said Nancy, "he got her password. That, or she didn't log out for some reason."

"Or couldn't," I said.

"What do you mean?" asked Nancy.

"The Christmas parade."

"What about the Christmas parade?" said Dave.

"Holy smokes," I said, realization sinking in. "Give me that list of everyone you interviewed after Mushrat's murder."

Nancy handed it across the desk.

I looked at it and felt a big smile spread across my face.

"I know who did it. I know who the killer is."

Chapter 36

"You were right, boss," said Nancy. "She's Hiram Frost's niece. That's the reason she stashed the wine in his basement. It was a nice, cool place, lots of room, and Ol' Man Frost was too feeble to go down the stairs anymore. She had no idea the bank was going to foreclose on the farm."

"Why didn't she stash it at her own place?" asked Dave.

"Probably because she doesn't have room," I said. "I've been in her apartment. It's not very spacious."

"Listen," said Nancy, "can we prove any of this?"

"Nope," I said. "She's done a very good job. There's no hard drive in the library computer, there are no eyewitnesses, the bullets that killed both victims were a match to the old barrel of *my* Glock, and there is no way to link her with LaGrassa."

"What if we find *her* Glock that has your old barrel on it?"

"It's long gone," said Nancy. "Probably at the bottom of Lake Tannenbaum."

"So, what do we do?" asked Dave.

"You know what I think?" I said. "I think that St. Barnabas being asked to host the relics of one of the Three Kings on Epiphany just as our killer's facade is crumbling is one heck of a coincidence."

"Huh?" said Nancy.

"After the tour was announced in England, the vicar of St. Hywyn's in Nantwich received a phone call identifying St. Barnabas as one of the wealthiest churches on the east coast of the United States. We all thought the bishop ratted us out. But it wasn't the bishop at all. He had nothing to do with it."

"She or LaGrassa made the call," said Nancy with a nod. "And they knew you'd take the bait. I mean, how could you resist? It's perfect. An easy target with no security to speak of."

Sal LaGrassa was into antiquities," I added. "If he set it up, she certainly could carry out the theft after she killed him. Then she could disappear into the mist to set up her business somewhere else."

"But why would she want the bones of one of the Three Kings?" asked Dave.

"Oh, she doesn't," I said.

"Then what does she want?"

"She wants the medieval reliquary. It's worth a fortune."

Chapter 37

Father Arthur Farrant was a smiling, affable vicar, apparently very happy to be out raising money for his beloved parish in Nantwich. When he and the accompanying priest climbed out of their rented car, they were both dressed in their ecclesiastical blacks—black pants, long sleeved black shirts, and accompanying dog collars. Arthur was in his early forties and had the look of hard work about him, his piercing blue eyes taking in the scope of St. Barnabas in a well-practiced glance. He took off a worn, blue cardigan, tossed it onto the top of the car, stretched, then ran his hands through a thick mop of reddish-brown hair before taking a moment to adjust his dark-rimmed, European-style, rectangular glasses.

Gaylen and I were on the front steps of the church waiting for them, having received a phone call from Arthur's cell a few minutes earlier asking for specific directions.

"Hayden Konig?" said Arthur, holding out his hand in greeting. "A pleasure. And this must be the illustrious bishop, Gaylen Weatherall."

I shook the priest's hand, but Gaylen rated a hug and a kiss on the cheek. "The pleasure is ours," she said. "Welcome to St. Germaine."

"Great weather!" said Arthur, looking around the square. "And what a lovely little town."

I smiled. It was thirty-four degrees out. "Thanks," I said. "We like it a lot."

"J.D. Overnight," said the other priest, an American, judging by his accent. We both shook hands with him. J.D. had an altogether different demeanor. His body language said "I don't want to be here, I'm much too important." I had him pegged as a would-be academic, someone who thought he should be teaching at a seminary, a bevy of adoring students hanging onto his every eloquent thought, but somehow (and through no fault of his own) he had spent his whole career working at a diocesan office. He was obviously pretty disgusted that he'd been the one to catch the assignment of ferrying around a box of bones. J.D. Overnight was a large, moist fellow, sweating even in the dead of winter, and had come to the mountains equipped with a houndstooth driving cap and a dark green, waxed-cotton jacket that he probably thought made him look like an English gentleman. I didn't envy Arthur Farrant having to be saddled with this guy for two weeks.

"You'll have to forgive my speech," said Gaylen, self-consciously. "I broke my jaw in a car wreck before Christmas. It's still wired shut."

"Nothing to forgive," said Arthur, giving her a big smile. "I didn't even notice."

"Could we go inside, please?" said Father Overnight. "There's no reason we have to exchange pleasantries on the front steps, is there?"

"No, of course not," replied Gaylen politely. A little too politely. She gestured toward the front doors. "Please come in."

•••

"This is beautiful," said Gaylen, looking at the Nantwich Reliquary sitting on the big wooden table in the conference room. Bev nodded in agreement.

The wooden box was ancient, eighteen inches long by fourteen inches deep and a foot tall. Each side, as well as the top and presumably the bottom (although we couldn't see it), was made of a single piece of very dark English oak. There were two-inch-wide silver straps that wrapped the sides, bottom to top, at the corners and every eight inches or so. Four straps in the front. Four in the back. Three on each side. Each one delicately engraved with climbing roses.

The top was carved with a medieval depiction of the Adoration of the Magi, each figure covered in gold. The sides were carved with scenes as well. Mary enthroned with the infant Jesus covered one side, the Baptism of Christ, the other. On the front of the reliquary were images of the apostles. On the back, a scene of the Last Judgment. These carvings had originally been covered in gold, like the lid, but now the gold was almost all gone, flaked away over the centuries. The ornate hinges and hasp on the top of the box had been fashioned of silver and were well worn. The lock and keyhole in the front of the box were oversized, and solid gold.

"The first time this reliquary is mentioned in the written record," said Arthur Farrant proudly, "is in 1470. Twenty-two years before Columbus set off for the New World. In England, the War of the Roses was in full swing."

"And are the bones of one of the Three Kings really in there?" asked Bev, astonished to be viewing such a thing in the conference room of St. Barnabas.

"Of course not," said J.D. Overnight with a smirk. "It's all superstition. Superstition and nonsense."

"Well," said Father Farrant, "it's a legend, of course, but there's no denying that Christians and saints have been coming to view this shrine since 1164, the year that the relics of the Three Kings made their way from Milan to the cathedral in Cologne. Can you imagine the prayers that have been offered up in the presence of these holy relics? Prayers for protection against the black plague, prayers for kings and monarchs and nations, prayers for family, for wealth and power, prayers for strength and courage in battle, prayers against tyranny..." Arthur took a deep breath. "It's a humbling thing to contemplate."

J.D. Overnight blew a puff of air from his oversized lips in disgust.

"And," added Arthur with a twinkle in his eye, "there is certainly the possibility that those bones are actually one of the Three Kings."

"Oh, I believe it," said Bev. "Have you ever looked inside?"

"Oh, no! The last time it was opened was in 1892, when it was rediscovered. But the priests did leave us with a written account of the contents along with a drawing of what they found inside. It's in the archives of the church."

Arthur traced his finger across the lid.

"There's a special compartment along the back of the reliquary," he said, indicating a space about half the width of the box. "It contains the remains of old rotten and molded bandages, most likely made of *byssus*. There are some pieces of aromatic resins and similar substances. There's also a lot of dust and other particles."

"What's byssus?" asked Gaylen.

"It's an exceedingly fine and very valuable textile known to the ancients. This was most probably made from the finest Egyptian white flax. Of course, there's not much left now."

"What about bones?" asked Bev.

"There are numerous bones," said Arthur with a smile, "and pieces of bones. But they're quite small and brown. You know the story of Ewen, our Welsh priest, and the caravan sent to Cologne by Emperor Barbarossa?"

"We do," I said. "I filled them all in."

"Well, we think that Ewen didn't want to get caught purloining any of the major bones. Of course, a rib here or there or a lot of little finger bones would hardly be missed. There are also two medieval coins in the box, both made of silver and only stricken on one side. They would be very valuable."

"Amazing," I said.

"I'd give anything to take a peek inside," Bev said.

"Sorry," said Arthur, shaking his head. "There isn't even a key that I know of. No worries. You're in good company. None of the thousands of pilgrims to St. Hywyn's ever saw the actual bones."

Chapter 38

"So where are the bones of the King being stashed?" asked Meg.

"They're locked up in Gaylen's office," I said. "When the service begins, one of the acolytes will carry the box in during the processional hymn and place it on the altar."

"Neat!"

"Then, after the service, Arthur Farrant will give a talk in the fellowship hall for whoever wants to stay—the history of the bones, relics in general, that sort of thing."

"We're staying, right?"

"I wouldn't miss it."

"What are we singing for the Epiphany service?" asked Meg.

"*Lo! Star-Led Chiefs*," I said.

"*What?*" said Meg. "We all thought you were making us sing through it as a joke."

"Nope," I said. "I'd never make fun of a composer named William Crotch."

•••

The twelve children who showed up for Kimberly Walnut's Cocoon lock-in were the same children that generally showed up for everything. Moosey, Bernadette, Ashley, and Christopher had been in Sunday School together since they were five. Dewey was the newest member of the gang, taking the place of Robert who jumped the puddle and became a Baptist.

Garth and Garrett Douglas (the twins) joined the church a couple of years ago. They were a pair of terrors, and I suspected that they were only allowed to attend Cocoon because their mother Emily had agreed to be a chaperone. Stuart, Lily, Samantha, and Madison were new to the church as well, having joined in the fall after their triumphant debut in *Elisha and the Two Bears*. Addie Buss was Benny Dawkins' thurific protégé, but, despite her growing reputation as a smoke-slinger, she was still just one of the kids.

I could see that Kimberly Walnut and Emily Douglas were going to have their hands full when I walked into the church at six o'clock. They were both in the kitchen putting together a fried chicken supper they'd bought from Piggly Wiggly. Kimberly Walnut had given the children the assignment of sitting quietly and drawing a picture of their favorite Biblical Christmas scene. The children had taken this to mean that they were to invent a game called "Hymnal Attack," a game reminiscent of "Space Invaders," in which the bombardiers (girls) dropped hymnals from the choir loft onto the targets (boys) who walked to and fro on the main floor, stiff-legged and as fast as they could.

"Hey," yelled Dewey, as one bomb found its mark. "No throwing! You're only allowed to drop it!"

"Oops, sorry!" called Samantha, her apology followed by a plethora of stifled giggles. "We won't count the points for that one."

"Just wait until it's our turn!" said Stuart.

"We have to get to a hundred first," called Addie, dropping another hymnal. Bang! it went, and knocked Garth to the floor. Cheers came from the balcony and the boys redoubled their efforts to walk faster.

I watched for a moment, shook my head with a smile, and headed for the kitchen. As I walked past the chapel, I saw Gaylen setting up for the vespers service. I stuck my head in.

"Hi. How's it going?" I said.

"Fine," said Gaylen. "Everything is going great. The kids are upstairs busily drawing pictures of the Christmas story and we'll be discussing their art during vespers. I think Kimberly Walnut's finally got a handle on this thing."

"I think that she does," I agreed.

●●●

Gaylen Weatherall's office was open. I stuck my head in the door and saw the reliquary sitting on the side table beside her desk. I walked over to it and checked the lid just for fun. Locked. I was sixty-eight percent sure that it was the reliquary that the killer was after. Nancy, Dave, and I would be up all night, but we figured that, if we could nail her for grand theft, maybe the feds could make a murder case later. They'd been collecting a lot of evidence over the years. They might be able to put something together.

I knew that Gaylen would lock her office when she left for the evening and I was going to make myself conspicuous until then. Then I'd retire surreptitiously to my own office and listen to the microphone that Nancy had hidden on Gaylen's bookshelf. I'd give her a call as soon as I heard our thief enter the rector's office. Nancy and Dave would arrest her as she walked out.

•••

"Jeez," said Nancy into her cell phone. "It's three o'clock in the morning. What's she waiting for?"

"I don't know," I said. "Maybe we've got this whole thing figured wrong."

"Yeah, maybe."

•••

At 4:15 my cell vibrated on the desk. I picked it up and flipped it open. "Yeah," I whispered.

"You gotta get down here," said Nancy, her voice full of urgency.

"What for?"

"There's been another murder! Over at Old Camp Possumtickle."

"The nudist camp?"

"Yeah. We just got the 911 call. We've *got* to go, Hayden."

"Where'd the 911 call come from?" I said.

"I can guess, but we don't know for sure. Anyway, Dave and I are going over there. Sorry. It might be a false alarm, but it might not. We've got to."

"Go ahead. I'm right behind you."

I stood and pulled my coat over my cast, and ground my teeth in frustration.

"Dammit!" I said under my breath.

Chapter 39

There had been no murder at Old Camp Possumtickle. In fact, there weren't even any people at Old Camp Possumtickle, it being January and Old Camp Possumtickle now being Camp Daystar, St. Germaine's Christian Nudist Retreat.

We spent an hour walking through the camp after Nancy picked the padlock on the gate.

"How about the 911 call?" I asked.

"I checked with Boone. It came from a cell phone. There was no number they could trace."

"Did they say if it was a man or a woman?"

"Woman," said Nancy. "Not that it helps much."

"Well, let's get back. I'm afraid I know what we're going to find."

"We could go pick her up," suggested Dave. "Maybe she's still got the box."

"I kind of doubt that she's still in town," I said. "But we might as well get a warrant and go on over to her apartment. Nancy, go ahead and give Judge Adams a call."

"Lemme wait until six, huh? Last time I called at five, he read me the riot act for fifteen minutes."

"Yeah, fine," I said. "Let's go check the church and then go get some breakfast."

•••

Gaylen's office was locked. I reached behind the copy machine to get the master key. It was gone. I looked at my watch. 5:45.

"The Slab will be open at six," said Dave. "You want breakfast, or do you want to call the priest and get the key?"

"We can wait a bit. She'll be in at about seven for those kids. We'll stop back then."

Chapter 40

"We want the organ contract for the new Cathedral," said Sophie Slugh. "The Slugh Organ Company will be the new standard in pipe organs for the 21st century."

"Is that your company, Sophie? I never heard of it."

"It used to be Peter Pooter's Penny Pumpers, but Peter's plan pooped out when he couldn't make the pumps plather. It was an engineering problem. We simply replaced Peter's penny pumps with Kooloobati gas-slugs. They supply all the air a pipe organ needs."

"Makes sense," I said. "Flatulent flatworms. Brilliant. But what makes you think I have anything to do with who gets the contract?" I asked.

"We know you've got the goods on the Queen Bishop. One word from you and she'll cough up that contract like Mr. Frisky on National Hairball Day. Then, once the Slugh Organ is installed, everyone will want one."

"Yeah, probably," I agreed -- as agreeable as the head underdwarf, Agrin the Agreeable, who, as I'm sure he would agree, owed me seventeen dollars (three-years' wages in Kooloobati), which was the princely sum I'd paid him to keep Sophie in the compost heap -- "but I don't think that's going to happen."

I narrowed my gaze and pulled a salt shaker out of my pocket. The air was sucked out of the room by a hundred slimy blowholes. It reminded me of the U.S. Senate.

"Didn't you frisk him?" Sophie burbled at a slug that looked suspiciously like Nancy Pelosi, but with better plastic surgery.

"I can't stand to touch a gumshoe," she (or he) squished back. "They give me the screamin' willies!"

And that's when the seasoning started.

•••

"I've got the warrant," said Nancy, walking up to our table. "Judge Adams is out of town. Judge Minton wasn't too happy, meeting me at 6:30 in the morning. Not only did I have to stop at Dunkin' Donuts and bring him a coffee and a cruller, but when he opened the front door, he was in his bathrobe." Nancy gave an involuntary shudder. "And it wasn't exactly tied shut."

"I know how you feel," I said. "Mrs. Crampkin did the same thing to me last month when I went over to help her get her cat off the roof."

"Mrs. Crampkin's a hundred and eight years old!" said Pete. "Maybe more."

"You just ain't whistlin' Dixie," I said. "I haven't seen that many wrinkles since Hannah dropped that case of prunes down at the Piggly Wiggly. Mrs. Crampkin looked like a bald Shar-Pei."

"Have some waffles," Dave said to Nancy. "They're delicious. We're meeting Gaylen Weatherall in a couple of minutes. Then off to nail the perp. Well, if she's home."

Nancy slid a chair out from under the table and bellied up to a plate of Belgian waffles.

"Perp?" I said to Dave. "Did you just say perp?"

Nancy laughed. "He *did* say perp."

Dave hung his head in shame.

"Can I come?" asked Pete. "I've got my Kevlar vest in the back of the truck."

Cynthia walked up to the table and began to refill our coffee cups.

"You've got a vest?" said Nancy. "Why? Why on earth would you have a vest?"

"I'm going turkey hunting with the mayor here," Pete said, smiling up at Cynthia. "It's not that she's a bad shot. It's just that she's the current beneficiary on my insurance policy."

"No," I said. "You can't come."

"You could deputize me," suggested Pete.

"Go ahead and take him," Cynthia said. "Maybe he'll get shot and save me the trouble."

•••

We met Gaylen in Marilyn's office at seven o'clock sharp. She was dressed for the day's work in a wool skirt and matching sweater. Her long white hair was tied back with a ribbon.

"What's the rush?" she said, when Nancy, Dave, and I walked in. "I had to be here anyway for the children's sunrise service, but you three look as though you've been up all night."

"We'll tell you in a second," I said. "Could we go into your office?"

"Sure," said Gaylen. She pulled her keys out of her sweater pocket and unlocked the office door. We followed her into the room. She walked behind her desk, sat down and looked up at us.

"What?" she said, looking around, then, seeing what the rest of us saw, or rather didn't see, *"Oh, my God!"*

The reliquary was gone.

Chapter 41

The sun was just breaking over the top of the mountains when we knocked on the apartment door. We'd all noticed the black Ford Explorer 4x4 sitting in the driveway. The door swung open and an attractive woman smiled at us.

"Come on in," said Diana Terry. "I've been expecting you."

"Here's our warrant," Nancy said as she handed a folded piece of paper across the threshold. "For your apartment and your car."

"Yes," said Diana. "So it is."

"Would you mind waiting with me outside?" I said. "While Dave and Nancy check your apartment?"

"Not at all. Let me get my coat."

"I'll go with you," said Nancy. She and Dave followed Diana into the living room. Diana appeared a moment later clad in a heavy, quilted overcoat and wrapped in a scarf. She had a stylish knit cap on her head.

"They won't find anything, you know."

"I'm pretty sure they won't, but we have to check anyway," I said.

"What made you suspect me?" Diana said. "Not that I'm guilty of anything, mind you. I'm just curious."

"A couple of things," I said. "The first was the computer at the library. You were on the internet when Big Mel shorted out the transformer and all the power went out. I talked with you and Rebecca right after it happened. Remember?"

Diana smiled, but didn't say anything.

"Rebecca was planning an author Skype that evening. When the power came back on, Donald Mushrat raced to the only computer hooked to a printer. He had to finish his sermon. That computer was still logged in to your email, since you never logged out. Sometimes that happens."

"Hmm," said Diana. "I can't imagine that's true."

"Mushrat couldn't resist reading someone else's email. He was like that. Then he read something that told him the recipient of the emails he was reading was a killer. He announced as much during his Bible study. 'We have a Jael in our community.'"

"I wouldn't know about that," said Diana sweetly. "I wasn't there."

"Well, you certainly didn't know I was in the choir loft," I said, "but you were there. I saw you. You just didn't stay with the others when I sent everyone to the fellowship hall. We got everyone's statement. Yours wasn't among them."

"Oh, right," said Diana. "I was there. Now I remember. But then I had an emergency and had to leave." She smiled again. "I'm sorry. I must have forgotten."

"We did some checking. You're Hiram Frost's niece. And you actually *are* an ex-nun. We thought that might just be a cover. You'd know the scriptures pretty well."

"Well, Uncle Hiram's side of the family is Catholic," said Diana. "I went to the convent when I was seventeen. I left ten years later. Priests aren't always as holy as they'd like you to believe."

"You've been taking care of Hiram for a couple of years, doing some shopping for him, picking up his medicine..."

"Oh, sure. I loved Uncle Hiram."

"You knew the house and you knew Hiram couldn't manage steps anymore. That's why you stashed Sal LaGrassa's wine in your uncle's basement. Of course, you had no idea about the bank foreclosing on the farm."

"I don't know anyone named Sal LaGrassa. And I was *shocked* that Uncle Hiram had wine in his basement. Shocked, I tell you!"

It was my turn to smile. "It is Nancy's and my considered opinion that Sal met his demise because you didn't really want him to come to my house, steal his wine back, and kill Meg and me."

"Well, I do like Meg. She's a nice person."

"That can't be the only reason."

"Well, hypothetically, if I *did* know this Sal LaGrassa, he may have been acting more and more erratically. Not sticking to the protocols. He might not have been able to have been trusted anymore."

"So, I suppose I owe you a debt of thanks," I said.

"Well, if any of this were true, you certainly would."

"Anyway, as soon as Mushrat announced that he'd uncovered a killer, you knew he needed to go. You'd heard your emails read aloud on Sunday morning and you knew he'd been copying them. What you didn't know is how much information he had. There could have been something in those emails that might have eventually led the feds straight to you. Something that Mushrat hadn't figured out yet."

"Interesting," said Diana.

"So you shot him during the hymn. And you used a Glock just like the one I kept in the organ bench. But, before you did—in fact before you killed LaGrassa—you switched the barrels in the guns. To throw suspicion on me, just in case something went awry."

"How clever!" said Diana. "Why didn't anyone hear the gunshot?"

"Oh, please," I said. "Do I even have to mention that you used a noise suppressor? A silencer? You probably shot him right through your purse."

"What's a silencer?" said Diana, innocently, then added, "You know, you really shouldn't keep a pistol in the organ bench."

"I've been told that before," I said. "By the way, about the other email that Deacon Mushrat read. I hope I don't have to worry about a twenty-thousand dollar murder-for-hire somewhere in this community."

"That is not something I'd worry about, if I were you."

Nancy and Dave came out of the front door of the apartment.

"Nothing," Nancy said. "No Glock. No guns of any kind. No reliquary either. We'll check the car, but I'll bet there's nothing there either."

"If it's not here, where is it?" asked Dave.

"Not that I know anything about what you're talking about," said Diana, "but, when I was up at the church last night with the kids, I saw an old box up in the choir loft."

"How much is that thing worth, anyway?" I asked.

"Well, it's priceless, of course, but I wouldn't be surprised at a private auction estimate of seven or eight figures," said Diana. "Or so I've heard."

"What's it doing in the choir loft?" asked Nancy.

I looked at Diana Terry and smiled. "Someone stole it," I said, "but then discovered she couldn't get it out of town. She couldn't leave it at her house, because the cops would be coming with a warrant. She couldn't leave it in her car for the same reason. She had to put it back."

"But why did she leave it in the choir loft?" asked Dave.

I looked at Diana and she shrugged. "Maybe," she said, "because that's where she found it. You know, after the kids were done playing with it."

"Really?" I said. "The kids were playing with it?"

"Maybe," said Diana. "Not that I'd know, of course."

"Of course, you wouldn't," said Nancy. "But I still don't understand why *someone* didn't put the reliquary in her car and drive out of town as soon as we were called out to Camp Possumtickle."

"Probably," said Diana, looking over at me, "because some smart-ass cop put sugar in *someone's* gas tank."

•••

We checked the car, but Nancy was right. Nothing.

"Can we lock her up?" Dave asked as we walked back down the sidewalk.

"Nope," I said. "Not yet. No evidence. No confession."

"Nothing," said Nancy. "Another hit-nun gets away scot-free. It's the story of my life."

"Oh, well," said Dave. "Maybe Pete's got some more waffles."

Chapter 42

"Were you kids playing with that old box in Dr. Weatherall's office last night?" I said.

I had all the children lined up in the fellowship hall, sitting in folding chairs. Kimberly Walnut came walking out of the bathroom and saw her little angels under interrogation.

"What's going on?" she demanded.

Emily Douglas came out of the kitchen a moment later. She glared at her two twins. "Spill it," she growled.

"It was Dewey!" said Garth, pointing a finger at the boy sitting two seats to the right.

"It was Moosey's idea!" squealed Dewey. "I just unlocked the office."

"It was Bern..." started Moosey, but then stopped. He sighed and slumped in his seat. "Yeah, okay," he said. "It was me."

"How did you get the key?" I asked.

"I found it behind the copy machine," said Dewey. "It opens everything."

"When did all this happen?" said Kimberly Walnut.

"When you and Mom were asleep," said Garrett. "We've been playing in the church all night. But we didn't take the box till almost morning."

"Let me get this straight," said Gaylen. "All you kids were running through the church all night. With the master key?"

"Yep," said Garth. The other kids nodded. "Mom and Mizz Walnut were really snoring up a storm."

Gaylen glared at Kimberly Walnut. Kimberly twitched.

"Let's have the key," I said, holding out my hand to Dewey. He dug into his jeans pocket and dropped the brass master key into my hand.

Nancy and Dave came walking into the fellowship hall and in Dave's arms was the Reliquary of Nantwich. He put it down on one of the folding tables set up to serve the children's breakfast.

"It was in the choir loft," said Nancy. "Sitting on the organ console."

I looked the old box over carefully and rubbed the old lock with my finger.

"Well, no harm done. Let's get it back to the office," I said. I pointed a finger at all the children, one at a time. "And not one word about this to anyone. You understand? Or I'll throw you all in jail."

The children all nodded vigorously.

"And that goes for you adults, too," I said, looking at Kimberly Walnut and Emily. "Not one word. Now you kids go back to your coo-coo thing."

"Cocoon!" said Kimberly Walnut. "It's called 'Cocoon!'"

•••

"So what's the deal?" Nancy asked. "You were very adamant that no one says anything."

"What if the Reverends Farrant and Overnight knew that a bunch of ten-year-old kids were traipsing around in the church, playing with a priceless relic from the Middle Ages?"

"They would not be pleased."

"No, they would not," I agreed.

Chapter 43

Most of the senators...er..."slugs"...made it out alive and plump. Some didn't. Sophie was one of those that didn't. The last thing she said to me as she was shriveling up like a piece of fatback in a sizzling frying pan was "Urrrgg hafrap!" Strong words.

"Get me outta here," called Pedro. "I'm as sticky as lawyer pudding. Them slugs had their way with me."

"Spare me the details," I said, snipping his bamboo shoots with my pocket knife.

"How did you know to bring the salt shaker?" Pedro said.

"It was the kiss," I said. "She could wear a disguise, but she couldn't change that kiss. It was the taste of wet feet mixed with marinated ham that gave her away. How could a man ever forget that?"

"What about the Slugh Organ?" asked Pedro.

"Seems to me we've got an in," I said, smiling like the cat that got the slug, then decided it didn't like slugs, spit it out, and got a canary instead. "We've got the technology, and none of these senators is going to mess with us anymore. They're running scared, as scared as Sarah Palin's book editors."

"So you're saying..."

"I'm saying that the Queen Bishop is going to award the contract to the Slugh Organ Company."

"Who is us," said Pedro happily.

"Who is us," I agreed.

•••

The twelve days of Christmas begin on December 25th and continue through January 5th. On the 6th of January, we celebrate the Feast of the Epiphany—the coming of the Wise Men to the Holy Child, symbolizing the revelation of God-made-man in the person of Jesus Christ. The Biblical Magi, traditionally named Caspar, Melchior, and Balthasar, represent the non-Jewish people of the world and paid homage to the infant Jesus with gifts of gold (the symbol of Christ's kingship), frankincense (symbolizing his priesthood), and myrrh (foreshadowing his death). The Feast of the Epiphany begins the season of the same name that takes us to Ash Wednesday and into Lent.

The children had finished their Cocoon program after lunch and had all gone home fluttering like the butterflies they had been born to be. Kimberly Walnut had taken the rest of the day off. I suspected that I wouldn't see her for the Epiphany service.

Meg and I got to the church about forty-five minutes before the service, and preparations were in full swing. Benny Dawkins was warming up in the aisle with his practice thurible. J.D. Overnight was supervising the embellishment of the litter on which the reliquary would rest—decoration that included boughs of fir and sprigs of holly. Two acolytes would carry torches, two others would carry the litter in procession.

Bishop O'Connell was busy chatting with Gaylen and Arthur Farrant, admiring the reliquary and asking questions about the history of the kingly remains. The Altar Guild was putting the finishing touches on the decorations, and the fellowship hall had been hung with greens and lit with candles for the reception and talk by Father Farrant following the service.

The choir wasn't meeting beforehand, having been instructed to be in place for the processional hymn precisely at six o'clock, but many of them had already vested and were helping by setting out bulletins and cleaning up stray pine needles.

About twenty minutes before the service, people started to come in. Word of the bones had gotten around town quickly enough, and there had been articles in the two local papers advertising the event. Except for the Wednesday night prayer meeting at New Fellowship Baptist Church, we were the only game in town. NFBC was also loaning us Brother Hog, Noylene Fabergé-Dupont, and their son Rahab, all perched on the front row.

•••

Edna Terra-Pocks began the service with one of my favorite Christmas organ pieces, *Bring a Torch, Jeanette, Isabella*, arranged by Keith Chapman. I was up in the loft with her, turning pages with my one good hand. She finished up and put the music for *We Three Kings*, our processional hymn, onto the music stand and began to play.

Benny Dawkins, his incense pot smoking, came in first. He was followed by the cross bearer, the acolyte carrying our Epiphany banner, and the choir. Benny was beginning to swing in the first of what would be an evening of truly memorable maneuvers.

The two torch bearers came in next, followed by the lay eucharistic ministers and the two acolytes carrying the reliquary. Arthur Farrant, J.D. Overnight, Gaylen Weatherall and Bishop O'Connell, all of them decked out in their finest raiments, completed the procession. Luckily we had five stanzas of the hymn to sing by the time everyone had to be in place.

When I was playing the organ, I was usually too busy pushing ivory to appreciate Benny's artistry. Watching him work without having to worry about what notes I was playing was a pleasure. About half-way down the aisle, a second thurible appeared in his other hand—where he had kept it hidden, I had no idea—and he began to spin both, one in each hand: the pots moving in a blur, crossing back and forth in front of his body in a symphony of gold chains and smoke. He was subtle and fantastic in equal measure. Truly a master.

"Blessed be God: Father, Son, and Holy Spirit," said Gaylen, when the procession had finished.

"And blessed be His kingdom, now and forever. Amen," said the congregation.

Edna played the introduction to *Glory to God in the Highest* and the congregation sang.

"O God," intoned Gaylen, when the congregation finished singing, "by the leading of a star you manifested your only Son to the peoples of the earth; Lead us, who know you now by faith, to your presence, where we may see your glory face to face; through Jesus Christ our Lord, who lives and reigns with you and the Holy Spirit, one God, now and forever."

"Amen," answered the congregation.

We moved smoothly through the service: the lessons, a hymn, a short sermon by Arthur Farrant about kings and relics, the creed, prayers, confession and the Peace. When the announcements began, Moosey crept up the choir loft stairs, peeked his head in and waved for me to come back and talk to him.

"I gotta talk to you, Chief," he said.

"Can it wait?" I said. "The offertory is coming up. I should really be up here to conduct."

"Nope. It can't wait."

"Okay, hang on one second."

I waded through the choir to the organ and whispered to Edna.

"No problem," she said. "If you're not back, they'll just follow me. We'll be fine."

I looked at Meg, sitting on the front row of the soprano section. She and Bev had been listening. They both nodded at me.

I followed Moosey down the stairs into the narthex. Dewey, Bernadette, and Addie were all waiting for me.

"We have to tell you something," said Addie.

"Yeah," said Bernadette.

"It was my fault," said Dewey. "Well, me and Moosey."

"What are you four talking about?" I said. "And keep your voices down."

"We got that old box out of Dr. Weatherall's office," whispered Addie. "We just wanted to look at it."

"So which one of you opened it?" I asked.

"How did you know we opened it?" said Bernadette.

"I saw the pick marks. I'm guessing it was you, Moosey. You use Bud's set of shims?"

"Umm, yeah."

"Well, what's done is done. We can't change it. I meant what I said, though. You all keep quiet about this."

I heard Gaylen say the offertory sentence: "Walk in love, as Christ loved us and gave Himself for us, an offering and sacrifice to God."

"I've got to get back upstairs," I said. "You kids go find a seat."

"That's not all," blurted Addie.

I froze. "What's not all?"

"When we were up in the loft, Dewey knocked the box over."

"*That* wasn't my fault," Dewey said. "Moosey hit my arm."

"Then what happened?"

I heard Edna Terra-Pocks begin the long, fourteen measure introduction to *Lo! Star-Led Chiefs*.

"Everything fell out of the box," said Bernadette. "It was all over the floor. There was a lot of dust and rags and stuff."

"Mostly dust," said Dewey.

"There were some brown sticks, too," added Moosey. "And some little chunks of tree sap. They were pretty small."

"So, you put it all back?" I said.

"We couldn't," said Addie in dismay. "Garth and Garrett thought it was so funny. They stomped it all into the floor with their big shoes. Then everyone ran off. It was just us four that tried to clean up."

I heard the choir begin to sing.

Lo! star-led chiefs Assyrian odours bring,
And bending Magi seek their infant King!

"So, what did you do next?" I asked.

"Well," said Moosey, "we cleaned up everything we could."

"What about the box? I know you locked it back."

"Yeah," said Moosey, "but it didn't have a rattle anymore, so we put some stuff in it."

"What?" I asked.

"Chicken bones from dinner," said Bernadette. "And some napkins."

"It all rattled about the same," said Dewey. "We didn't think anyone would notice."

"What did you do with the dust and stuff you cleaned up?"

"Umm..." said Addie, nervously.

"Umm..." said Bernadette.

Marked ye, where, hovering o'er His head,
The dove's white wings celestial glory shed.

I looked hard at Moosey. *"What?"* I demanded.

"We put everything into one of the organ pipes. One of the ones in the front."

"You *didn't!*"

Moosey shrugged and tried his gap-toothed grin, but it fell flat.

"Not the rags," Dewey said quickly. "We put the rags in the trash."

"Here," Moosey said, reaching into his pocket. He handed me two silver coins, ancient and struck only on one side. "I wasn't gonna keep 'em."

I snatched the coins from his hand and dropped them into my pocket. "Not a word!" I hissed at the four children. "Not one word of this to anyone. You understand?"

"Yessir!" they said in unison, relieved that I wasn't going to shoot them.

"Now get on into the fellowship hall and see if there is anything you can do to help Mrs. Sterling."

They took off out the front door and around the outside of the building like rabbits just as the choir was heading into the final page of the anthem. The anthem ended with a quiet organ postlude, but if I knew Edna, and I was sure I did, she had decided to rewrite the ending and go out with a splash. I raced up the stairs just as the choir finished and signaled to Edna, with my good arm, to keep it down. It was no use.

Just as I knew she'd do, she put the expression pedal to the floor, opened all the stops, and came down on the last chord with all the juice she had.

The great noise went up. "Pa-toomph!" went the pipe, then joined the cacophony of its brothers and sisters. The dust of the king shot up into the air, played in the light for a moment, and then settled gently on the heads of those sitting in the back of the church. Several people thought they felt some small particles land in their hair, but they brushed them away without a care. The choir didn't know what happened, but they'd heard the popping sound and seen the explosion of dust.

"Huh," said Marjorie. "Ain't that something? We oughta swab them pipes out more often."

Postlude

Diana Terry decided to leave town, as we expected she would. When I told Meg about her, she was horrified, but still grateful.

"If it wasn't for Diana, you'd be dead," she said.

"Well, you, too."

"Probably," Meg agreed, "but let's not forget that she did kill Deacon Mushrat."

"I'm not forgetting it for a moment," I said. "Even though we had no evidence to arrest her, I gave her name and picture to the FBI. They'll keep an eye on her. But I have a feeling we'll see Diana Terry again."

The Nantwich Reliquary and the chicken bones made their way back to England after a highly successful tour that raised over thirty thousand pounds for St. Hywyn's church. Father Arthur Farrant was more than pleased and sent us a lovely note upon his return. Our sexton was a little perturbed with all the dust that had suddenly appeared in the nave, but a good cleaning took care of everything.

The two coins from the reliquary ended up in my desk drawer, right under my typewriter, until I could figure out what to do with them.

Gaylen's jaw healed within a couple of weeks and, when the wires came off, she was back to her old self. The same could be said of my arm. Edna Terra-Pocks stayed on through January but then found another part-time organist position closer to home. I was glad to get back, but it was a few weeks before I could get my fingers to move the way they did before the accident.

Brother Hog and Noylene decided to get married. Noylene went ahead and added Brother Hog's moniker to her own, becoming Noylene Fabergé-Dupont-McTavish. Little Rahab got his little tail snipped off the same day he was circumcised. Two weeks late, Brother Hog said, but Noylene got a two-for-one from the doctor, and she never could resist a bargain. Dave Vance was sad. He'd been hoping to watch little Rahab get dunked into the baptismal font by his tail.

Big Mel continued to win trophy after trophy, and became even more of a legend than the St. Germaine Christmas Parade had made her. She published a book on the Big Mel philosophy of "winning through intimidation" and went on the tour circuit of toddler beauty pageants.

Mr. Christopher Lloyd got his own show on HGTV called *The 14 Layers of Style*. It was cancelled after four weeks when Mr. Christopher was caught on tape by Entertainment-TV flogging his chintz with Raoul the cameraman.

Nancy Parsky had a wonderful vacation, returning from her holiday bronzed and happy. Dave (whom she decided to take with her at the last minute) didn't come back either bronzed or particularly happy. In fact, Dave came back the color of a boiled lobster and had some rather shocking tales to tell about being repeatedly strip-searched in the Belize airport.

Marjorie never did start her blog, technology being what it was and Marjorie being who she was.

Brother Hog retired from New Fellowship Baptist Church, un-retired his revival tent, found himself a new Scripture Chicken, and hit the back roads with a will. His reputation preceded him and he had no lack of offers of a place to pitch his tent and preach the gospel.

Bud went back to school to major in business. He had a new goal, a business plan, and a dream to open his wine shop. I'd guard his investment until he was ready. Elphina, privy to the knowledge of his eventual windfall, vowed to wait for him.

Pete and Cynthia went turkey hunting. Both survived.

St. Barnabas turned its sights toward Epiphany, Lent and Easter, the seasons rolling by like clouds across our beloved Appalachians—days turning to months, and then to years. People would come and go, clergy and musicians would come and go, fashions would come and go. St. Barnabas would endure.

•••

"Marilyn," I said to my secretary. "Pack your bags. We're going on vacation."

"Really? Where are we going?"

"Kooloobati. I hear it's lovely this time of year."

"Isn't that where the chockobats live?"

"So I hear, doll-face."

"But I don't have anything to wear."

I smiled. It was good to be a detective.

About the Author

Mark Schweizer lives and works in Tryon, North Carolina. He tells people he's famous, but they don't believe him.

The Liturgical Mysteries

The Alto Wore Tweed
Independent Mystery Booksellers Association "Killer Books" selection, 2004

The Baritone Wore Chiffon

The Tenor Wore Tapshoes
IMBA 2006 Dilys Award nominee

The Soprano Wore Falsettos
Southern Independent Booksellers Alliance 2007 Book Award Nominee

The Bass Wore Scales

The Mezzo Wore Mink

The Diva Wore Diamonds

The Organist Wore Pumps

Just A Note

If you've enjoyed this book—or any of the other mysteries in this series—please drop me a line. My e-mail address is mark@sjmp.com. Also, don't forget to visit the website (www.sjmpbooks.com) for lots of great stuff! You'll find recordings and "downloadable" music for many of the great works mentioned in the Liturgical Mysteries including *The Pirate Eucharist, The Weasel Cantata, The Mouldy Cheese Madrigal, Elisha and the Two Bears, The Banjo Kyrie* and a lot more.

Cheers,
Mark